MURDER BY ANCIENT DESIGN

A WILLI GALLAGHER MYSTERY

MURDER BY
ANCIENT DESIGN

KAT GOLDRING

FIVE STAR
A part of Gale, Cengage Learning

GALE
CENGAGE Learning

Detroit • New York • San Francisco • New Haven, Conn • Waterville, Maine • London

GALE
CENGAGE Learning™

Set in 11 pt. Plantin.
Printed on permanent paper.

LIBRARY OF CONGRESS CATALOGING-IN-PUBLICATION DATA

Goldring, Kat.
    Murder by ancient design : a Willi Gallagher mystery / by Kat Goldring. — 1st ed.
        p. cm.
    ISBN-13: 978-1-59414-748-7 (hardcover : alk. paper)
    ISBN-10: 1-59414-748-5 (hardcover : alk. paper)
    1. Gallagher, Willi (Fictitious character)—Fiction. 2. Women teachers—Fiction. 3. Aztecs—Exhibitions—Fiction. 4. Museum curators—Selection and appointment—Fiction. I. Title.
PS3607.O47M87 2009
813'.6—dc22   2008043354

First Edition. First Printing: February 2009.
Published in 2009 in conjunction with Tekno Books and Ed Gorman.

Printed in the United States of America
1 2 3 4 5 6 7 12 13 11 10 09

This book is dedicated to Texas high school professional teachers who are in the classroom day in and day out, teaching and nurturing our state's richest resource, our children. For you who are truly "in" the classroom, you are the ones who should be honored for your courage and perseverance each day.

You fight against such tremendous odds about which the public has no inkling. It is my hope that some day the powers-that-be will realize a simple equation: TEACHERS IN THE CLASSROOM + STUDENTS IN THE CLASSROOM equate to consistent learning and achievement. So, for those of you in the trenches each day, working and implementing standards and procedures to instill needed skills, knowledge and values within Texas youth, thank you. Thank you for continuing to fight such great odds. Bless you all.

ACKNOWLEDGEMENTS

Many thanks to friends and family who allow me to call them with the strangest questions, who help research the oddest bits of trivia, and who sustain me through the process with their humor, their graciousness, and their presence: Hollyanna Shaffer, Aunt Norma and Uncle Steve Stevens, Claudia Bennett, Mac and Shirley McKee, James D. Morton, Cathy Brown, Truman Bates, Karon Carter, and Linda Barton, whose special insight and bright light will be missed, but always remembered.

Special gracias to Shirley Jean McKee for assistance with some of the rhymed quotes for *Book of the Ancient Ones.*

To the gifted and creative Writerie folks—Squirrel, Rocky, and Peggy—who continue to help me hone writing skills, blessings on you for your patience and shared knowledge.

For the most wonderful gift of the Monday night sessions and the needed interludes of laughter and fun through this process, hugs to James Doyle, Tom, Shirley, Mac, Jamie, Tyler, Jackie, J.T. and Patsy McDaniel, Cliff, and all others who have joined our pickin' 'n grinnin' night. *Pilamaya ye—thank you.*

ACKNOWLEDGMENTS

CHAPTER ONE

With the gods my heart will e'er remain
After those with hearts untrue are slain.

—Ca'nunkas'ah
The Book of the Ancient Ones

On the thousand-foot squared-off top of the pyramid Willi Gallagher stared, eyes widened, unable to breathe easily. She rested her hand on the ancient stone with the embossed Mexica hieroglyphics, the coldness of the pillar creeping into her skin, up her arm, and worming down her spine until she shivered. This was one of many groupings of pillars—a circle of three for each corner that supported a roof over the pyramid. Within the shadows of the trios she could remain hidden. Willi blinked but could not tear her gaze from the horror before her.

A three-foot-high marble-smooth rock sat atop this pyramid. Four priests in plumed headdresses grasped a limb of the sacrifice—a girl of dewy skin, eyes glistening with tears—eyes peering into Willi's own, beseeching her to help.

But Willi dared not call attention to herself. She had no desire to be spread-eagled and awaiting the fifth priest who now approached with knife upraised. The helpless victim—in the grip of horrific inevitability—did not cry out, did not struggle. The four pulled on her arms and legs, arching her back, exposing the tender breasts thrust sharply above the ribcage. Willi was so focused on the breath cycle—the vulnerable in and out of life—within those ribs, it took her a moment to register the action of the fifth priest when he slashed downwards and sliced open the girl's left side. As he drew forth the

9

beating heart, Willi offered up a silent scream of shock, of denial, of . . .

Her mind erupted then into purest fear.

She clutched her hand over her own heart. Yes, still there, beating, beating so fast it would burst out of her. Dear God, the pain. Struggling to draw air into her lungs, she sank to her knees. The roar of her own blood gushed, swirled and cascaded through her, and she swayed. Yet, she kept her gaze on the scene upon the cold, cold stone. She caught a few words over and above the tumult of her own body.

While the priest held the pulsating muscle aloft for all gathered below on the many steps to revere, he intoned, "Our bones, our flesh." From many of those richly robed and bejeweled spectators as well as triumphant warriors rose a joyous undulation. The many hundreds— who awaited the same fate—hung their heads, screamed, fainted, wet or soiled themselves.

The stench of urine brought Willi sharply back from the dark void. She gasped. Tears stung her eyelids and covered her face.

The regal one repeated, "Our bones, our flesh."

Willi was shivering now. Dear God, don't let them see me. Don't allow this to continue. This shouldn't be happening. Not in the modern here and now. No, no, no.

Still with the sweet girl's heart held high, the Priest of the Knife strode across the flat top of the pyramid toward the larger-than-life stone depiction of Chacmool—he of the lounging figure, resting upon one elbow, one leg bent at the knee in relaxed repose. In one chiseled hand rested a bowl. Into this rough receptacle, the priest squeezed lifeblood from the heart before dropping the organ into the rich liquid.

With each victim—man, woman or child—the process was repeated. Willi's mind only registered terror, horrible unmitigated and never-ending terror that reached down into her bone marrow. Terror that chilled her own blood. The rushing of that same blood in her ears again drowned out even the squawks and skirls, the whines and wails of the mutilated. Except for one horrible scream, a shrill howl that pierced even the miasma of her terror.

"Ah-oooooooooo!"

A wet, sandpapery cloth brushed across her face. No, no, not a cloth. A moist, rough tongue.

"Willi? Are you okay? Here. Let me help you stand up."

"What? What—"

Someone helped her get up. She blinked and her breathing returned to normal. Now the dog's tongue seemed plastered to the nylons covering her leg. She looked down. "Ludwig?"

The pug-nosed boxer licked her again, sneezed and howled.

Willi swallowed and peered into Anastasia Zöllmer's clear blue eyes. Being the same age as Willi—thirty-two—Anastasia's eyes had no lines around them, but she would garner crow's feet early if she kept looking that worried.

Willi straightened up. "You're late."

Anastasia glanced at her watch. "Maybe three minutes."

"Oh, really." Willi tried desperately to still her shaking knees. She glanced at the first of seven displays around her in the new Nickleberry Museum—a scenario depicting the top five steps of an Aztec pyramid used for the sacrifice of war captives. She shook her head. Damn her ability to transform in time and place through what Quannah called her *daydreams* and through what her white witch neighbors, the Kachelhoffer sisters, referred to as her *precognitive visions.* Whatever they were called, she'd learned through the years to recover fairly quickly from their effects and respond to the real world in a moment or two.

"Are you okay? Even your face, tanned as it is, seems pale. Not that the look doesn't make your green eyes stand out, but there are ways to get a look and *ways* to get a look." Anastasia Zöllmer repeated, "Are you okay? You had Ludwig and me worried."

Willi tasted bile and rubbed her throat. "Sorry about worrying you. Guess I was . . . uh . . . zoned out to the limit, thinking about all the decisions to be made before choosing the curator. Also, I've got to meet Quannah at the Nickleberry airport right after our meeting."

"I suppose," Anastasia said, "you could call a couple of hangars for private planes and one airstrip an airport." She ran a hand through her spiky blonde hair. "I love it. Caught you daydreaming. Tch. Tch. Tch. I could go along and let Quannah know he shouldn't be taking you up into any clouds. You can get there all by yourself."

"You will not mention this lapse which was *not,* absolutely not, daydreaming." Willi shut her eyes for a moment to send a prayer upward. *Great Spirit, allow me enough brain cells to get through today's interviews without falling apart.* Sleep deprivation and the worry she'd been under the last few weeks was more than enough to down a Texas Marine.

"I love it. Yes, this and my sighting you, sweet English teacher that you are, yesterday at—now, where was that—the shooting range—might be something I'd need to talk over with Quannah."

Willi straightened her skirt again to give her time to think of a response. Dang, she'd hoped no one had seen her. "You might have been mistaken, or I must have a double wandering around." She crossed her fingers and asked mentally to be forgiven for the white lie. She seemed to get away with them, perhaps because she had had such examples as her Nickleberry High sophomores. This fall break in mid-October was a welcome respite from the good, the bad, the bright and the dense, bless them all.

"Nothing going on with me," Willi said. Right, nothing except what was keeping her from a good night's sleep. She blinked her eyes. She had to focus on her role as chairperson right now.

Anastasia took out a silver cigarette case, tapped out a filtered cigarette and said, "I won't light up until we get to the patio outside my office. Even though the museum won't be open for months to the public, I would never smoke inside. We have to be careful of our artifacts and art pieces." She tapped the unlit cigarette. "Guess I'm a bit anxious. Shouldn't be nervous with you on my side." Anastasia smiled at her. "No other contender can count the head of the museum's subcommittee for curator appointment as a best friend, right?"

"Anastasia, don't say that."

"Why not? We've been friends since high school."

"Sure, but I can't let that influence my choice. The committee has set guidelines, and we're going to consider each candidate fairly and equally according to those guidelines."

The acting curator smiled and her eyes lit up. "Willi, I'd expect no less of you or the other members. I'm the best one for the job, and I'll prove it to you before the decision process is finished."

"Your getting, or not getting, the position isn't going to change our friendship for me, I hope."

"No, no. It won't change things between us except you'll never get another one of my homemade piña coladas, and, of course, those afternoons in my swimming pool—hmmm—those might disappear."

"You are *so* bad."

"But good for the job, Willi Gallagher, good for the job."

"You've certainly got perseverance."

With a wink, her friend said, "I love it. Speaking of job and duties, guess it's time to officially meet the others."

Willi straightened her cobalt-blue jacket over her skirt, adjusted her black pantyhose, which had twisted enough to develop a tiny run around her left knee, and wiped a smudge off her two-inch heels. "Yes, I can't wait to meet whoever set up the . . . uh . . . pyramid display. All the magnificent jaguar figurines placed up and down the steps—are they real or replicas?"

"All items are replicas in the displays unless they're under or behind specially sealed glass. We won't place those prime items into the displays until just before the opening."

"Makes sense. Let's go meet the others. Sooner we start, the sooner the day can end." Hell's bells and Texas toads, Willi couldn't wait for this day to end. She willed herself not to blink her eyes so much. Probably looked like a startled owl. Talking would help keep her brain cells alert, so she asked, "Who is the person responsible for the Aztecan pyramid?"

Anastasia raised an eyebrow. "That would be Dr. Ernesto Etzli."

"You've already met, I suppose?" Willi asked.

"No. When he arrived, his aide, Yadotle, Yahdodle, or something like that, picked up the keys. The two have only come after dark to work on the scene and set up a temporary office. Each of the candidates is allowed a private cubbyhole, something your subcommittee insisted upon. Gives everyone office space for chores such as ordering, working with their assistant, and for relaxing when possible."

"Hmmm," Willi said, "and you don't like that, huh?"

"Okay, so I'm double bad." Anastasia reached to run her fingers through her hair, instead lowered her hand and tapped her cigarette in the palm of the other hand. "Know what his name means?"

"I speak a little Spanish, but I don't know what *Etzli* means."

"It's the old Aztec language—excuse me—Aztec was the white man's name. The ancients referred to the race as Mexica and the language as Nahuatl. Anyway, his name is not true Spanish."

"So? What does it mean?"

"Blood."

"Blood?" Willi glanced over her shoulder at the statue of Chacmool and the large-fanged jaguars with eyes that seemed to follow her. Ludwig's nails clicked on the sandstone surface behind the two women as he waddled after them. A shiver ran from the nape of her neck down her backbone. "*Blood.* Great. Just great." When she and that word came into close proximity, it never brought anything good. "I'll try not to hold it against him."

"Oh, I don't mind," Anastasia said, and grinned.

"You are so bad."

Willi tapped on her watch face.

"Stop that. You're not on a school bell schedule. When have you become so time conscious on your days off?"

Willi patted the side tendrils of her upswept chignon. Good grief, she would not worry her friend with the frightful facts; she settled for a half truth. "Quannah's been out on horseback for a day and a night on a manhunt, and I'm worried about him. I've not slept well."

"Ah, your Texas Ranger—"

"Special Investigator for the Texas Rangers."

"Excuse *me.*" Anastasia locked arms with Willi, and pulled her through to the office and out into a private side patio, where she at last lit up her cigarette. She waved the smoke out of her own face. "I know how you feel. It's the same with Ramblin' and me. I hate it when he's out of town, like the last few days. Not to worry. I'll be very businesslike and stop the meeting as soon as possible. No reason for you to talk more than necessary with the other candidates anyway."

"Not that you have an ulterior motive in that sentiment," Willi said.

"But—" Anastasia eyed Willi.

"But?"

"Willi Gallagher, you are on edge about something else, not

15

just because you want to meet Quannah." She dropped the stub of her cigarette. Ludwig immediately pounced on the lit end and stamped it out before grasping the butt, and gulping it down.

"You shouldn't let that poor pooch swallow that." Willi bent down and scratched behind Ludwig's ears. "Can't believe you trained him to do that."

"Okay, avoid the real issue—something between you and Quannah, perhaps—if you must. Go ahead and pick on me and poor Ludwig."

Willi grinned. "Well, his . . . uh . . . cleaning up talent did make it easier to convince the museum members to allow Ludwig to act as the official mascot of the museum, and if you get the final okay and move out of acting curator to full curator position, there'll be no problem with having him here as one of your 'official' duties. This isn't like a Dallas or Fort Worth metropolitan museum. We can still flaunt a few Texas independent mannerisms. Show me the entrance you've been bragging about before the interviews start."

"You bet. Maybe your tension will ease, and you'll share what's really going on with you," Anastasia said, and walked toward the foyer.

Willi wanted to avoid telling Anastasia altogether. Within the foyer she studied the water treatments flowing over inlaid ceramic tri-levels of azure and green tiles. "The waterfall," Willi said, "is exquisite."

The sound, muted and relaxing, welcomed visitors to sit in the semicircle spanning sixty feet before forming into a cascade of half a dozen sunken seating arrangements. Willi sat and breathed in deeply. Each two-hundred-foot section featured comfortable nooks and crannies to view the massive art of each area. "Lovely."

Anastasia suddenly grabbed Willi by the shoulders and looked down at her. "I saw you walking out of the License-To-Carry building, the one at the edge of Burleson. It was you. No mistake. On Thursday. You were carrying a package. What's going on, Willi? Please tell me."

Willi's face suffused with heat; she stood to move away from Anastasia's grasp, and scrutiny.

"Goodness, you're making chili out of one *jalapeño*. Thursday. Of course, now I remember. I took my daddy's ancient firearm to be appraised." Her shoulders slumped. Oh, great, now she'd gone past a simple evasive white lie, to an out and out fib, and she was supposed to be someone the community looked up to, hence their trusting her honesty and integrity as chairperson. She walked out toward the center of the four-story foyer where sunlight streamed through a skylight to fall upon a twenty-foot bronze sculpture in front of a mirror just as tall. It was a depiction of a frontier family braving the Llano Estacado—Staked Plains—wind and heat.

"We were so lucky to get a genuine Shelton," Willi said, peering at herself in the mirror a moment. The better to check for little red horns atop her head, perhaps accompanied by a swishing pitchforked tail. Nope. Only dark tendrils escaping to frame her face. She nodded her approval of the Texas sculptor's work.

Anastasia sighed while following in Willi's footsteps. "You always could keep your own counsel. Have it your way, but if you ever want to talk about . . . about your daddy's firearm, or anything else bothering you, I'm here. You're one of the strongest and most intelligent ladies I know, but I still worry on occasion. Could be all those peccadilloes we got involved with in high school. You do recall the train track incident, the papering of the principal's house, the street race night, and—?"

"Enough. You know too many secrets." Willi placed cool fingers to her cheeks to dissipate some of the heat. "Nothing to tell really about Thursday. Now, how were we so lucky as to get this Shelton masterpiece?"

"This was one of the items yours truly convinced the state's foremost sculptor to donate."

"Works beautifully against the sun and water background as if those pioneers stood on the grasslands of Texas. He's got such feeling etched into their worn but proud visages. And it's so huge at twenty plus feet."

"Yes, it definitely sets the tone for our art displays."

Willi raised her chin. "I'm so glad the founders decided on having both the art and the natural science under one roof. Really, it's awesome."

"Shelton has just sent another smaller piece, but it's in the meeting room." Anastasia retraced her steps through the five art enclaves and around the waterfall behind which elevators stood with a stained-glass door leading to the hallway of offices opposite of Anastasia's large one. A door, marked with a plate as MEETING ROOM ONE, swung open when she waved a hand before a wall sensor.

"Ah, last I was here the sensors weren't operating correctly," Willi said.

"Still aren't, but we're getting the bugs worked out."

"Anyone can open it with a swipe of the hand?"

"Right. We have the option to also set it so only particular staff members can use the inner doors. Right now the outer doors have keyed entry cards or they can be opened with traditional keys. With all the displays being set up and people coming and going, it's driving Tattoo crazy."

"Somebody calling me? I can do it, whatever it is. Give me the time, the space and the inclination." A young woman in black pressed overalls with a Clorox-whitened turtleneck beneath adjusted her leather belt tooled with the name TAT-TOO on it. She bent down and scratched Ludwig behind his ears, a ploy that sent his stub tail into happy gyrations. She repeated, "Yes, I need the space and the in—CLI—na—tion."

Willi grinned at the Texas twang and stressed words Tattoo used. "You're looking sharp."

"Thanky kindly. Trying to dress nice enough I won't scare the customers when I have to wander among 'em, and reasonable enough I can still do my job. I keep a pair of grease-monkey suits in my office for the real dirty work."

Anastasia ran a finger through her blonde hair. "She hasn't let anyone forget she now has an office."

Tattoo grinned and the red rose tattooed beside her left eye closed into a bud. "Might be out in the warehouse boonies, but it's an office, by darn, and I'm getting it fixed up between chores." She pulled the sleeves of the white turtleneck down over her hands where the tips of her arm tattoos, ivy vines on one and the tail of a snake on the other, slithered. "Just thought you might like to know, Ms. Zöllmer, that old Mexican woman set up her storytelling stuff right in front of that nasty pyramid." As she said *mess-cun* Willi cringed. "I moved it all out again. That's like the third time."

Anastasia rubbed her hands together as if she were making a great effort not to put them around someone's neck. "Tattoo, remember our talk about respect for all the cultures represented here and—"

"Oh, yeah, sorry. Mex-*i*-can woman. Tell you what, I've never been in the state pen, but knew lots of folks like that coming through my mama's house. I sorta picked up some rude speech and rough ideas, but I'm working on them, I am."

Anastasia patted her on the shoulder. "You're doing great. I'm proud of you, Tattoo, and appreciate your efforts to develop a . . . a uniform of sorts for your job. Like Ms. Gallagher said, you look sharp."

Tattoo grinned, and Willi nodded. Yes, no doubt Anastasia had attributes that went far beyond the paper shuffling and brouhaha-ing with the ritzy patrons. She managed to enlist decent help for low wages, she had proven herself an efficient money-manager through the new construction, and she kept in-house squabbling between workers to a minimum. The financial contributors to the museum wanted to pay for all the visual bells and whistles, but it was difficult to get them to part with enough funds to get more than minimum help, and certainly no uniforms. Hmmm, might be interesting to see Anastasia handle the rather pushy Mexican lady, Drianina Manauia. Willi tucked a tendril of black hair back into her chignon, and nodded again. Yes, Anastasia might look like a runway model, but she also had the panache of a business executive.

"Tattoo, we'll try to compromise with Mrs. Manauia," Anastasia said. "She reveres the old Aztecan gods and feels her stories would be better heard while in the presence of the great pyramid."

"I don't like that old woman, and it ain't because she's Mess . . . uh . . . Mexican." Tattoo pulled at her sleeves. "Gives me the heebie-jeebies with them bloody tales of hers, and she just gets an evil *de*light, I mean a real evil *de*light out of scaring the bejesus out of folks. Come out from behind that pyramid the other night, doing some high screeching at the top of her lungs. That old lady said she was invocationing—"

"Invoking?" Willi offered, the English teacher in her taking control for a moment.

"Yeah, that's it. Invoking the gods. Telling gruesome stories about little boys who snuck into caves to smoke and were found deader than a sprayed roach because the gas in the cave mixed with that dang smoke and killed them. And like their bones rattle and smokes comes out between their ribs when they dance on top of their graves on some dang celebration. Yeah, invoking the gods. More likely devils with that noise."

Anastasia bent toward Tattoo. "What a wonderful opportunity

for you to . . . to look past what you don't understand and make a grand gesture—one to show her you're willing to accept she has the right to her own beliefs—by helping her create a special area for her storytelling."

"Yeah. Okay. I could build a tri-fold divider that would blend with the pyramid, like it was part of the jungle growth or something." Tattoo sighed. "Couple tables around made out of stuff to look like boulders. Yeah, I *could* do that. Give me the time and inclination. But I ain't listening to any more of her stories about mean old men who change to coyotes, or maybe it was bats, and drag off children and stuff. Do kids really need to hear those tales? That's what I'm wondering."

Anastasia smiled. "Oh, I knew you'd think of something." To Willi she said, "Besides helping out on unloading new inventory in the back warehouses, and working as our fix-it person on minor plumbing and electrical and such, Tattoo has a wonderful bent toward creativity that's beginning to serve us well."

"More'n likely, she ain't gonna like whatever I do, the old battleaxe."

Anastasia bowed her head.

"Little by little, step by step," Willi said.

Rolling her eyes, Anastasia said, "Baby steps."

A beeper on Tattoo's overalls went off. "Aww, stuff for display number six is ready to be unloaded soon as I get my rear in gear and check off inventory. Gotta scoot. Ms. Gallagher, hope to see you and your Mr. Investigator down to the Oxhandlers Barbecue and Emporium soon. Enjoyed our visit the other night." She did a quarter-step turn and added, "Anytime you want, I'd be glad to meet you at the pistol range. The one you went to last Thursday, that's the same one I practice at, you know."

"Really?" Willi studiously avoided Anastasia's look that had *I love it* written all over it.

Grinning, Anastasia asked, "Tattoo, you're into antique firearms, also?"

"Antique? No way. The .357 Magnum, which is a .40 caliber handgun, yes ma'am. It'll blow a pretty decent hole in someone. Same as Ms. Gallagher's. I'd really better scoot now. I'll check with you when the inventory's done." With a last rub down Ludwig's form, she sauntered away, tennis-shoe clad feet splayed outward in a no-nonsense swagger.

As Anastasia led the way into the meeting room, she pushed a remote button to open the draperies. Willi shut her eyes for a moment, awaiting the inevitable question. Anastasia, however, said something she didn't expect. "What's Quannah doing out riding horses, now?"

"He's helping track down three escaped convicts from the Huntsville Prison."

"Yes, I saw some of those men on Channel Five last night."

"Lady officers, too," Willi said, "but he was in the lead." She lifted her chin. "That trio is a nasty bunch."

"Not embezzlers, I take it."

"Hardened criminals due up for numerous counts of murder—two right near the outskirts of Nickleberry."

"Good grief, Willi, do you think they'd come this way? Do they have relatives here? That's why you—"

Willi smacked her lips and cleared her throat. Fine. Let Anastasia believe she'd purchased a gun because of the fear of the escaped cons. Oh, if only it were that simple.

She rushed to say, "That's part of what Quannah is checking out. My last cell phone message from him was short, clipped, businesslike, so there's been no success." Willi glanced at her watch. "I want to meet a few minutes with the other curator candidates this morning. I hope they'll be on time."

"Not to worry. Another two hours and you can drive over to

the airport and pick him up. In more ways than one, maybe. Whoo-hoo."

"You are so bad."

"Sometimes it's good to be bad." Anastasia pulled out a chair at the head of the oval table. "Here's your place for the day, Ms. Willi Gallagher."

"Shouldn't that be yours?"

"Normally, but I'll sit to the side with the other contenders." She flashed a smile to rival the sun streaming in through the window behind Willi's chair. "Yes, somewhere here with the other contenders."

"Ladies." A Bostonian voice greeted them from the doorway. "Parker Nolan here." He held a silver-tipped cane with which he tapped his very New England hat brim before he twirled the hat and caught it in his left hand. "Posh surroundings I must say for a place I was informed would not be at all metropolitan. However, I was expecting the simple amenity of a hat rack."

Anastasia walked forward with her hand held out, and introduced herself and Willi, before saying, "Here, let me take your hat and cane."

"I prefer to keep the cane, if you don't mind, but the hat, of course, please."

With it in hand, she turned around, pushed a button on the wall that opened a large closet with full-length mirror. "Perhaps this amenity will serve."

"Yes, quite. Thank you."

"Please have a seat," Willi said. "I'd like to get to chat this morning with each of you running for the post of curator for the Nickleberry Museum."

Nolan pulled out a chair and gestured for Anastasia to sit. She shook her head. "Thank you, but I'll go check on refreshments before everyone arrives. I'll be right back."

With a bow of his head, Parker Nolan took the chair, crossed his legs, hooked the head of the cane upon the table edge, and steepled his fingers before him. "What details do you need? Thirty-nine."

"I beg your pardon." Willi raised an eyebrow. Great, seconds into the interview and she'd already lost focus. "Thirty-nine?" she asked.

Parker Nolan leaned forward. "My age. Thirty-nine . . . I mentioned my age—being as I am one of the youngest candidates—just to get that out of the way. Stereotypical Bostonian and just as blue-eyed as my English ancestors. Three percent more body fat than I should have despite four days a week at the gym. I do like my own gourmet cooking and enjoy sharing food and home—entertaining, you see. Interest in art and history with majors in both, hence my desire for the position. Most of this, naturally, is in the application."

Willi leaned her head to one side. "Yes, Mr. Nolan—"

"Parker, please."

"Parker, what piqued my curiosity was what wasn't in the typed info."

"Such as?"

"Such as your family background. For example, who are your parents?"

Parker Nolan unwound his fingers and fidgeted with the jaguar-headed cane. "I felt they, and their interests, would have no bearing."

"Maybe so, maybe no. Your father is a judge, I've come to learn, and your mother an interior decorator."

He brushed at the blonde stubble of mustache under his nose. "You employ detectives?"

She ignored that question and said, "As far as I'm concerned the information lets me know that you come from a family with strong work ethics, a sense of community and values befitting leaders. If you're chosen for this position, you'll definitely be a leader in Nickleberry politics."

"That is true." He settled the cane upon the table edge again.

Willi hoped for more, waited a few seconds to allow silence to force him to speak and peeked at her wristwatch. Where in the heck were the others? Professor Stöhr and Dr. Etzli? She sighed and waited another five seconds, but Parker Nolan remained quiet. She said, "Was your first artistic interest engendered by your mother's involvement with designs and fabrics and such?"

"Actually, no. Quite the other way round. Since I broke away from the tight talons . . . from hearth and family wealth, to seek my own way through university, she decided she could also continue her education, although she opted to stay with the Judge. But even that bit of her independence upset the Judge, no end, that did."

"I see." She smiled and tried the silent tactic again. Let him boil in the bean juice a moment.

"Do you?" Parker Nolan reverted to his steepled-finger body language. Sun glinted upon his manicured nails.

Willi brushed a knuckle across the tip of her nose. Okay, so he hadn't even come to a slow simmer. She needed new tactics. Ah well, the pause gave her a moment to think about why a son would call his dad the Judge. Could be a sign of respect. Or not. Maybe His Honor, Judge Nolan, was rather overbearing, family- and money-conscious and ruled with a New England spine of tempered steel, in which case, she could only admire the son for having an equally strong demeanor and character to give up money and comfort for hard work and accomplishments in his own field. She nodded. Parker Nolan, self-made man, could hold his own counsel even under pressure. He'd certainly need that ability in dealing with the supporters and patrons of the new establishment, the general populace of visitors, and certainly the detractors.

She changed the subject. "What's your favorite meal to prepare?"

Parker blinked as if the question took him by surprise. "A particular culinary delight which is one of the reasons I want to settle in Texas."

Willi leaned forward. "Please don't tell me this has anything to do with local pinto bean dishes."

He laughed for the first time, and his eyes lit up as he opened his hands in a relaxed gesture. "Cooking on the grill, preferably outdoors, the Texas barbecue, as it were." He, too, leaned forward in his enthusiasm. "It's a completely different culinary adventure in each area of the country, but Texans seem to have a special corner on the delectable diversion. I'm being quite optimistic and searching now for a home in this area, and insist that the Realtor find a location where I can build my dream outdoor kitchen. And, yes, beans are part of the fare accompanied by a wonderful grilled salmon and honey-glazed vegetables with a steamed-in-foil pilaf that a queen would savor." He raised an eyebrow in a question every female past the age of fifteen recognized, in this case, might she be the queen who would like a taste?

She bowed her head a moment, smiled, and said, "My heart-mate, Quannah Lassiter, and I would love to partake sometime. If you're chosen I hope you'll remember. We Texans tend to be neighborly, given every opportunity."

He acknowledged her status with a slight nod, and said, "Even if not chosen, I'm settling in this area. I'll find something to turn my hand to until the position reopens. I'm the best for the job, I assure you. Proof is in the procurements I've done freelance for other museums. Have your Special Investigator for the Texas Rangers check those things next time he looks into my familial background."

"I didn't say he was a—"

"His name is often in the local papers. As part of my pre-training, I've subscribed to both the town newspapers and the county sheets. As you know, not only does he appear in many law-related articles but also general involvement in the community. One of the last articles was concerned with an Irish Fling Festival and his dancing abilities. And you're often mentioned in the same articles. So . . . I thought you might consult with each other seeing as how you're solving cases together on occasion."

"Very astute of you, Parker. Then you know about many of the supporters of this new museum, too."

"I'm learning of them and the detractors, who think this"—he waved his arm to encompass the museum—"is a waste of city monies and federal grants. However—"

"However?"

"However, I wonder if I might impose when needed to ask the indomitable *Miss Marple of the Range* questions as needed?"

"Guess you read that in the papers, too. Touché, Parker Nolan, touché." She grinned, beginning to like the easy repartee and the gentle wit of this displaced Bostonian with his bent toward barbeque and beans. Yes, Parker Nolan knew how to work with people, and had the deftness to turn the tables sideways, backwards or upside down, she'd bet.

Now, where in Blue Blazes were the others? Being late did not speak well for them. Despite the momentary relief from worry, before she met with Quannah, she needed to get some time in at the gun range. The mantra ran through her mind. *Practice makes perfect. Practice makes perfect.*

Rather than checking her wristwatch, she glared at the bronze sun clock on the wall. *Make hay while the sun shines, folks, and be quick about it.*

A screech from the hallway brought her out of her chair. She beat Parker Nolan to the door by a millisecond, and he must have moved like a souped-up engine. He not only carried his cane, but had retrieved his hat.

The banshee caterwauling grated worse than sharpened claws on an old blackboard. Willi reached into her shoulder bag and gritted her teeth. Hell's bells and damn it, she had left the pistol in the car trunk.

CHAPTER TWO

Beware the words that bring one fear;
Such fanged creatures are ever near.

—Zatiio
The Book of the Ancient Ones

With a deft movement of his cane, Parker Nolan held the door open, and Willi rushed out. Ludwig's howls joined the cacophony and sent a jolt through Willi's spine. Running as fast as her heels and skirt allowed, she rushed around the waterfall, down the hall toward the pyramid and Chacmool. Willi broke through a crowd of two of the cleaning staff, Tattoo, Anastasia Zöllmer, and another gentleman who was rotund of tummy, short of stature, but loud of voice.

"Pick up the mongrel!" he yelled. He would not have needed a microphone in a normal-sized auditorium.

Willi studied his features. Oh my gosh, he had to be kin to the Oxhandlers minus the tallness and broad shoulders. He definitely had the Oxhandler stentorian voice, and something about the features, even in the puffy face, bespoke of the Nickleberry Oxhandler lineage.

"Get that nasty-footed beast off the floor!"

The Hispanic cleaners yelled out, too. *"La sangre. Dios mio, mire la sangre. Pobrecito perro."*

At the perplexed look upon the large man's face, Willi translated. "She said to look at all the blood and poor puppy."

"The mutt! Pick him up!" yelled the Oxhandler look-alike.

Anastasia scooped Ludwig into her arms, and with anger seething from every fiery glance, she ground out the words, "Don't refer to Ludwig again in such a manner."

Willi quieted the two Hispanics—one a young man, another a woman of perhaps fifty—Mexican laborers under Tattoo's tutelage. These two helped with the heavier work as part-timers.

The woman held a hand over her heart. *"Madre de Dios."*

Willi patted her arm. "Are you okay, Mrs. Oñadiz?"

"I don't know. Maybe now okay."

"What happened? Why were you screaming?" Willi guided Mrs. Oñadiz to a settee in front of the pyramid display.

"Look. You look here and *allá*. I think maybe it's the jaguar of the old tales. See?" She pointed to the floor.

Red paw prints formed a pattern that crisscrossed upon itself three or four times going up and down the pyramid steps and circling the small gathering. Willi said, "I don't think we have to worry about it being a big cat of any kind."

"Certainly not," the round gentleman roared. "Ridiculous! Here is the culprit. This mongrel in the arms of his mistress." The gentleman patted his paunch and raised a hand before Anastasia could open her mouth. "Not meant as derogatory comment upon his lineage, madam, merely descriptive of his actions." He reached out and rubbed behind Ludwig's ears, causing the silly mutt to grin and slobber.

Parker Nolan stepped up. "Is the little fellow bleeding? Had an accident, perhaps? Here, Ms. Zöllmer, let me hold him for you. You're shaking."

Between him and the Oxhandler kinsman, they oohed, ah-hed, and finally he of the ripe vocals announced, "Not hurt, no. Neither cut nor bruised, it seems." He took a handkerchief out and wiped Ludwig's paws.

Mrs. Oñadiz said, "Me. I think it is me."

"You're bleeding?" Willi asked.

Assured her precious Ludwig was enjoying the attention and not in the least harmed, Anastasia rushed toward Mrs. Oñadiz. "Where are you hurt? What happened?"

Mrs. Oñadiz patted her forehead with the palm of her hand. "No. I make the dog do the barking. I scream when I see all the blood. The dog, he barks and runs through it. No, no, now I am so confused. The dog, he was growling, up at the top like he was chasing someone away." She pointed to the apex of the pyramid where the backstage, as it were, was covered with billowing orange and red curtains. "Yes, then I come and he really starts the barking. He no leave all the marks, I don't think."

"Blood?" Willi exchanged a glance with Anastasia. "I thought maybe it was paint that Tattoo had brought in for the storyteller's divider."

Tattoo bent down, studied the stains, and said, "I've had the inclination since we talked, but no time to chew on the job. Me and Ignacio here heard the screeching and barking. We come running. You know what I know, but this ain't blood, and it ain't no regular paint."

Parker Nolan, cane resting in the crook of his arm, handed the pug-nosed hound to the rotund gent. "I'm Parker Nolan. Sorry. Don't know your name, sir."

"Hmph. Professor Stöhr. I was setting up the train displays on the tracks leading in from the old warehouses of Nickleberry Station. Shall I hold him while you inspect the paint?"

"Quite right." He bent down with Tattoo. "Not blood, but rather a wash of some sort, probably tempera paints, wouldn't you say, sir?"

Professor Stöhr handed off Ludwig to his mistress. He straightened a green brocade vest over his ample tummy, twisted a gold button and smiled. "No doubt, no doubt. It comes in dried form. Little mutt might have slobbered in it, then tromped around, giving us the impression of a wild beast's paws. Animals are smart. He then sets up a fuss so he won't be blamed for it, but rather some beast of the shadows. Ah, yes, he is a smart one. Ah, I wish to apologize to all and to this fellow—ah—he is so cute. I myself get a bit excited when others do, you see? Like an old teakettle set to the boil, off I blow steam, and then all is over, yes? Yes, I believe you are right, Mr. Nolan, it's paint that merely resembles blood."

Willi sighed. Thank Great Spirit for that. She glanced at her watch. "Professor Stöhr, you're the one I'm to visit with next." She rubbed her hands together. "But, we do need to stay and find out who was so careless as to leave tempera paint out. Luckily, it cleans up easily, right, Tattoo?"

"Hope so. We'll see."

Anastasia rubbed Ludwig's short body, and smiled. "You go ahead and chat. Tattoo and Ignacio will locate the *who* and *why* behind . . . this." She locked one arm with Parker Nolan's and guided him back toward the offices.

"But—"

"It's up to you," Anastasia said over her shoulder. "Now when does that biplane land? Didn't you miss breakfast and the brunch? You'll have to do the interview and get something to eat before you meet the investigator, right?"

"But, Dr. Etzli—"

"I'll find out what the delay is with Dr. Etzli and have him call you on your cell phone, okay?"

Willi swallowed. If she talked with Professor Stöhr, she could get away to the comfort and advice of Quannah, and perhaps ease the fear tagging along in her wake. With that reflection, the tightness in her neck and shoulders eased. The thoughts about the shooting range slunk farther back in her mind. Yes, a pow-wow with Quannah would do wonders for her. The sooner the better.

"Madam Chairwoman, that is you, Ms. Gallagher, yes? I have a suggestion," Professor Stöhr said, both hands splayed open upon his chest. "I myself will take you to a delightful luncheon if first you will ride to the train sheds with me. I have something most important to show you inside one of them. A situation deserving of your attention." He swung one hand outward to show her a golf cart, one of three used to maneuver quickly through the museum, from the old Santa Fe depot and rails and back.

Tattoo, hands on her hips, stepped up to Professor Stöhr. "Shouldn't be anything more in those sheds you need, sir. My crew and I had all the big items moved up weeks ago."

Stomach to stomach, the two glared at each other. Professor Stöhr smiled benignly. "And an excellent job you did, too, I must say. All my instructions were followed to the dotted 'i' and the crossed 't' in every detail. Thank you. No, this is just a . . . a tiny discrepancy of which those in administration need to be made aware."

"Yeah? Well, I'll just drive you both, then."

"Tattoo." Willi opened her eyes wide and said, "Why don't you take care of this emergency? Your supervisory skills are needed here."

Already the professor had seated himself, turned the ignition and waited. As he drove away, Willi cocked her head to hear Tattoo. "Anything wrong out that-a-way, I'll see to it. I'll do the fixin', you hear?"

He kept the vehicle to the right side on a darker area of stone which marked the section used for the carts' travel lane. He drove past the entire half block of the pyramid display, around three others of ancient times, and finally rode through a dank tunnel of walls made of railroad ties. Just the scent of the treated wood transported Willi to an older time and place of the 1800's.

"This," Professor Stöhr said, waving his beringed fingers at a

33

locomotive attached to a diner, sleeper, and caboose of that age, "is part of my display. But, later, we look later. Now, I wish to show you something farther along."

As they careened through the swinging doors and into the old above ground depot area, Willi grew a bit concerned. After all, she didn't know beans—limas or *frijoles*—about this man, other than his application info and references. And, references could sure be tampered with. But, she had no real reason to feel such uneasiness, and he did say there was a problem in one of the train storage sheds. How else could he show her? The reason for her gun practice which she wouldn't explain to and therefore cause worry for her friend Anastasia, loomed for a moment in her own mind. A stalker had been following her, leaving threatening notes. This rotund man, whom she'd never before met, could hold no dangerous intent toward her, surely. Still, she'd be careful. She inched as far away on the seat as she could. The situation necessitating her trips to the gun range affected her thinking about everyone. She preferred to call it a healthy paranoia. No one could hear even bloodcurdling screams from this far down the old Nickleberry Santa Fe tracks. Belatedly, she said, "Perhaps we should look at this with all the other committee members."

"No, no. Madam Chairperson, you may report to them. None but you were to come today. Only you, Ms. Gallagher. What a shame they leave such a lovely young lady as you to do all the dirty work."

"Yes, that it is, a shame."

Oh, Great Spirit, please, don't let this be the one, the man I've feared to meet for over a month now. The one who's been leaving less than benign messages in my pathway at school, out in the community, on my car.

She wasn't ready; she'd confided in no one, only prepared herself as best she could. Oh, sure. Prepared. Right. She was as prepared for a battle as an overturned turtle. All those hours in target practice and the self-protection classes seemed silly at the moment. She wore heels, not her tennis shoes, and her precious, loaded pistol was locked away in her car trunk. Good place for it.

Her tongue dried up like an old gym sock. She covered her mouth and blew into her hand to test her breath. What in Hades was she doing? Who cared if her breath offended if she were laid out upon one of these forsaken and seldom visited tracks? Or worse. Maybe locked into one of the twenty-seven or so warehouses on both sides of the multilane tracks?

"How much farther?" she asked, while she got ready to throw off her shoes and sprint if needed. By daggum, she'd have no trouble outrunning the stout man. Yeah, she was fine. Everything was fine. At least, she was on orange alert and could react if something did happen. Beads of perspiration moistened her skin, yet she couldn't work up a hint of moisture to make more small talk.

"Madam Chairperson, are you all right?" He didn't wait for an answer, but swerved the cart into the pitch-black interior of shed number seventeen. This workspace, like all in the old complex, meandered through a quarter mile, at least, of soaring ceilings, numerous huge storage areas where a phalanx of eighteen-wheelers would feel right at home.

Willi's heart dropped a beat, and she managed to croak, "Watch out! You can't see—"

He clicked on the headlights. "Be not alarmed, Ms. Gallagher. Ah, it is just down here. Yes, I am sure this is the area."

A sharp right turn, another left and he stopped the vehicle. "Back there. We will have to walk a few feet. The cart cannot maneuver through the smaller aisles, you see." He went over to a breaker unit on a center pole and flipped a switch. Yellowish light swathed one end of the warehouse. Overhead, ancient fluorescent bulbs, most of which needed to be replaced, glared down on her.

Willi's hair stood up on the nape of her neck, and she rubbed her wet palms against her skirt. Everything about this moment shouted *red alert* which meant she should not, absolutely should not under any circumstances be following this man through tunnels of rusted machinery which had probably not been put to use for the last couple of decades. And yet, she marched onward. As Quannah had taught her, she quieted the inner turmoil for one moment by counting and breathing consciously.

Okay, she was not a fool. With that many alarm signals, why *was* she still pursuing Professor Stöhr? After a moment's pause, she allowed the knots in her shoulders to ease, as that inner knowing reached her conscious thoughts. The signals making her nervous weren't directly from Professor Stöhr. She grinned at his rounded rump bending over in front of her. No, she did not feel threatened by the gentleman. *This area.* That's what was making her as jumpy as water hitting hot grease in granny's skillet.

Moving aside so she could look around his generous rear, he said, "See, Madam Chairperson? This we cannot allow. Even in these far reaches. So much of the equipment, which will take years to restore for the museum, could be damaged by such things. It is good that I survey constantly, yes? Since my arrival three days ago, I have been through all the warehouses, all the sheds, every nook and cranny. And this I discovered this morning. What do you think?"

Willi's temples throbbed as if someone tapped an old rail spike just above her left eye. She kicked aside some of the debris—red cardboard packs of French fries, cartons from which tumbled half-eaten egg rolls, take-out plates from Catalina's Mexican restaurant with blackened guacamole dip left in one corner. "Good grief, this is absolutely not acceptable on the premises. I *will* see the workers know they can't leave the remains of lunches on the floor. I'm truly flabbergasted."

"Me, I do not think this is caused by the staff. They have a lounge and often eat out in one of the café pavilions around the museum." Professor Stöhr stood up, straightened his vest and splayed his wide fingers across his ample frontage. "Bums. Street people. Even the smallest burgs have them nowadays. Ah, but they cannot set up squatters' rights. This is not the 1800's."

"You're right, Professor Stöhr. Do you have a guess as to how they got in? These warehouses are old, but the committee has noted how very secure they were." With index finger and thumb she shifted aside and dropped an orange cloth covered in mechanic's grease. Hmmm. Not flannel. More like thick cotton. Underneath lay bits and pieces of metal. "Wonder what they were looking for here? Are these parts of something mechanical on one of the old engines?"

He bent down, picked up a handful of the broken shards of metal, and peered closely. "I think not. Not old parts, anyway." He laid the bits in her upturned palm.

A beetle scuttled over her foot. She jerked backwards. "Oh my gosh. That garbage is drawing the varmints. I'll talk to Ms. Zöllmer, and she'll get Tattoo to clean and disinfect this area." Willi retreated, tripped over the shredded orange material, picked up the cleanest piece and wrapped the metal collection inside.

"Here, let me dispose of that for you," he said, grabbing it away and dumping it inside a large bin on rollers underneath the fuse box. "You must not get your pretty hands dirty with such refuse." He moved behind one of the monolithic pillars. "There may be more vandalism over here."

She frowned at his peremptory action. She could damned well make up her own mind as to what she'd get her pretty hands on, thank you very much. Before she joined him, she reached in the bin, and tucked one small piece of cloth in the side pocket of her purse. She couldn't retrieve any of the metal pieces. She muttered, "Too far down."

That had been the first negative response she'd had about the professor. Certainly not a biggie, if that attitude didn't again rear its head. He peeked around the pillar and said, "I brought this to your attention because your committee is responsible for security and safety matters."

"We are until the permanent curator takes over."

"And, me, I would be happy to have that responsibility. No one else discovered this breech. Ah, no. Just me. I will keep a watch on all things and guard it like a papa protecting his darlings."

"You have children?"

"No, I refer to the train cars, each with a different story, each with a special mystery, yes?"

"Well, that's some lady's loss. Maybe you'll find the right one in Texas."

"Traveling the world, I've met many lovely and worthy prospects, but alas, no one has accepted my offers. I am blessed with many lady friends to go about to concerts and public functions. Perhaps, as you say, a Nickleberry lady may suit." With thumbs tucked inside his vest pockets, he bounced on his feet. "First priorities first. This beautiful museum. She will be my most cherished darling. After you view my display, and get to know me as a businessman, a creative connoisseur of southwestern art, an able administrator of funds, staff, and buildings, you will know that I, Professor Stöhr, am the best choice. I will stay in Nickleberry until the position comes to me for I have family in this town. The Oxhandlers. You may know them."

"Everyone knows them, but I'm not the only one you must please." She softened her comment with a smile.

"But you hold much power in your hands, and you report all the details, yes?" He rubbed his hands together. "Come now, as promised, let us go to a local eatery of your choice and my treat."

"It's the committee's treat. We Texans wine and dine our contenders right fine, as we say. Each one of you is special. Enjoy while you can."

"As you wish, Madam Chairperson, as you wish." He switched off the warehouse lights, climbed aboard and swung around to pick her up.

A flutter of movement attracted her attention. With one foot in the cart, Willi blinked and narrowed her eyes. "Use your high beams and light up the far corner beside that small door."

"Ah, I believe that leads to an old dismantling shop for smaller parts."

Willing the shadows to dissipate, she peered harder into the gloom. Again she caught movement. Her stomach made a sick little roll. "Looks like . . . oh my gosh . . . like someone collapsed." The stash of old rags and what might have been a tarp, budged to cause a few of the tattered cloths to rustle.

"You wait. You wait here." He straightened his vest and inched out of the cart.

Willi couldn't fault him for lack of courage, but ignored his warning while copying his actions. To the lump of rags that shifted to the left and more into the shadows, Willi said, "Are you all right? Who are you?"

The professor placed a hand on her shoulder and moved around her. "Get up and explain your presence on these private premises."

More shuffling ensued and a distinct odor drifted from the bunched cloth. Willi sniffed and beads of sweat broke out and ran between her shoulder blades. *Oh my gosh. That stench.* "Pro . . . Profes . . . Professor, just quietly back away."

"Lady Chair, I will just—" He reached to grab the man's shoulder.

"*Don't*. Come on. Now, now, *now.*" Willi grasped the professor's arm, propelled him around and shoved him into the passenger side. In the driver's seat, she hit the gas and reverse, backing around columns, doing a one-hundred-eighty-degree turn while the wheels slid across an old grease spot, and finally got the cart going toward the outward doors. As the last of the headlights swung across the recumbent figure, Professor Stöhr gasped. "Oh, my God. I see him clearly. This way. Faster. He is coming after us."

Willi dug her foot into the floorboard, whizzed around a hideous collection of gears the size of a Tyrannosaurus rex, and scooted outside into the sunshine.

Hanging on with one foot dangling on the ground, Professor Stöhr roared. "Stop. Madam Chair, stop. We are safe. He has taken a more scenic route."

Hands a-tremble, Willi stomped on the brake, came to a halt and caught sight of their pursuer as he swung his black and white striped tail around the corner of shed number seventeen.

He said, "That could have been a most unpleasant encounter."

"Do tell. Hell's bells, we have more than one type of unwelcome skunk entering the premises. Tattoo has her work cut out for her."

Seated across from Professor Stöhr at a window table at Catalina's restaurant, Willi closed her eyes for a moment to enjoy the Mexican music, then opened them to admire the tile work, the muted lighting, and the golden stonework. A soft background rendition of *Tú Solo Tú* wove its way through the lively conversations. Professor Stöhr peered around the room and asked, "Did you not say Dr. Ernesto Etzli and his aide, Mr. Yaotle, were to meet us here?"

"Yes, that was another reason I wanted to eat here, but his aide did say there was an expected shipment, and they might have to reschedule." Two former students, Johnson Skall and Leonard Bishop, bustled around the table.

"More chips, Ms. Gallagher?" Leonard asked with a grin. "You don't even have to give us extra points."

After introducing them to the professor, she said, "It's been a few years since you've needed extra points on anything. How's UT at Arlington treating you?"

"Super," chimed in Johnson, the tallest of the duo by a head and a half. He set Professor Stöhr's beer down. "Both of us tested out for credit for Freshman English and for two semesters on our Spanish. Be sure and tell Mrs. Kartman, okay?" He placed a fresh set of the restaurant's pepper shakers—ceramic skunks with sombreros—on the table.

Oh, great, skunks. Hairs rose upon her arms. If Quannah had encountered a trio in one day—three *signs*—three *lessons*—he'd call them. This was her second opportunity with the black and white critters today. So what in Hades was there to learn from a skunk? Certainly there was a skunk of a person with a malicious bent stalking her for the last month, leaving messages. Since the first notes had been at school, she figured it was some pettiness on a student's part for a low grade. But the notes had escalated to volatile, and had bothered her enough to get her to the firing range. As if that would do any good, since she couldn't, and wouldn't even if she could, carry a gun to school. She'd overreacted to the first notes, had absolutely no clue as to why the silly things had frightened her so badly, but . . . she had trusted her instincts. She rubbed her head. Just what she needed on top of everything else zipping around in her brain today—ponderings upon the skunk meaning, and did she count the salt and pepper shakers as one or two signs? If things came in at least three's as Quannah insisted, had she had three or only two encounters? Why was she even worrying about it? She answered herself. *Anything served to get her mind off watching constantly over her shoulder, constantly wondering if the next note would come with a face-to-face confrontation.*

"Ms. Gallagher?"

"Yes?"

"You'll let Mrs. Kartman know?"

"Of course, of course. I'm proud of you boys. She will be, too."

When they moved away to place the orders, Professor Stöhr blew the foam to better reach his brew, raised his glass to her, then tapped a finger on the sombrero-clad shakers. "Ah, these might have seemed cuter a half hour ago before our close encounter."

"Indeed." Her cell phone rang. She checked the ID—LASSITER. "Sorry, I usually turn off the ringer when eating."

Quannah quickly explained he'd get one of the men in the field to bring him and the horses to Nickleberry during the late afternoon instead of coming in the official biplane to the Nickleberry Airport. "Sorry, Gallagher."

"I understand. I hear the dust and grit in your voice, Lassiter. You and your eagle eyes took the last-sweep position, didn't you? You *are* taking lunch breaks and drinking plenty of water, right? And—"

"Gallagher, you know me." With that less-than-clear answer, he hung up.

"Ms. Gallagher." A sophomore, Selma Hazeltine, came up to the table. Dressed all in black down to her nail polish, she sneered the greeting.

Willi said, "Hello, Selma. How are you, Edie?" The well-dressed lady accompanying Selma nodded at Willi and the professor. Willi said, "Professor Stöhr, Selma is an exchange student from Germany."

"Ah, where my own forefathers came from, yes. Nice to meet you, young lady."

"Yeah, sure."

Professor Stöhr snapped to attention and peered at Edie. "You are her hostess here in the United States?"

"Yes, and it's so nice to meet you. I read an article in *National Geographic* that had a photo of you in Mexico or South Texas, perhaps."

"Both, I have been to both. You have an interest in our historical artifacts, then?"

"She is one," Selma said.

Willi cringed at the teen angst. Thank goodness the girl had failed her class for two of the grading periods and had opted out for the rest of the year, choosing to take a correspondence course instead. And thank Great Spirit that Edie had to deal with the girl's attitude and not her. Willi said, "Edie Rivers is a master teacher the rest of us try to emulate. Her junior English classes are both fun and challenging."

Edie, gracious as ever, thanked her, but with red spots tinting her cheeks giving testimony she was embarrassed by Selma's actions, chose a booth close to the rear of the restaurant and guided Selma in that direction.

Willi's phone immediately rang again. She said, "It's Dr. Etzli. I'd better answer. He might need directions." A moment later she closed the phone. "He's asked that I meet him at his bed and breakfast on Fetchwin Way this evening."

Willi gave Professor Stöhr points for merely shrugging, when he might have preferred to make a derogatory comment about a competitor being late and changing a meeting twice in one day.

"Tell me," she asked, "about the interesting travels you've had through Mexico and Texas concerning certain historical items."

He talked for a few moments with enthusiasm. He patted his gold chain peeking out of his breast pocket. "You understand, Madam Chair, the significance of those procurements?"

"Uh, yes, absolutely." He referred to some fine silver swords and conquistador helmets.

Focus. Listen to the man. Stop thinking about the crazy jerk.

"This," he continued, "was a couple years back. So, you see, already those items have increased in worth."

"Wonderful. Again, you purchased them where?"

He frowned and leaned forward, his eyes flashing. Then he nodded, a grin creasing his rounded features. He shook one finger at her. "Ah-ha! I see what you are doing. Observing how I handle different ways of coming at a subject, how I maneuver through the constant questions my position—my possible future position—might provide."

Feeling chagrin at her lack of attention, she said, "I don't know what to say to that."

"You can say you appreciate my bravery in traveling through dense jungle areas of Mexico, traveling through its driest climates and up into the mountains to follow the trail of mere whiffs of tales told by the Indians there. Tracking down the silver by some of the conquistadors—that was, yes, a true adventure. There is much more in some of the small pueblos. Pueblos you might think had nothing but the few burros and the dirt upon which their hooves trod. But not so. There in the villages and the haciendas spread around them, many artifacts are guarded, just as the old sword hilts and helmets were. More to be had, yes, for the Nickleberry Museum someday."

"Perhaps. So you've actually stood upon some of the ancient Aztecan pyramids?" Her earlier morning vision sent a lightning flash of blood dripping through the priest's fingers and down into the bowl of Chacmool.

"Oh, yes. You are aware of the recent archeological finds in

Texas which seem to prove the Aztecs resided here, or traveled here often to trade. That is the article to which Mrs. Rivers alluded."

"Ms. I don't believe Edie's ever married."

"Indeed. Perhaps that explains why she gives her time to help with the exchange program."

"Perhaps. Go on. Tell me more, Professor."

"I did some most interesting studies with the descendents of members of the Jaguar clans who believed they could shape shift. Also, I became privy to some of the ways they—meaning the ancient members of the clan—did away with enemies. Quite a sanguinary study that was."

"Bloody—sanguinary—yes. I can . . . I can imagine."

"They had more subtle ways, too. A gas found in the caves of Mexico, probably all over the southwest, was used most ingeniously when less violence was needed."

"They gassed their enemies?"

"No, Madam Chair. It seems this gas was harmless unless mixed with smoke. So they reduced the gas to liquid form, coated the cooking bowls or pipes, and voilá, they were able to be many miles away before the smoke mixed with the gas and killed the enemy. Not always foolproof. I suppose in ancient times they might not have had the sophisticated measuring devices, so sometimes they only sent their victims into a faint." He rubbed his hands together. "So, you see? I have many interests and possibilities to bring to the museum now and in the future as my circle of southwestern contacts increases."

"And the committee will decide in due course, but I will keep all of this in mind and share with the other members."

"I wish to talk of you and the community for a moment, if I may?"

"Of course, you deserve to know what you're getting yourself into if you get the Nickleberry post."

"Quite obviously your students like and respect you. It is a perk when one is dining, yes?"

"It gives you that warm and fuzzy feeling and much needed confirmation that your pulling them along through Hardy, Melville, Frost, Shakespeare, verb conjugations and essay writing might have left some lasting impressions upon them. My colleague, Mrs. Kartman, will be thrilled to hear she did such an excellent job they both tested out of two levels of Spanish." Willi ducked her head and drank greedily from the rum and pineapple concoction.

Johnson Skall placed a steaming plate before her. "Two onion and cheese enchiladas, light on the sauce, no beans, no rice, right?"

"Thanks, Johnson."

"Most welcome, Ms. Gallagher. And for you, sir, tacos with guacamole on the side. And here's more salsa for both of you. Enjoy. I'll be back to refresh your drinks."

Professor Stöhr said, "Tell me more."

"More?"

"About school. I will be dealing with this community and must know how to meet its needs. Great ideas come from airing views and getting the problems out in the open, yes?"

"I suppose it could work that way, ideally." She took a moment to chew her enchilada. Ah, hot and cheesy and seasoned just perfectly. She drank her piña colada. The sharp ice burn at the bridge of her nose made her wince. She grimaced more as Quannah's face seemed to float before her and his voice intruded into her rum haze. *"Indian woman drink rum, gonna be talking dumb."* She lifted her retroussé nose in the air.

After taking a bite of his guacamole, the professor leaned forward. "Why do you stay? Why do you teach? How do you function with all the negatives we hear about in the news?"

"I stay, like Edie Rivers and others do, because we're good at what we do. Despite all the obstacles and the silly, silly politics, I enjoy the students. Despite the watered-down courses, I work hard to get the information through to them. We get only minimal support from immediate supervisors, so that most of us have had to develop some strange survival philosophies."

"Yes, Madam Chairperson, yes? Your eyes are twinkling. Share, please."

"Many of us have for this year the philosophy that we don't care if students come in buck naked, swinging a machete, guzzling from a bottle of Dos Equis, and are high on marijuana, we don't bother to write them up." She sighed. "If we do write them up, they will only receive a slap on the hand. The rules are not enforced because the administrators don't do their part of the job."

"Ah, ah, ah. I think perhaps you exaggerate a bit, but, even for the moment, it feels good, yes, to take back some control. That is what is lacking on all levels, isn't it?"

"You're very astute. Sharp and quick as a Texas roadrunner, you are, and I'm speaking too freely. Please forgive my interview style today." She shoved the piña colada back.

"No, please. You make me feel like an old friend. Now, this roadrunner sounds most interesting. In fact, all the Texas flora, fauna and fowl intrigue me." He tucked into his food for a few minutes. "Just one more quick question while you are graciously indulging my curiosity about the community. All the teachers make life good at work because they are supportive of one another, yes? I believe my Oxhandler relatives—two cousins of mine—teach at the high school."

"Dan and Neeper Oxhandler. They are supportive and, for the most part, others are, too."

"Ah, so some are trouble makers?"

Willi waved her hand in the air dismissing her words. "Uh . . . just one teacher who's acted strangely lately. Broke into my room a number of times, went through my worksheets. The instructor never explained what was wanted, why there was a break-in. It was very odd. One day the teacher is friendly, the next the idiot won't speak or is out and out nasty in all responses." If she'd confided this to Anastasia, she would have had to give a name or an hour of going down a list of everyone else at school and all the possibilities would have ensued, not to mention that it might have gotten out to the community at large before Willi could truly figure out if this was the stalker. Anastasia wouldn't have intended that to happen, but sometimes the most innocent of remarks could lead to the greatest rumors in a town such as Nickleberry. And, somehow, Willi instinctively accepted that this rotund man she had feared at first was going to be one of those who had tight lips.

"Well, do not fear my speaking to anyone of this, until you resolve it as needed, Madam Chair. But, tell me, what did you do? Try to reason?"

Willi grinned. Yes, he would keep her confidence. "Oh, conferences did no good. After one of our visits together, the janitor caught the snooper in my room again, lifting papers. Finally, I approached the principal and vice-principal, and suggested they take the master key away. They swore five different ways from last Sunday no one but they and the trusted janitorial hall leaders had one, and that I had to stop making unfounded accusations."

Willi frowned. Maybe those notes hadn't come from a student, maybe . . . but, oh, surely, surely not from a teacher . . . a professional. She shook her head.

"At any rate," she finished. "They did talk to the instructor about my concerns, and I suppose that frightened the sneak away."

"Teaches the same subject?"

"No. Three hallways away, in fact." Willi again shook her

head. Good grief and fried jalapeños. What in Hades was she bringing that up for at this moment? *Guess that ugliness had niggled and bothered more than I realized.* "A friend knowledge-able in psychology told me to stay away from further confronta-tion. Said the erratic behavior might presage a personal emotional crisis and worse actions. So that's what I've done."

She shook her finger at the professor. "I repeat you are very astute, and no more piña coladas for today, thank you very much. You've made me as gabby as Elba Kachelhoffer."

"And she is?"

"Beloved friend and neighbor. She and her sister, Agatha, practice white witchcraft—herbal remedies and such—and with their friend Viola Fiona, operate the only teahouse in Nickle-berry. Elba is known for her penchant for trio comparisons and voicing her opinions whether asked for or not. Neither of the other two is shy about that, either, and all three have hearts of gold. Just to let you in on the know, Agatha and our Sheriff Tucker are seeing each other. Now, that's all the local gossip you'll get from me. When you visit your cousins, I'm sure they'll fill you in on more."

"Ah, Madam Chair, I appreciate the relaxing atmosphere and the opportunity—"

He shoved back his plate. "Forgive me. There is reason to my curiosity." He splayed his hands across his brocade vest. "What I can do to alleviate problems in the community and school, I do not *yet* know, but be assured, I will actively start to work on it now. Furthermore, I say to you and your colleagues: Please, do not give up your good fight in the trenches. Just the two former students whom I've met today attest to you doing much right despite the provocations to do otherwise. Keep your chin up, Ms. Willi Gallagher, and stay with the work. It is so important. So very important." He opened his hands. "I will not batter you with more questions now. I appreciate the relaxing atmosphere and the opportunity—"

He broke his speech off as a boy of about twelve ran up to the table, slammed down a crumpled envelope and ran outside. Willi grew lightheaded and knew it had nothing to do with her rum drink, but everything to do with the pristine white eight-and-a-half-by-five envelope in front of her, just like the others she'd been receiving for the last month.

Willi gasped. "What in the world? Grab him!"

CHAPTER THREE

By the dark of night the blood will flow
And the gods of life their power will show.

—Cod'ahco
The Book of the Ancient Ones

"Go!" Willi yelled. "Grab him!"

Leonard Bishop, first out the door, raced around the corner. Johnson Skall cut through the kitchen. In less than two minutes they were back with the boy neatly keyholed between them. Johnson said, "You shouldn't be bothering Ms. Gallagher. When she says stop, you stop, you hear?"

When the boy didn't answer, Leonard Bishop must have put pressure on his arm, because he shouted. "Okay. Okay. Whatever. What's it to you guys?"

Willi waved the envelope in front of his face. "What's your name?"

"None of your—" He grimaced at Leonard, who smiled sweetly while obviously applying more attitude adjustment to the kid's arm. "Kit, my name's Kit Destlerson."

Professor Stöhr tapped on the brown paper. "Ah, it is addressed to you, Ms. Gallagher."

She nodded. "Yes, and I want to know why you delivered this here, who told you to, and—"

"—Nobody tells me nothing."

"Anything."

51

"Like I said, lady, like I said."

Willi narrowed her eyes, slapped the envelope on the table, and in a steel-magnolia voice dripping with sweetness and cool-ness, accented each of her words. "Who? Why? I want to know now. Right now."

"Don't matter to me. Some guy." He glared up at Leonard. "Loosen up your hold. He gave me five dollars to run in and give it to you."

"You knew who he meant when he said Ms. Gallagher?" Willi asked, leaning closer to him.

"Gallagher. Don't know no Gallagher."

"Any."

"Whatever, lady. He pointed you out through the window. Give me the five. I ran in. Did the deed. So, can I go?"

"What's his name?"

"Duh-uh. What idiot would identify hisself—?"

"Himself, you little—"

"—Whatda ya? An English teacher? Chill it off, lady."

Leonard gave one of his sweetest grins. "We could dunk him in the toilet before they flush, Ms. Gallagher, you say the word."

"I still like the way you think, Leonard." To Kit Destlerson, she said, "Ponder before you speak, and describe him like you were doing it for . . . for your English teacher. All details count."

"He's black. Skinny. He smelled."

"Smelled as in dirty? Did he smoke, smell of marijuana? Dirty, how?"

"Like old mops and too strong aftershave. He drew out four five-dollar bills and slid me one. Lady, that's all."

Johnson Skall spoke up. "You've got Dockers and an ironed tucked-in shirt. You look as if a rich mama dressed you to look like a grown-up, so what'd you need five bucks for from a stranger?"

"Duh-uh. To get cool duds, not this crapola. It's embarrassing. Lady, that's all I know. Can I go now?"

Willi couldn't believe there wasn't some tidbit more, something to help her identify this black man who was stalking her and leaving ugly notes throughout her personal space whether at school or community. "What *exactly* did he say?"

When he balked, Leonard said, "Round and around in the bowl he goes, 'round and arou—"

"Okay. Give this to that woman. That one there with the man in the vest. He pointed through the window, okay? He said to hand it to you personal like and run." Kit sighed as only preteens and teens can sigh, as if everything in life is such a gargantuan effort the most common emotions must be expressed in **Rockwell Extra Bold** font in sixteen-point size. "And then, lady, he said, 'I'll give you part of . . . uh . . . five dollars.' I said, 'I want the whole five,' and he pulled out four and handed me off one. Ain't nothing else."

"There's nothing else."

"Lady, you heard of Valium?"

"You heard of high school?"

"I'm only in seventh grade."

"Well, Kit Destlerson, you'll be seeing me in sophomore English when you get to Nickleberry High. Before you arrive, I hope you improve your attitude, your language and your acquaintances."

"Shall we set him free upon an unsuspecting world until then, Ms. Gallagher?"

"Yes, let him go."

They escorted him to the door while Professor Stöhr again tapped the brown envelope. "What is it?"

Willi closed her eyes a moment and swallowed. "Let me see." With index fingers she twirled it around to see the writing. "Hmmm. Cut out of magazines, no doubt."

"Perhaps a surprise from some of your students."

Willi put warm hands to suddenly chilled cheeks. *Good grief, I must be paler than cream gravy.* "Yes," she managed. "Might very well be from a present-day student." Goose bumps cascaded over one another racing down her arms. With her unused knife, she slit it open. A folded sheet slid out. "Again with the cut-out magazine letters."

"What does it say? Ah, it is your birthday, perhaps? What a . . . uh . . . novel way of delivery."

"No, I was a December baby, not a Halloween urchin."

The one sentence blasted out in a mosaic of red, purple and orange letters, some upper case, others lower case.

YoU **WILL sUfFEr for What** *U* dID **b**itch.

The goose bumps raced each other into a chill that made her shiver. "It . . . uh . . . doesn't say anything important. Silly prank." She slid the half sheet back inside, tried to muster up a cheery face, and said, "Yes, silly prank by kids. Perhaps a clue to some surprise planned in my sophomore English class." Her hand trembled as she shoved the envelope into her purse. She peered at herself in the metal water pitcher. Eyes as round as Minnie Mouse, she blinked. She'd think about the crazed stalker later. She could not imagine anyone of that description who would have any reason to do something so . . . so . . . crazy.

YoU **WILL sUfFEr for What** *U* dID **b**itch.

Here, she'd almost been hoping it was the erratic co-worker, but this incident seemed to give lie to that idea. She wished she'd saved the first messages begun a month ago. Not until the third and fourth one did she take them seriously. Those two had included that nasty appellation: bitch. Perhaps it was a popular pseudonym, even self-imposed by today's raunchier youth, but she found it repulsive and . . . and embarrassing that anyone would apply it to her. But the word had been on the note taped to her door at school, another on her windshield after she came out of Whataburger right after a football game, and now, this third one. She would add it to the other two at home. She'd not told Quannah about the first notes, because she'd really thought they were a student prank. She'd signed up for gun practice after the one found on her door. By then, she'd decided she was a strong woman, used to taking care of her daily problems and refused to go whimper and whine to him. She peered over at Edie and Selma. Yes, perhaps a sick kiddo with attitude out the wazoo, but not Selma. Edie, thank goodness, kept a tight rein on the girl, and Selma did have her bright moments in that she was president of the Science Club, a member of the ROTC. Willi much preferred her in her Wednesday dress uniform than her black attire. No, these attacks had the acid taste of embittered adultness to them.

Again, she envisioned Quannah's features, his hooded eyes, his calm—most of the time—demeanor, his pony tail tied back with a leather thong, his Stetson hat. She and Quannah had not gotten together as so many couples did, simply for co-dependency. A mutual respect, a growing and constantly tested trust, a deep love had drawn them together—along with a couple of murders. Quannah had little respect for crybabies who made themselves victims and refused to fight back. Hence, her buying the handgun, renewing her license-to-carry and her practice sessions at the range.

A shiver rippled down her back as condensation rippled down the water pitcher turning her visage into a watery distortion—a frightened woman who wanted more than anything at the moment to run to her man's arms for protection. Well, she could at least, at the first opportunity, give him the facts and ask for his law officer advice and viewpoint. She took a sip of water, then gulped down the entire glassful. Somehow, she got through more conversation with the professor and talked to Johnson and

Leonard about their upcoming fall exams.

When she'd paid the bill and left a hefty tip, she said, "I can say I've truly enjoyed my time with you, Professor Stöhr. I'm sure we'll be talking many times through this process."

"It will be my pleasure. Now, I know you have other . . . concerns . . . and places to be. I myself will walk through this part of town and perhaps meet some of my distant cousins, Ozzie Oxhandler and his sons, before making my way back to the museum." He tapped his fingers on his vest. "Perhaps I will encounter a dark, skinny man who smells of strong aftershave and old mops."

"And you would do what? Call me? The police?"

"Me? I would ask him *who* paid *skinny* the twenty dollars to deliver the envelope. The little boy let that slip. He only got five, but the real contact received twenty. That's what I would ask, yes."

Willi hit her head with the palm of her hand. Damn, fear could stop the most basic thought processes—well, fear and a hefty draft of rum. She smiled at the professor and said, "I like the way you think."

But, she sure as hot Hades didn't like the way the creep thought.

YoU Will sUfFEr for What U dID bitch.

Now, wait a cotton-pickin' minute, as her granny used to say. No reason why she couldn't go along and hunt down the varmint with the professor. Quannah's phone call left no doubt that he'd not be available at least until this evening. From experience, she also surmised that emotionally he might need some down time before he helped her tackle her particular threat. She didn't want to take his focus away from what was most important—protecting the citizens from a couple of killers. And, he certainly would do so if he thought his lady—his Winyan—was in any danger. So, with Quannah out in the fields—literally out in the fields on horseback—searching out three escaped convicts, he'd be busier than a summertime's hornet's nest for awhile. Sure, there'd be no reason she couldn't go investigate with the professor. Nothing other than the queasiness of her legs upon standing, the doubtful sloshing of her stomach, and the distinct repeat taste of the rum. She could chase after the five-dollar cheapskate or finally do what she wanted to earlier in the day. If she went with the professor, her professionalism as chairperson would certainly be compromised by bringing him into a personal situation. If she went to the range, she'd be giving in to her fear of the stalker.

Really, the dilemma wasn't the most difficult in her life, yet she seemed to stand like a Shelton statue, albeit one with a light covering of rummy perspiration, while pondering upon the two fingers she had held up to help her decide. At last, she moved outside the restaurant foyer. To the left, only a few feet across the parking lot, sauntered Professor Stöhr, and to the right her car and range practice beckoned. She took careful steps until the pineapple aftertaste subsided. By then she had her hand on her door handle and the professor was far down the street. So, she drove to the next county over to the pistol range. The AC had done a commendable job of drying the alcohol from her skin. She knew as a lady of the south, that should have been referred to as her glow, and she could have made that leap if not for an encore of Quannah's visage and statement.

"Indian woman drink rum, gonna be talking dumb."

She didn't bother to change to jeans and tennis shoes. In her cobalt blue jacket, black skirt and heels, she was the most overdressed one on the range. A couple of low wolf whistles did not in the least deter her. In fact, she grinned as she placed the required ear protection over her head. The pull of the gun, the satisfying spray of bullets in the target's chest area, allowed her a moment of reprieve from the fear that had overtaken her since the third note. Nasty swine, whoever they were. By damned when she discovered who they were—and she would find out—they better hope they looked good in Huntsville prison orange. *Big words, sure, while she was safe on the range, with a gun in hand.* She rolled her eyes at her own bravado.

She paused in the middle of reloading. Wait a minute. She pulled out the scrap of cloth from the side pocket of her purse. Maybe those were tatters of . . . nah. She set the pistol on the stand in front of her and rubbed her temples. No, these scraps had grease and oil on them. What had possessed her to even pick them up, she had no idea. Yeah, sure, there were three Huntsville escapees, but those vermin were cornered out in the boonies according to news reports and the cryptic messages she'd received from Quannah. Willi grimaced. Her curiosity and her imagination did sometimes . . . uh . . . maybe on a very few occasions . . . but not often at all . . . might, just might lead her down a daydreaming trail. With the idea of the convicts in her head, she'd immediately jumped to the wrong conclusion. They'd been nowhere near Nickleberry proper, or near the warehouses of the old Santa Fe tracks in back of the museum. She stuffed the pieces back into her purse.

After an hour and a quarter, she reloaded her gun for the last time, placed it in the holster and into her purse before she walked out to a most satisfying clamor of whistles and compliments, not all to do with her shooting skills. The time at the range had clarified her mind. She *must* tell Quannah as soon as possible about the threats. She didn't want to face such a crisis alone anymore. She had a strong, compassionate, and most loving *hombre*. With nose in the air, she decided those qualities up beside his hardheadedness, his bent toward overprotecting her, and his penchant for making her learn more and more about Indian lore even when she balked, stood up just fine.

The chimes of her cell phone rang. "Yes?" Her smile and the

lilt in her voice disappeared as she repeated what Tattoo said on the other end of the line. "Missing? Anastasia, too? Nonsense, Tattoo. She's probably taken a well-deserved long lunch, perhaps at home with Ramblin' if he returned early from his business trip." Willi adjusted her phone as she got into her car and peered at her appointment calendar. "Now stop worrying." *There were definite things to be concerned about, like nasty letters and a stalker, but thank goodness, she didn't have to add sensible Anastasia to the list because she might have taken a long lunch.*

On the phone, Tattoo said, "Did I say I was worried? I'm not worried. Just thought somebody ought to see she ain't where she's supposed to be. She's a stickler about *me* being on time and where I'm supposed to be. Maybe someone ought to worry, but it's not gonna be me."

Willi raised an eyebrow. Good grief, if Tattoo didn't care why even call? Hairs on the nape of her neck rose, a sure sign she might need to figure out the reason, but a glance at her calendar for the week took her completely away from that thought. "I'm going to see the second professor on my list, Dr. Etzli and his assistant, Yaotle. I'll check back in a couple of hours. I'm sure Anastasia will be in her office by then."

She noted the 4:45 p.m. time on her readout, disconnected, shot a sharp glance at the rich red hues of the leaves mingled with the golden, and sighed. The displays of skeleton bones, witches, scarecrows and bloody-fingered vampires in the front yards of the Victorian homes gracing the beautiful old residential area of Nickleberry's east side, in particular the street named Fetchwin's Way, seemed to reach out and touch her with icy fingers. Rather than the AC, she turned on the heater and searched for the Dalrymples' place which Dr. Etzli—Dr. Blood?—had chosen for his stay. It'd been years since she'd taken piano lessons in that old house.

She patted her purse where the reassuring heft of her loaded

.357 Magnum offered security and then adjusted her side mirror. Had that green vehicle been there a moment ago? Seems like she'd seen that same make and color all over town lately. Or . . . or . . . was it the *same* vehicle? Her heart danced a little jig in her throat; she swerved the car to the curb and glanced over her shoulder. It felt like someone was watching her. She checked over the other shoulder. Damn her imagination and curses on that nasty note-sender. *No one is following me. I'm fine. Just perfectly double-damned fine.* She eased down another block to 279 Fetchwin Way, found the four-story Victorian with white gingerbread and paused to calm herself before getting out. About an hour with this Dr. Etzli fellow, and by then perhaps she could meet up with Quannah.

She walked along a curving brick path lined with grimacing pumpkins, pots of bubbling green ooze and giant spiders. She peeked back over her shoulder for a third time in as many minutes. The green car, black windows disguising the occupant, moved slowly past the house toward the 300 block of Fetchwin Way. Willi glanced at her own car. No note fluttered from beneath the windshield wiper. The person in the car was probably some perfectly innocent driver who maintained proper speed for this quiet residential area. She counted the steps up the old porch. An even twelve, thank goodness, not the unlucky thirteen. She wondered again for the umpteenth time why her daddy Phidias Gallagher, who'd been a respected lawyer, left her with an everlasting legacy of superstitious lore concerning the number thirteen, black cats and such.

She eyed the iron rose vine surrounding the doorbell. She gave two firm punches. Petite Miss Ubbie Dalrymple opened the door. Like a shadow, her twin brother, Mr. Ustin Dalrymple, nodded over his sister's shoulder. After he had been widowed a decade and a half ago and neither had had children, he had come back to their childhood home from which she'd never

moved. Of an age and stature similar to Willi's tiny Aunt Minnie, the two looked like cherubs that might need to be carded
on nights out if not for the white hair. Lively brown eyes atop
inquisitive little noses twinkled as they said together, "Willi Gallagher, please come in. It's been so long." Willi grinned at their
ability to speak in unison at times.

"Do you still keep up with your piano?" Ubbie asked.

Ustin, in a voice two octaves lower, said, "Practice makes
perfect, you know."

"I've not played since I was thirteen."

Two little mouths turned downwards. "Tch, tch, tch."

"I've been teaching for years at the high school. Sophomore
English."

Ustin faced his twin. "Working with youth. That has to count
for something. Come on in. You're out of school for this
afternoon?"

"I took this Friday as a personal day to start the informal
interviews for the curator's position. We do have all of next
week off for fall break."

"Good for you. You got an early start." Ustin ushered her
inside.

Behind her Ubbie said, "And we've kept up with you through
the years. Ustin was teasing you. We know all about your teaching career, and your second career."

Willi stopped, faced her and asked, "Second career?"

"You are our local Miss Marple of the Range, you know."

"Oh, yeah, that. Well, I've not been stepping on the sheriff's
toes on any cases lately, thank goodness." She stepped into a
foyer of buttermilk yellow and peered down a long hallway of
four-foot wide curved doorways segueing on the left side into
open kitchen and family room, with an immense living room to
the right. "No more dark wainscoting and flowery wallpaper?"

Ubbie smiled. "One must move with the times. Ustin has

remodeled in the metroplex for the last decade or more. We figured it was about time to do up the old home place while we still could. We'll be leaving it to a nephew, the only living relative left after our Vermont—our oldest brother, you know—passed away two years ago come next month." She led the way to the family room where flames glowed within the stone fireplace. "Please, be seated."

Willi had a hard time choosing. Comfortable couches, sofa chairs, and ottomans offered enough spots to host thirty people. Two baby grand pianos placed one curve within the other sat on a raised oak floor at one end. Pot lights glowed down on the polished surfaces. Scents of cinnamon and apples wafted over the butcher-block island separating the kitchen from the room. A double set of French doors with spring-hung cream sheers let in the October light.

She snuggled onto one of the chocolate ottomans in soft chenille. Before she could say *boo,* Ustin handed her a cup of spiced cider and Ubbie gave her a plate of chewy brownies. She said, "With lots of our pecans. Get them right out there." Ubbie nodded toward the giant pecan trees outside the French doors. "Our latest boarder doesn't appreciate Texas pecans."

"Humph," Ustin offered. "Kept mispronouncing *pecan,* too."

"Finally," Ubbie said, "we had to let him know a *pee*-can was something you'd find under your great-great-granny's bed. A pe-*can* is what's in these delectable delights."

"You're preaching to the choir," Willi said, "but I think one is my limit as I enjoyed a substantial lunch with one of the contenders for the curator position."

In unison they said, "We're great supporters."

"We gave three performances to help raise the funds to get the project started years ago."

"Yes, I know, and it was so appreciated. You all are aware that one of your boarders is one of the applicants?"

"Ubbie knows a lot about him." Ustin winked.

"Pardon?"

"She's got an eye for Dr. Etzli, she does."

Ubbie glared at her twin. "You say the most foolish things in your old age. Thought you had to take the meals on wheels today. Get along with you, now."

He chuckled on the way out. Ubbie said, "Silly thing still acts like we're children." She settled her short frame by tucking one leg under her in the corner of a sofa. "Now what can I do for you, Willi Gallagher? Something about this Dr. Etzli from South Texas, who by the way, holds no interest for me whatsoever. The man is ten years my junior."

It was Willi's turn to wink. "Why, Miss Dalrymple, I think the lady doth protest too much. Actually, he's fifty-seven, and as I recall you're just now touching that sixty mark."

"Come January, yes. So you want to talk about this Dr. Et-zli?"

"Uh-huh. Just three years your junior. A mere thirty-six months."

"I can see I'm not going to get any mercy in my own home today." Her cheeks pinked up nicely, and she said, "But, seeing as how I clean the guest quarters, I have to burst a romantic bubble for us both. I've seen a photo he keeps in his bedroom of a beautiful Latina lady. Gorgeous, dang nab it."

"Could be a sister? His mother's picture, even. Or perhaps a long-lost love who a lady such as yourself might easily help him forget. Hmmm?"

Ubbie waved away their silliness with a flutter of her fingers in the air. "Now, what do you need to know?"

"I'm supposed to interview him. He'd left a message earlier that he'd prefer to talk in his rooms. Is he here?"

Ubbie leaned out of her comfortable position and shot a sharp glance past the sheers of the French doors, the patio and the pecan trees to a guest house at the back of the Dalrymple property. "Not yet. Only two spots for him and his assistant to park. They'll be in soon. How about we catch up on community and friends while we wait?"

Willi nodded. Why not? She'd gained more information in the past from just talking with folks than some of the toughest interviewers could get with all their more worldly tricks. A while later, Willi glanced at her watch showing 7:15 p.m. A Texas hen fest could last a right long time before getting to the real kernels of info. She tightened her lips. Let's see, Dr. Etzli. A no-show for the morning interviews. A cancelled meeting at lunch. Now, two hours late for a third opportunity for the informal interview. Yeah, guess who was last on the list for high recommendations today. Shades of gray presaged the October sunset outside the curtains when she gently maneuvered Ubbie back to the topic of Dr. Etzli.

"He's a gentle-spoken man," Ubbie said, "and well-read and can discuss books and philosophy for hours. Has such an open mind. I do like that about him."

"Do I hear a 'but' in there?" Willi asked.

Ubbie shifted position to place both feet on the floor, elbows resting on her knees as she leaned forward. "He wears sunglasses."

"Lots of folks in Texas do, and almost year around keep them in the car."

"But we don't wear them unless it's sunny."

"True." Willi tilted her head, encouraging Ubbie to offer more.

"We invited him and Yaotle—that's his assistant, if I didn't mention that before. We invited them for stew and cornbread and music one afternoon out on the back patio. I asked him if he had a black eye. Told him that was something we Texans showed off."

"What'd he say?" Willi asked, mimicking Ubbie's forward leaning stance.

"Said he worked so much under bright lights and microscopes and studied such fine details in old manuscripts, he chose to rest his eyes as much as possible. But this was on a cloudy day beneath a covered porch. He didn't take them off when we came inside for the music."

"And what color eyes does he have?"

"Dark, dark brown with little flecks of golden—" Ubbie sat up straight. "That's neither here nor there, Miss Snoopy." Her grin and rosy cheeks took the sting out of the words. "And he—"

"Yes?"

Ubbie sighed, and snuggled back on the couch corner. "He usually only goes out during the evening. I'm surprised he went out today. Him in that beautiful red, sleek sports car, and his assistant in a beat up old pickup that's seen better days. I'll give the young man this, he keeps that truck shined like it were the most expensive wheels on the road."

The vibration of a motor hummed outside the French doors. As if a vicious jungle cat had crept from the rainforest fronds, the motor's purr sent shivers down Willi's spine. The glint of metal against bright red caught in a flash of the sensory security lights that came on as the car drove past. She blinked and rubbed the chills away. Good Lord and rabid raccoons, she needed to follow that kid's advice and seek Valium if even the sound of a motor sent her into a paranoid reaction.

"Oh, come here to this side, and you can see Ernesto." Ubbie and she both jumped up and pulled aside the sheers to see more clearly.

"Ernesto?" Willi asked.

"That *is* his first name. There," Ubbie said, "isn't that odd?"

Willi peeked at Dr. Ernesto Etzli's black suit pants and jacket.

"His dress shirt is like those in the 1800's."

"Yes, high-collared. Long-sleeved."

"Good grief, Miss Dalrymple, he's not only got sunglasses, but some sort of scarf underneath his black hat brim. Sort of like—"

Ubbie grinned. "I know what you're going to say. Sort of like 'The Shadow,' right?"

Willi nodded. "That thought had crossed my mind."

A few minutes later, Willi sat in the guest quarters on a burgundy corduroy loveseat across from "The Shadow." Honey-gold walls surrounded the two other chairs, both leather recliners, placed in front of a high-tech TV ensemble. The Dalrymples had obviously extended their renovations to this outward region. Muted lights glowed upward, washing the ceiling and cascading the illumination in provocative pockets to accent Southwestern artwork, mostly sixteen-inch ceramic squares, depicting such subjects as cacti and coyotes, calves and chili peppers in the brightest of palettes.

Etzli, without his black "Shadow" bandana and hat, spoke to her in mellifluous tones. His hooded eyes opened wide as he expressed his thoughts about the possibilities for the museum. "It is grand, Ms. Gallagher, and will be grander as each year passes. I will do good things for the museum. You'll see. Nickleberry heads will spin."

"Yes." Willi felt the hours wearing into her reserve energy. Well, she would just ask as few questions as possible. Before a visit with Quannah, she might need first a double dose of aspirin, a shower, and a couple of quiet minutes with no vices, no interviews, no assessments—just peace. "Spinning heads, huh?" She needed to get a feel for the man beneath the cape of command, which he presented quite well, having been a curator of a privately owned museum in Mexico City as well as assistant curator in San Francisco. "Your credentials are darned impressive, Professor Etzli. Nickleberry Museum might very well be the place to shine your stirrups."

He grinned at her Texas slang. "Ah, stirrups or not, please just Ernesto or Mr. Etzli. I've never used the title *Professor* and do not feel the need for it."

Willi tapped her purse. Interesting choice of words. Not *I don't feel comfortable with it.* Just simply *do not feel the need for it.* Willi said, "Of course." That was good. One professor in the running was plenty. Where Professor Stöhr was vertically challenged and rotund, Etzli was lean, tall—extremely tall. Where Professor Stöhr winked and became charmingly excited, Etzli was polished and in command. When the phone rang, he lifted his six-foot-six frame with grace and assurance. He approached with a worried frown, opened his mouth to speak, and hesitated, as if he might have bad news about the museum display.

Willi leaned forward. "Problems?"

He smiled and swept his hand in a theatrical arc. "On the contrary. That was Yaotle. I'd left him to work with the exhibit. At darkfall, I will join him. You will want to meet. I insist he be part of my team, as you know."

Crossing her legs, Willi leaned back in her chair. Bullshit. She'd thwarted enough sophomore students in mid-fib than you could shake a crooked stick at, and here he was telling her all was okay. Well, maybe it was simply a tiff between boss and worker, not something she really needed to be privy to at the moment. She said, "The committee noted and appreciated the detailed résumé you sent about him, along with yours. His name is Tommy Balboa." She quirked one eyebrow up in question mode.

"He is a devout follower of the old gods and chooses to go by the one name, Yaotle. Yaotle's name means 'warrior'. He was given it by priests who practice the old religion. He's a seriously *spiritual* warrior, and does not manifest the meaning in the physical."

Willi nodded her understanding. "I know your name in the old Nahuatl language means 'blood.' "

"Ah, you have done your homework."

"Actually, the acting curator, Anastasia Zöllmer, enlightened me."

"Really? A formidable adversary, Ms. Zöllmer. A good friend of yours, too?"

Willi hesitated. "Yes, as Tommy Balboa is to you, I suppose." Willi narrowed her eyes. He could go hit piñatas until the room was covered in candies, if he thought he was going to draw an apology for a long-standing friendship. And how dare he think that would in any way influence her choice.

"You have a certain frostiness about you when you think someone has questioned your integrity." His hooded lids shadowed his eyes for a moment before he cleared his throat. "My mention of your friendship was not meant as any such inference; I know you are a professional in every sense."

She smiled by way of conciliation.

After a half-hour of comfortable chit-chat, Willi wanted to ask him about his own strange attire, but something in the man's attitude when she broached personal subjects shut her out. Okay, no *problemo*. It wasn't a necessity to know every little detail about each applicant. She just wanted enough to understand their basic values, how they might handle the museum patrons and supporters. Ernesto Etzli offered outstanding and well-deserved accolades within the field. When asked about marriage and family, he'd discussed the relevance of the family life—Anglo and Hispanic—in the pioneering days of Texas, his area of expertise. His display centered around a typical Texas ranchero, inside and out. When questioned about hobbies and pastimes he merely turned the tables and got her to discuss the activities available in Nickleberry and the surrounding areas, never once giving a concrete fact about his own personal interests.

Willi's cell phone rang. "Do you mind?"

"Please, answer it. I must put a casserole in the oven to be ready to take for tonight. You may go through to one of the bedrooms if you need more privacy."

As he went into the kitchen, she opted for the largest bedroom, obviously his since the black scarf and hat hung on a rack by the door. She sat on a curved metal chair by the bed, reached in her purse, touched the velvet cover and then the cold metal of the gun, finally grabbed and pulled out the phone and clicked it open. Dang, the call had come from Lassiter and he'd hung up. Despite what Big Chief claimed was his hunter's patience, that man refused to wait more than two rings. She pushed his speed-dial number and glanced at the one photo on the bedside table. A gorgeous knockout of a lady—Hispanic with smoldering eyes and cascades of dark hair—stared out at her. Ah, so Mr. Etzli did have a love interest. She'd have to ask about the lady, find out if she were local or someone from one of his past positions.

When Quannah answered, he said, "Stay calm. I didn't want you to hear this over the news."

"You caught the escaped convicts?" She pictured his proud warrior stance, the Comanche blood showing in his high cheekbones, the wide grin of strong white teeth, his raven-black hair. "You got them! Yes!"

"I wish, Gallagher, I wish."

"Well, what, then?"

He used her pet name and softened his tone. "*Winyan,* there's been an accident, and I know the car belongs to your friend Anastasia."

The pineapple taste rose to her throat. Finally, she swallowed, took the phone away from her ear and stared at the cold metal. Maybe she had misunderstood?

"Oh, my Lord. Where? Did she get up on a ladder at the museum? What?" She took a few steadying breaths. "Perhaps you're mistaken. Probably it's one of the hired help . . . well . . . because . . . she wouldn't be clambering around the displays."

Quannah said, "Not at the museum. A car accident, *Winyan.*" He gave her the location, and hung up. No mistake.

To the empty line, she said, "I'm on my way." She stumbled back into the living room.

Returning from the kitchen, Etzli said, "Would you like to continue this at the museum tonight? We'll gladly treat you to this simple meal."

"Meal? No, no . . . I . . . there has been an accident."

"May I be of help?"

"No. It's my friend. It's Anastasia."

"Indeed. What a pity. Please let me take you to the location. You should not be alone."

"I'll . . . I'll be fine. Another friend is going to meet me there."

Etzli took her by the elbow and guided her outside and around the Dalrymples' house. Nightfall's shadows blanketed the driveway. He placed her gently in her car. "Are you sure you'll be okay, Ms. Gallagher?"

"Yes, I'll call the museum later to let you know. I've got to hurry." She shoved in the key and turned on her headlights.

Dear God, please, please let Anastasia be alright. Ramblin'. Had someone called Ramblin'? Willi's heart revved faster than her engine. When she glimpsed the dark-colored vehicle behind her, she merely frowned.

Just coincidence. I'll worry about it later.

The interviews didn't matter. The curator position was of no concern. The threatening letters were silly. Nothing was as important as a friend's welfare. *Oh, how life twisted and horrible events kaleidoscoped into less important designs when the really explosive hit you.* She turned right, left, and slammed down on the gas pedal to leave the now familiar green car on Fetchwin Way.

CHAPTER FOUR

Above the prey the vultures swarm
Ancient truths will do the harm.

—M'ima
The Book of the Ancient Ones

Minutes later she arrived at the local HEB supermarket parking lot where Quannah helped three city policemen push the crowd back out of the way. She rolled down her window. The triple set of cruiser strobe lights pulsated, washing the scene with red and blue. It was all the more eerie because the sirens were off, so the horror unfolded in hushed tones of clipped sentences from the bystanders. Willi slammed on the brakes and skidded to a space just off the cordoned parking lot. Only then did the ambulance's presence along with the EMTs' register. She ran toward the prone figure covered in blood.

Quannah grabbed her and twirled her around. "Nothing you can do right now, *Winyan,* nothing." His leather-thong–tied ponytail whipped in the evening breeze while his black eyes seemed to pierce into the very marrow of her being. Even in as traumatic a moment as this, the intensity of his gaze created a little thrill that ran the entire five-foot-three-inch length of her. He leaned down, adjusted his Texas Ranger's badge on his belt loop and repeated. "Nothing. Let the NPD take care of this."

She swallowed and licked her dry lips. "But . . . how badly . . . how—" She tried to gulp in more air. This wasn't her first rodeo as far as bad car scenes went, heaven knew, so she had to get her emotions under control. More calmly, she asked, "So what does the Nickleberry Police Department know? Why are you here? That . . . her car looks crushed. Is that all her blood?"

He moved to her left to block the view. "It always looks bad at the scene. I'd just gotten in from the field. We got a tip that the convicts have come closer into the city."

His eyes showed such anguish as he stared into hers, her heart did a flip-flop. She reached up to touch his face. The warmth of his skin somehow eased her fear, and she nodded, taking courage from his strength, from his presence.

Quannah eyed a reporter with camera in hand. "Hey, no pictures right now while they're working with the victim. Have a little compassion, okay? Back up, back up."

"Hey, man. I got rights here. EMTs saving lives. This sells papers, man." Flashes ripped through the dark.

Quannah, jaw squared, took the photographer by the elbow and moved him aside. "Pretend you're human, okay? Give some privacy here, some respect."

"Hey, I know better than to get my lens directly on the victim. Lighten up, man."

Willi's eyes riveted on the unobstructed scene. Anastasia's body writhed upon the parking lot. "Oh my, look! What? Oh my . . . what's . . . what's happening to her?"

Anastasia, her spiked blonde hair matted with blood, thrashed upon the tarmac. A horrible crowing sound erupted from her throat. Then with head and heels touching the surface, her torso bucked upwards. Slap, slap, slap upon the blood pooled beneath her. All three paramedics formed a circle around her.

"Why aren't they doing something?"

"*Winyan,* they are. Her airway is blocked completely. I'm sure they're getting it cleared."

Willi fell against his broad chest. "Sorry. Don't know what's the matter with me."

With a hand splayed across the small of her back, he turned her away from the carnage and walked her toward the edge of the lot. "Adrenaline rush. Acute anxiety about your friend. Understandable. Scenes like this are pure terror. This reporter is going to make himself useful and escort you back to your car. Wait there for me."

"Man, I wanna stay with the vic, you know? If she dies . . ."

Quannah went so quiet when he turned his hooded gaze upon the photographer, he whispered the words. Whatever Quannah said caused the photographer's face to blanch, but the journalist nodded.

"Okay, man, okay. Guess you're right. I'll relay the news to the Fort Worth reporter to catch pics at the hospital."

After Willi sat on her car bumper, she took some deep breaths and sniffed sternly. No more histrionics, by daggum. She couldn't help if she couldn't think straight.

"Friend of yours, Ms. Gallagher?" The reporter for one of the local papers—*Nickleberry News*—faced her. For a change, the young person wasn't one of her former students, but she had worked with him many times for publicity gigs for the new museum. He might be on the crime beat, but he also had to cover the garden clubs, the FFA, and whatever else the paper sent him to report on.

"Yes," she whispered. She studied the stout figure—all muscle she'd bet—who probably served as a linebacker in high school, or maybe he was one of those weightlifters. But there was still that hint of baby boy about him that most females seemed to want to nurture. Willi had no problem fighting that impulse.

"I'm Elliott Grimes, covering crimes." He tried to be jovial with the rhyme, but the effort made her frown. "Sorry, ma'am, but that's what I do." He brushed at his hair, brown bristles tipped with peroxided ends.

"Crimes?" She shook her head. "Then why are you here? At an accident? And why aren't there any cars in front of the store?" She got up, wrung her hands and started to wander away.

"Ma'am, I don't think that officer with the pony tail would appreciate either one of us over there."

"He's a special investigator for the Texas Rangers."

"Wow. Really? What's he—?"

She eased back down on the bumper. "His uncle is Brigham Tucker."

"Our sheriff?"

"Yes. Seems you'd know that." She ran her trembling hands through her hair at the temples and back.

"I'm new to Nickleberry. Been here two months. So, he's a special investigator?"

"He's been out searching for those escaped convicts."

Elliott Grimes pulled out his pencil and pad. "The Huntsville convicts? Why did he come back to town? Have they already caught them? Gosh, I hope I didn't miss that."

Willi rolled her eyes. "Yes. Just now. No. You haven't missed it. Now may moss grow on your damned pencil if you ask one more question." Ah. She smiled. That felt good.

"Yeah? Thanks. Uh . . . could you spell his name for me?"

"Perhaps I should have put a green-snail-slime curse on that pencil, you insensitive little snot." The grin at the end of the sentence took all the fun out of it for her.

"Last thing I'll ask. Promise. Then maybe he'd give me some info later."

"Maybe. It's Q-u-a-n-n-a-h Lassiter. Double n's and double s's. He's cooperative with those who know when to approach and when to stay out of the way."

"Yeah. I kind of got that message."

"Actually you're not quite as bloodthirsty and morbid as the usual ones they've had on such calls." Willi eyed him again.

"Like I said, I'm new. I really want the sports beat, but . . . some old local geezer, a former coach, will have to die off before I get that chance. If I miss some gruesome details here, it's no skin off my nose as long as they don't turn TV cameras on me, not that it's likely any would show for this."

"Wouldn't be good if your boss saw you comforting, huh?"

"You got that straight."

Now, what was it *she* wanted to ask? She couldn't stay focused. Something important about . . . about the accident. Just that word—*accident*—sent goose bumps dancing from elbows to wrists. In her tiredness, in her after-drinks mode, in the fright, she wasn't able to grasp something important about that damned word. Like a wisp of a spider's web, it hung suspended in her mind—tenaciously strong, but wafting out of reach with each new sensory detail of the horrific scene around her.

Out of the corner of her eye, she caught sight of a familiar figure, rotund of shape and still sporting his vest and rings. She gave a halfhearted salute, but Professor Stöhr turned to the person beside him, and didn't see her. Ah, Parker Nolan. Guess the committee would appreciate them taking an interest in the present curator. Odd that both would be shopping at HEB this time of the evening.

Elliott Grimes pointed to motorcycle cops at the entrances to the store lot. "You're lucky to have snuck by them. They've made most of the customers leave and won't let others in. Leaving a big space for CareFlight to set down."

Ah, finally the question surfaced. "No, no. The ambulance is present. Aren't they transporting her to the hospital here in Nickleberry?"

"Ma'am, I believe CareFlight has more state-of-the-art equipment which she might need to keep . . . her . . . uh . . ."

"Stable?"

"Yes, ma'am. Before that macho Indian officer—" He mouthed his pencil. "Uh . . . that Texas Ranger found me too close—uh . . . before you got here . . . I heard Henry Hardee, one of the EMTs, tell another that she'd probably lost something like forty percent of her blood. Transfusions are necessary and quickly in such cases. Henry has a voice that carries, or I wouldn't have gotten that much."

"Transfusion?"

"—And there were other complications. Maybe a broken larynx, other body trauma. But, ma'am, they can work miracles. And they got here fast. Not even two minutes according to the lady who called it in."

"And that was?"

"Some lady who spoke Mexican."

"Mexican?" Willi glared at him. "That's the nationality. Spanish is the language."

"Yeah, whatever."

Willi rubbed her temples. Exactly. Right now with a friend's life in the balance, what did it matter? Not one *papa frita*. "Is she still here, the lady who called in?"

"First thing I checked out with a call down to the PD. No way they could tell who it was, other than it came from a pay phone over at the service station across the street."

Willi sighed. "Just some Good Samaritan, I imagine. Where are the other victims? Already been lifted out?"

"Other victims, ma'am?"

"Her car . . . her car is all twisted up against that pole in the middle of the parking lot. Where's the one that ran into her?"

"That's why I'm here." He scratched his head. "Another car was near her, but according to witnesses never made contact, just swerved to miss her as she drove into the pole. I call that a possible hit-and-run. Of course, when she T-boned around the pole, she knocked two cars out of the way." He checked his notes. "Those belong to a cashier and one of the managers. Guess they feel lucky she swerved into this almost empty area rather than close up to the front third of customer parking. Lot of pedestrians going in and out."

"But . . ." Willi stood on knees that were as weak as if they were full of water bubbles ready to burst and leave her legless in a wavering sea. She swallowed and reseated herself. "But, she would have had to be going—what?—seventy, eighty miles an hour to wrap that car in such a way?"

"At least seventy, yes ma'am, at least. And I think—"

"What?"

"That other car was chasing her, maybe made her wreck."

"Oh my gosh, no. No one would want to hurt Anastasia." But even as the words came out of her mouth, her face broke out in a sweat, a sweat the brisk October breeze couldn't negate, a sweat that grew sickly sweet in smell as it dried and was replaced over and over. To heck with feminine southern shine.

"Well, somebody wanted her scared or hurt."

Willi swallowed back bile and peered around for the one person that should have been at Anastasia's side unless he had reverted to his former ways. He might want to scare or hurt her. Ohmygod. Where in Blue Blazes was Ramblin'?

She peered across the street at Curry's Service Station on the corner, where a red sports car pulled up. A tall man dressed in black minus his hat-à-la-Shadow, got out of the car and walked to a rattletrap of a pickup, where he leaned into the passenger side to release the door and got in. Willi frowned. Guess Ernesto Etzli had called his assistant, Tommy Balboa—Yaotle—to meet him here. Willi shook her head. She didn't remember telling Etzli where the accident was, but she'd been so shaken, she might have done so. Yes, she must have. Otherwise, how would he have known? At least, she could honestly say the contenders weren't such bloodthirsty piranha that they didn't support a downed colleague. About the only one missing right now was Tattoo. No sooner had that thought winged its way from her head than Willi glimpsed the girl, nose against the inside of the Curry's Service Station window, both hands framing the sides of her face, and she looked as stricken as Willi felt.

Willi searched the macabre scene around Anastasia. "Where *is* Ramblin'?"

The whirr of helicopter blades overhead made more talk impossible. The front of solid blue gave way to orange and white stripes with *CareFlight* emblazoned on the bottom and the side of the flying emergency room. She discerned three people inside. Did everything tonight have to be in three's? What a silly thing to focus on. Something was so off kilter. Duh-uh, and triple Hell's bells. The EMTs, having turned Anastasia's care over to the flight team, stood back while they strapped Anastasia into the special Stokes gurney and wheeled her over to the helicopter. Willi again ran her fingers through her hair, stood and clenched both hands to her chest.

Once they were airborne, Willi unclenched her fists. Elliott Grimes tapped her on the shoulder. "Who is Ramblin'?"

"What . . . uh . . . ?"

"You asked out loud about where he was."

Willi peered around. Skin around her eyes stretched so tightly a whole jar of moisture cream would not alleviate the strained skin. She answered Elliott Grimes, who covered crimes, by way of a second question.

"Even more important, where is Ludwig?"

After two hours in the emergency waiting room, Willi slumped into the plastic-molded torture module some referred to as a waiting room chair, a chair that hit her mid-thigh, a chair that with its slick surface made her constantly slip, slide and shuffle.

So, now she leaned her head on Quannah's shoulder. "Thanks," she said.

"For what, Gallagher?" His cell phone burbled, he checked the readout and ignored what must have been the seventh or eighth contact.

She gently pushed his ponytail and leather strapping aside, and hugged his arm. "For getting rid of the reporters. Good gosh, they became as thick as fleas on a shaggy dog. Why so many for just a simple accident?"

Quannah shuffled. "An eyewitness called all over town before they got the facts straight, that's all. Some little Mexican lady all excited about being that eyewitness and wanted everyone to share in her fifteen seconds of glory. Usually, they're happy with just telling the police, but she called the newspapers and even Channel Five."

Willi shrugged and held on more tightly. "And . . . thanks, too, for . . . for talking me through this ordeal. For all the calls to friends and such. For . . . for . . . *being* here." If his shoulders weren't slumped, she'd unburden her worries about her personal nemesis, the nasty note-sender. She wanted to be clear-headed when she did so, and certainly that wasn't the condition she was in now which was about as fresh as a week-old enchilada. One part of her also ached to be at the museum to find that short-legged, smoke-sucking Ludwig.

Hell's bells, she ought to be triplets. She also desperately needed to touch base with Ramblin' Anders, but her constant cell phone calls had garnered only a canned message. She hugged Quannah closer, caught the scent of horse and leather, wild wind and sage. "You're a good man to take off from the hunt for those three escapees to take care of me."

He kissed the top of her head, then her forehead and eyelids. "Not a problem."

"Big problem," Willi said. "I know in this kind of all-law

endeavor, the Texas Rangers are the ones to step in and take over the manhunt from the local sheriff's department and the NPD."

"Only if we see a need to, Gallagher. Sheriff Brigham is coordinating with the Nickleberry Police Department and—"

"All six cruisers of them, huh?"

"—and with the law in the surrounding counties. There's no reason for me to have to head the assignment. I'm here to check, see if they need the help, maybe go when they close in on the scumbags."

"So that's why you've been on horseback the last eighteen hours beating the bushes, wandering down arroyos, and—"

Quannah placed a finger over her lips, and grinned. "Don't tell anyone, but that's the fun part."

Willi raised an eyebrow. "Big Chief Sit-In-Saddle, they wouldn't believe me, if I did."

A nurse—her ID a bit askew—stepped into the room. "Anastasia Zöllmer's family?"

"The closest she has to family that's here," Willi said. "We told the last shift her parents are flying in tomorrow morning. We don't know where Ramblin' Anders is."

The nurse tapped her metal notebook. "Her husband-to-be?"

"Yes. Has there been any change? Can we see her yet?"

"I'm sorry. You've been so vigilant, but . . . you're not allowed. The doctor did say to let you know she's stable and in ICU. Until we contact a next-of-kin, that's all we can say."

"So? So, what do we . . . do?"

"Go home, Ms. Gallagher. Contact Mr. Anders. He *is* on the list of ones who can visit."

"So," Quannah said, "If . . . *if* we can locate Ramblin'."

"Exactly."

The nurse handed Quannah a cell phone. "Some lawman calling you. I guess yours isn't working here in the hospital. Just take it back to the nurses' station when you're finished."

Quannah sighed. "Lassiter. Yes? I've napped for about two hours is all. Right. Okay."

Willi sat up. "I know that tone. You've *got* to go?"

"I'll grab a fast-food feast and head back to check in with Uncle Brigham. There was some mention of a stakeout. At least, they've got the Beast set up out there."

"That huge travel trailer?" Willi said, standing as he did, not yet able to turn loose of his arm.

"Makes a decent field station. Will you be all right, *Winyan?*" As he repeated the tender word in Lakota meaning *woman,* he touched the edge of her chin.

She smiled up at him to show she appreciated the tenderness, which offered a way to show an honoring of all her womanly aspects from intelligence to attractiveness, from curiosity to out-and-out stubbornness. Each time he used the endearment it showed an underlying sense of devotion on his part.

"I'll be fine." She glanced at her watch. "Not even nine-thirty yet. I think I'll swing by the museum to see what's on Anastasia's calendar for tomorrow. Perhaps I can reach them tonight. Folks hate last-minute cancellations. I'll check the premises for Ludwig, too."

"Gallagher, the police are on the look-out for the pooch and for Ramblin'."

"Maybe for Ramblin', but with this manhunt going on, they're not sparing anyone to look for one frightened puppy dog. I've got to do something."

Quannah grinned. "Okay, but . . . I need to borrow your car. Remember, Uncle Brigham brought me from the field hunt. I'm without wheels."

"Not a problem. Lots of folks I can call, then I'll go hunting, too."

Quannah's dark eyes bored into hers. "Hmmm. Guess you

can't get into trouble with dog-pound duty. I'll call you as time permits. Rest easy. Great Spirit's going to take care of Anastasia, and the law's going to handle the hit-and-run driver if there was one."

"I still find that amazing, that fifteen people claim to have heard the screech, the crash, but no one saw how she ran off the road and into the parking lot center pole. Unbelievable!"

"Someone—like the little lady who called in—may still come forward. Leave that," he said with a narrowing of his eyes and a gaze that seared her skin, "to the police. If there is one, they'll find the perp. You find the pup." He pulled back from her and crossed his arms.

She gave him a dazzling smile and yawned. "Excuse me. Too early for that. Goodness!"

"Listen to your body, *Winyan;* you've been through enough emotional upheaval today to tire you physically. Go home. Rest under *Wakan Tanka*'s stars. You'll need to be fresh to support her parents and Ramblin' when they find out what has happened."

"You may be right, Big Chief, so uncross your arms. The little woman will soon head to the teepee. Promise. Unless I can tempt you to go eat with me first?"

"Sounds great, but . . ."

"Well, at least, go by FreshMart and get healthy fast food."

He growled, ducked down and nipped her on the neck. "Nice to know you care enough to watch out for your warrior."

The warmth of his nibbles sent shivers to her nether regions. What kind of person was she to have such thoughts when one of her friends lay so near death's door? With heated cheeks she pulled away. "Now, you just go be on your way, Big Chief."

He grinned and kissed her sweetly on the mouth. "Life goes on, Gallagher. Anastasia's and . . . yours." He winked. "When you look out and see that star twinkling, remember that's me thinking about you."

With cell phone in hand, she did a mental check of those co-workers who hadn't rushed off for faraway vacations this week, pushed in the preset numbers for two teacher friends—Hortense Horsenettle and Dan Oxhandler, then after receiving no answer, tried the Kachelhoffers, her white-witch neighbors. Well, dang and double damned if they weren't eyeing their crystal ball or working with the deck of tarot cards. They always turned the answering machine off during such times of concentration, so she left a message about where she was and what she needed. Realizing how late it was, she didn't want to call others less close to her. Maybe a few minutes of quiet prayer time was called for. She shut her eyes and prayed for Anastasia, for that dang beloved hound of hers, for . . . a ride away from the hospital. That last selfish idea made her blink.

As the clock clicked to half past ten, she blinked again. Good grief, she'd been out to the world for an hour? And dang if she'd accomplished anything this evening. In fact, she'd failed miserably at every turn. Not one word had crossed her lips about her stalker. Ramblin' and Ludwig hadn't been located, and she'd been left without transportation. She offered up another self-serving prayer—one begging Great Spirit to send someone to give her a ride. She concentrated on the Kachelhoffer sisters, willing them to close their natural remedy cookbooks, stop sipping herbal tea, and come pick her up.

About to head to the nurses' station to ask for an update, she was stopped by the sight of three of the last persons she expected to see again this night. Patting his round belly and pulling his watch from his vest, Professor Stöhr nodded. "Madame Chairperson, I came as quickly as I could. Please let me offer condolences about the demise of your friend and our colleague, Ms. Zöllmer. What can I do to help you?"

Willi opened her mouth to protest, but before the words

came, Parker Nolan tapped the end of his cane on the antiseptic-clean linoleum. "Dreadful business. Not good at all, no. I, too, offer sympathies. What may I do for you?"

Professor Stöhr faced Parker Nolan. "I thought that was you out in the parking lot. Wasn't sure, though, so I headed on inside."

"Yes," Parker said, removing his short-brimmed hat, "Perhaps you hurried to be the first to lay your Sir Raleigh cloak before a damsel in distress, the more easily to make an impression on the committee chairlady?"

"I beg your pardon, sir. How dare you—"

At that moment the third—Ernesto Etzli—who Willi had noted standing in the shadows, swept off his black hat and bowed before her. "Forgive these two for petty bickering at such a time, Ms. Gallagher. Any arrangements, I'm sure, will be made by Ms. Zöllmer's family. In the interim, if you need an acting curator at the museum, be assured, I would gladly—"

"Gentlemen!" Willi removed her cold fingers from her heated cheeks, crossed her arms and stood as an ancient Aztec warrior might before enemies, shoulders squared, eyes boring holes through each of the three before her. "You have been misinformed."

"How so, Madame Chair, how so?"

"Indeed?" asked Parker Nolan.

"Not possible," intoned Etzli.

"Anastasia Zöllmer, acting curator, will be on a short leave of absence, in which time she will still be considered for the position as permanent curator by the same standards as you yourselves will be considered."

Parker Nolan lifted and caressed the head of his cane. "She is not—?"

"Dead? No."

"Ah, Madame Chairperson, that is good news. Forgive my

obtuse blunder. I meant no—" Professor Stöhr held out his hands and shrugged. "Please, may I offer my apologies for what must have seemed a crude statement considering the true circumstances? May I offer you a ride, perhaps a late evening snack?"

"I believe Ms. Gallagher," Ernesto said, "would prefer the comfort of my sportscar over your van full of train parts."

"I, too, will certainly offer you a ride," said Parker Nolan. "No working van, no sporty Jag, simply a comforting waltz across the roads in my Delfin. Much like you—gracious and classic," Parker Nolan said, while offering her a bent elbow.

Well, fried bats and ringworms, damned if she hadn't got what she prayed for—a ride away from the hospital. She considered each of the three while managing to offer a smile of sorts. Goose bumps rose on her arms. Maybe the men would attribute them to the frigid setting of the hospital AC. God, don't let the panic show on her face. At the moment, she could find nothing more terrifying than to jump into a vehicle and be closed up with any of these three quite obviously desperate men. Oh, good Lordy, one of them—one of these three contenders—could well have been the jerk to run Anastasia into a pole. In which case, it wasn't an accident, but cold and calculated attempted murder.

She wanted nothing more than to escape from all three, run screaming to the elevator and away from them and the twisted minds that conjured up death. What was she thinking? She swallowed and tried to speak. She couldn't leave Anastasia alone. *Not now.* By a rattlesnake's buttons, she'd not leave her friend with these three sidewinders. But now there grew an erratic chittering of her nerves goading her to find answers, and the only way to find answers was to leave her friend. What to do? *What to do?*

Chapter Five

Inked markings hold a message dark
Where death may stalk its innocent mark.

> —M'ima'kimimi
> The Book of the Ancient Ones

Quannah sighed so deeply the aquifers must have rippled hundreds of miles beneath the 700 block of Fetchwin Way. He snuck a glance at his trigger-happy partner of the evening as he edged the rust-ridden rattletrap to the east side of the block and two driveways from 757 Fetchwin Way. Willi should appreciate the fact that he didn't bring her car, but chose one of the undercover vehicles. He never would use hers. There was always the chance the hunted might realize who stalked him, and later come after that particular car. If he'd had any other way to the vehicle compound, he wouldn't have taken her car. He knew she'd be in safe hands with the Kachelhoffer sisters. In fact, knowing Willi, she might be tempted if she had her wheels to follow him and see what was going on with the stake-out. Her curiosity had been known to lead her into danger. He grinned. At least, he could never fault her for courage. He sighed. The neighbors would get his lady home safe, she'd be snug in bed and waiting for him as soon as this stake-out ended. In a quiet voice, he said to his partner, "Guess this northern end of the street hasn't seen the renovations of those old homes closer to the center of town."

Around a mouthful of chocolate and peanut butter candy, Officer Smitty Parva, mumbled, "Guess not. Lots of rich folks bought them. They got money to pour into fallen down rat traps. Me? I'd bulldoze and start fresh. Yeah. Modern. That's the way to go." He sipped on his third cup of coffee. "Gonna see action tonight, don't you think? Bet you a fiver, spot you a ten. We're gonna see action." He patted his gun. "I'm ready."

Quannah inhaled the scent of peanut butter, ignored the proffered cup of caffeine and sat up straighter. He adjusted his bulletproof vest fitted with breast cover, back inserts and sections slid into the pockets beneath the armpits to protect his sides. Even though he had only inserted the front chest piece, the vest made him sweat buckets. "Hopefully, we can do so without bloodshed." Why for all of porcupine's quills did he get paired with a rookie on the Nickleberry PD? Guess it had something to do with the new directives of all branches of law enforcement working together on this high-profile case.

An October breeze wove in and out of the car. Peering in the rearview mirror at the renovated houses to the south, he said, "Those fussy Victorians, refurbished, look like elegant ladies with flounces on skirts and flimsy parasols. Probably scented with lilac and rosewater."

"Ain't you just the poet," Smitty said. "So where does that leave the run-downs of the northern end of the street?"

Quannah grinned. "Why, they're ladies-of-the-evening, hiding in the shadows of overgrown oaks, dense oleanders. Their skirts are tatters, their petticoats of peeling paint revealing the rot of neglect."

Smitty sat up, shifted in the seat, and said, "Special Investigator Lassiter, sir?"

"Yes, Officer Parva."

"Don't never share that kind of crap with me again. Save it

for Willi. Women drool over someone what can express their-
selves pretty."

"Gotcha." Nothing would suit him better right now than to
head home to a hot shower and that sweet-smelling Gallagher
woman—his *Winyan*—his lady in every sense of the word. He
rubbed the bridge of his nose. Of course, she had a hell-bent-
for-leather attitude about getting herself into the worst predica-
ments. At least he wasn't having spiders of doubt crawling over
his skin like he did sometimes when she was into trouble. He
hadn't even had any visions of her doing crazy things. So why
was he as antsy as Smitty Parva? Not anxious to get his gun out
and start blasting at the three convicts . . . just not settled. And
the sensation had nothing to do with the stakeout—something
likely to be very boring—if the young officer didn't do
something they'd all regret.

Smitty Parva tore open another candy, sucked on it in silence
a moment before taking a swig of coffee and letting the roasted
liquid melt the chocolate. He offered the second chocolate
concoction in the package to Quannah. "No, son. It's all yours."

"That's right," Smitty said, "Willi made you eat healthy. Yeah,
little woman calling the shots, huh?"

Quannah merely smiled. Dang kid was spoiling for a fight,
nervous, ready to pick on anyone just to get the boredom of the
evening to dissipate. "You mostly do the midnight shift, don't
you?"

Smitty cleaned the inside of his cheek with his tongue,
smacked his lips, and said, "Yeah, but they called us all in for
the duration. So, you and me, we got the head spot on the stake
out. We're gonna be the ones to take L.T. Nadge, Edwin Heberly, and Iago Rios. Bet you a fiver, spot you that ten. They're
going down and we two are going to be the ones in the middle
of the action."

"How you figure?" Quannah stifled a yawn, adjusted his bulletproof protection, and eyed Smitty in the lamppost light.

"Stands to reason. Yeah. We're not stuck in the surveillance van across the street, not around the corner in the old pickup camper up on blocks. We're in the driver's seat. Right here, two doors down. You oughta should put those back and side inserts on your body armor. Bullets start flying, you can't never tell. I rather have chafed armpits than lead between my ribs."

"You keep that gun holstered, I probably won't have to worry about that."

Smitty shoved his gun back in the leather. "If Nadge, Rios or Heberly move in or out of that house, we'll be on them faster than a six-legged bobcat. That sorry Heberly ought to be killed. Damned black ass. Doing in them white girls what were simple mental cases in the rehab homes."

Quannah sighed. "You are aware that our newest council member is one of the finest men in the city, and he's African American. Might not appreciate insensitivity, even with a killer like Heberly."

Smitty took his gun out for the fifth time in half an hour, checked his clip and snapped it back in. "Yeah. The captain said I needed to work on that affirmative action thinking. Damned murdering asses."

Quannah noted movement in the shadows around the dark house, narrowed his eyes and went into his on-point red alert, but said nothing to Smitty. Might just be the breeze blowing tree branches. He said, "This trio is a multiracial cross, Officer."

"Huh?"

"Edwin Heberly, a black from East Texas piney woods, originally L.T. Nadge is a white boy out of El Paso. He figured he and his bank-robbing, guard-killing girlfriend were going to be this generation's Bonnie and Clyde."

"Glad that didn't happen." Smitty tapped his foot on the floorboard. "They'd never make a movie called L.T. and Amber. Yeah. That wouldn't fly."

"Last one, Iago Rios, is the most dangerous. Most devious. You have to tread careful with someone like that, Smitty. If you'll ever need that pistol, it'll be for him. He's already said he won't be taken alive, but—"

"—but nothing. We need to acco-mo-date his macho ass. Raping a twelve-year old to get back at her sister who wouldn't date him. Pistol whipping that sister to death, then going in the house and—oh, God."

Quannah nodded. "Yes, he walked in, shot the bedridden granddaddy between the eyes, and raped his little seventy-three-year-old wife. Left Mrs. Hidalgo as the only survivor of her family."

Even in the dim light Smitty's face reddened. "Damned animal; that's what he is."

"No," Quannah said. "The *Wamaskaskan*—the Animals—do not behave hedonistically. They are to be honored. Iago Rios is in a group shared by nasty societal refuse like Dahmer—humans allocated to a subspecies—evil ones." Quannah decided nothing roamed in the shadows by the house and relaxed back into orange mode, allowing himself a moment to roll his head to release tension in his neck and shoulders. He executed a few breathing exercises, and for a moment a vision intruded.

Willi grinned and showed off a tattoo around her navel. Some evil hand held a knife to the translucent skin of her belly, and Willi continued smiling, unaware of the danger. The knife changed to the claw of some animal. Willi smiled and said, "Nice kitty."

"Damn, Gallagher, move it!" He blinked and the momentary flash was gone.

Smitty said, "What?"

Quannah rubbed grit from his eyes. He swallowed around dry lips. Damn that woman. This was not a time for her to get into any situations. He seldom got such visions, merely feelings about her impending escapades. And now the hair stood up on his arms.

"You talking about Gallagher or evil ones?" Smitty said, a perplexed look on his face.

Quannah cleared his throat, and said in what he hoped was a calm and reasonable voice. "Yes, the evil ones. Just remember, though, we are not of that subspecies." He glared at Smitty until the young officer looked him squarely in the eyes. "We *will* follow the proper procedures. Above all, Officer Parva, remember that you and I both want to go home to loved ones this evening. And tomorrow we want to walk with honor."

Smitty maneuvered his holster around. "Yeah. I got it. I'm blowing a lot of hot air. But . . . if it means I've got to take out one of those sorry asses so's I can get back to Emmy, then that's what I'll do."

"You and Emmy back together, huh?"

"Yeah." Smitty grinned. "I might borrow that silly crap to impress her one of these nights."

"About the ladies on Fetchwin Way?"

"Yeah. Stupid stuff, but she'll go for it."

"Don't let me stand in the way of true love. But, Officer Parva?"

"Yeah?"

"You didn't hear any of that stuff from me, okay?"

"Got it." Smitty Parva licked the last bit of chocolate off his lip and grinned.

Quannah peered through the rearview mirror. In the 600 block, a speeding vehicle swerved to a halt in a short driveway, brakes squealing in protest.

Smitty reached out the window and adjusted the side mirror to see behind him. "Some damned fool of a beer-gut finally getting home. Lots of drunk and disorderly that turn to spousal-beating domestic calls on these blocks. Sure-fired idiot burned half the rubber off. Smell it? Probably thinks he's sneaking in quiet like."

Hairs on the nape of Quannah's neck made him shiver despite the sweat beneath the heavy shield. "Yeah, sure. Might be just a drunk. Might be more." Ah, well, as long as it wasn't Willi getting herself into some scrape, he could handle whatever happened on Fetchwin Way tonight.

At 609 Fetchwin Way, Agatha Kachelhoffer, at the wheel of her sister Elba's old pickup, screeched to a stop in front of an old Victorian, divided into a duplex.

Willi, knuckles white and hands with a death grip on the passenger window, wondered not for the first time this evening why she had imagined she would be safer under Agatha's vehicular shenanigans than she would have been with any of the curator contenders. She wrinkled her nose at the stench of burned rubber. Maybe she should have waited until tomorrow, gotten her own car back, and come on her own steam. After this crazy drive, her legs would be too wobbly to go searching the long corridors of the museum for one butt-gulping Ludwig.

Agatha, in her typical attire that always reminded Willi of cockatiels and parrots, swept her begonia orange long skirt up as she stepped from the pickup. Her turquoise blouse cinched in with Pueblo Indian silverwork shown in the dim light with bits of silver thread used for embroidery around the neck. She pushed a gray curl into her chignon. The silver earrings caught no more of the moonlight than did her sparkling eyes, youthful despite their sixty years of use.

"Now, get along, Miss Willi. Sister said you were in a hurry to talk to someone here." Coming around to the passenger side, she loosened Willi's fingers from the window frame. "Don't be worrying about your friend at the hospital. Sister won't let anyone bother her tonight, especially those three vultures hanging around the waiting room. That's what's worrying you and making the color drain out of your face, right?"

Willi swallowed, opened the door and sort of let what was left of her limp body slide to the ground. "Yes, Agatha, that and the effect of centrifugal force upon one's body."

Agatha patted her shoulder. "You choose the strangest moments to philosophize. Guess that's why Sister says you need watching so much."

Willi took a moment to study the old house that had one side—609A—with a newly painted exterior including a door and window frame. The other side looked abandoned and was probably on some city planner's demolition list. Taking hold of the brass knocker of 609A, Willi banged the metal against the peach-colored wooden door. A light came on in the derelict side. Tattoo's face appeared at the backlit window. A moment later she opened the five or six layers of peeling paint that was the door.

Willi pulled Agatha away from the delicate peach display toward Tattoo's door. She said, "This is my neighbor, Agatha Kachelhoffer. Agatha, this is Tattoo . . . uh—"

"Just Tattoo. Come on in over here."

"I thought—" Willi began.

"That no one could live on this dump site side?"

"Well," Willi began but was saved from offering polite platitudes when three police cruisers, sirens loud, lights revolving, raced past to screech to a stop at the next block or so up. "I wonder what's going on?"

Tattoo sighed and waved Willi and Agatha inside. "Another drug bust. Get 'em all the time on this end of town, you know. Maybe a domestic disturbance. Lot of that going around the neighborhood, too. You won't find Mr. Rogers in this part of town."

Agatha, orange skirt swirling, silver twinkling around the

turquoise blouse, said, "Shame. Wish folks would do more renovating, like Ubbie and Ustin Dalrymple have, and like you . . . uh . . . Tattoo."

Willi blinked. "Yes, this is really beautiful, warm and welcoming. Listen, I hate to rush you, but I really just came for the museum keys. Anastasia said you were having a set made for me, and I really need them tonight."

A noise came from the kitchen. Tattoo glanced toward the door. "Tonight? Let me go check. You all make yourselves to home."

Willi gritted her teeth and forced herself to study Tattoo's decorating talents. Golden walls boasted niches filled with greenery and folk-art knick-knacks. Curtains of soft yellow and toffee covered the blinds. Fluted floor lamps offered a flow of light. The furniture looked like old wooden garden pieces but glowed beneath a coat of chocolate enamel.

Before Tattoo opened the kitchen door, Agatha fluffed a pillow and said, "Lovely. Damask?"

Tattoo hooked her thumbs in her back jeans' pockets. "Yeah, from the remnant tables. Other side is just plain cotton, though." Tattoo had chosen for after-hours a cap-sleeved T-shirt, the better to show the twining ivy vines down one arm and the snake down the other. Its bright greens and golden tones somehow managed to seem right at home in the small but elegant surroundings.

"Why, young lady. You ought to do one of those decorating-for-pennies shows for TV. Quite innovative, this room. Perhaps you could design a cozy reading corner for Sister and me at our tea shop."

"I do odd jobs, I do. With time and inclination, I can do what I set my mind to."

"No doubt," Willi said. "Did I mention I came to get the extra set of keys Ms. Zöllmer said you'd had made for me?"

China clanked behind a closed door. Tattoo flinched. "Be right back." She grabbed the doorknob. "Uh . . . please, wait here."

In the swift opening and closing of the door, Willi caught a glimpse of a tiny kitchen in soft greens to complement the buttery golden tones of the living room. Muted voices and more china and cutlery tinkled. Willi, nose in the air, eased closer, just to check out an artifact niche, of course. She could hardly help it that in order to admire an Aztecan arm bracelet, her nose almost touched the kitchen door. In fact her shoulder did, opening the door just a sliver so as to make the muted voices more audible.

A man said, "I ain't leaving yet. You know I can't. Not 'til all that's cleared up the way. And I need money, cousin. Money."

Tattoo said, "Here's all I got."

"Ain't near enough."

"It's all I got for now. Rest will take me a couple days, but when I get back tonight, you be gone. You can't stay here. Now give me those."

Willi picked up the bracelet. Obviously, being here in Tattoo's home, it had to be a replica, but it was a convincing one. Willi eased away from the door just as Tattoo entered with a plate of cookies. She frowned at the bejeweled trinket in Willi's fingers. Willi set it back in the niche. "Beautiful copy."

"Copy? Yeah. Not like I could afford the real stuff. And, I ain't got nothing but grocery store buy-of-the-week china to serve with, but it's a right pretty pattern, don't you think?" She held out a key ring. "Here's the extra set. There's a key card, too. It'll open the outside doors; rest are for the individual doors. A master for each of the hallways and the office area."

Willi frowned. Had Tattoo just retrieved those from the man in her kitchen? He sure didn't sound like a co-worker—in fact—rather more like an unwelcome guest. What would someone like that be doing with the keys? Dang. She couldn't ask without revealing she'd been eavesdropping.

Agatha admired the green, gold and black motif, and the chocolate chip cookies. "Delicious."

"Thanks." Tattoo bounced on her heels again. "Made from scratch this afternoon after work."

"About work. Well, after work," Willi said. "Didn't I see you at the Curry's Service Station across from the HEB grocery tonight?"

"Me?" Tattoo set the plate of cookies on the coffee table, an ottoman of pieced goods, probably from the remnant box, too, but pleasing to the eye. Willi said so.

"Thanky," Tattoo said, and repeated, "Me?"

"Yes, when the helicopter came, you were looking out the window. I was in the parking lot."

"Oh, yeah. Wonder what was going on?"

"Anastasia. Anastasia Zöllmer. There was a horrible accident."

Tattoo stuffed her hands in her jeans' pockets and rocked back on her heels. "Guess that explains why she didn't get back to the museum this afternoon."

"About that," Willi said, "you called me after lunchtime, and seemed worried about her. The car accident happened hours later. Between two and seven o'clock, she never dropped by the museum?"

"Not that I saw." She nodded at the plate of cookies. "Want another?"

Willi shook her head. "Why were you worried about her?"

"Wasn't. Told you that. Just wanted you to know she wasn't always Johnny-on-the-spot, you know? What with all these new choices to consider, seemed only right all facts ought to be out on the table."

"Was there some personal animosity between you and Ms.

Zöllmer? Some reason you wanted to shed light on her negative side? You must have had some driving force more than what you've said."

Tattoo peered at the art niches, at the lamps, and finally at the floor. "Think what you want. Told you what I told you, and that's that."

Agatha wiped crumbs from her hands onto her napkin. "Might have been this young lady simply had a premonition about events to come, Willi. Lots of folks don't want to admit to such things in a small community."

Tattoo snapped her fingers. "That's it. Hit it right on the nail head, yes ma'am, Ms. Kachelhoffer. Just a feeling I got."

Willi stared hard at Tattoo as if she were one of her sophomore students trying to explain why all the answers on the book report matched those in the Cliff Notes rather than the novel version. "A feeling?"

"Yeah, sure."

"I think not," Willi said. "If so, why make up that you wanted her to be seen as unprofessional in her attendance at work?"

Deep frown lines creased Tattoo's forehead, she shivered and the snake slithered ever so slightly upon her arm.

With a flourish of orange skirt, Agatha stood. "Perfectly reasonable."

"Excuse me?" Willi and Tattoo both said in unison, although Tattoo's utterance came out in a squeak.

"As I said before," Agatha repeated, "lots of folks don't want to admit to such things in a small community. Easier just to make some tarradiddle up to cover up any premonitions or second sight visions."

"Works for me," Tattoo said.

"Not for me," Willi said, "but we'll let it drop for the moment." *Darn, Agatha. She knew I couldn't argue about visions, daydreams or intuition, seeing as how I use them so much in my own daily drill.* She frowned in Agatha's direction and then smiled at Tattoo. "So where's the museum van? That old beat-up thing you use for tools and wood and such? Don't you bring it home each evening? I didn't see it parked outside. In fact, I didn't see it at the Curry's Service Station, either."

"Oh, sure, it was there. I gassed it up. Guess in the excitement you might have missed it."

"So, where is it now?"

"I left it outside the sheds tonight. Yeah, to sort of ward off any intruders. Every once in a while, I park it—mind you, beneath plenty of lights—so sorry butts don't go thinking no one's around the premises. We don't have a full-time guard, you know."

Willi sighed, got up from the sofa, and said, "That makes sense."

Agatha grabbed hold of her arm, guiding her toward the door. Willi frowned at her. "One more question before I go."

"Whatever." The snake rippled; the vine came alive.

"How will you get to work in the morning?"

"Got a bike I use sometimes."

"Willi, dear, why don't we give her a ride now to the museum, and she can pick up the van there. Weren't there others you wanted to talk with tonight?" Agatha, her head held at a perky-parrot angle, shot her a beady-eyed look. "Shall we all three depart?"

As she got into the rattletrap pickup, Agatha gunned the motor. Willi grabbed onto the dashboard for dear life. A gun shot ripped through the evening; a second shot reverberated a millisecond later, rapidly followed by another two bursts. Yet, when they studied the street, nothing seemed to be happening. No sirens blared atop police cruisers, no dogs suddenly started barking. Tattoo, in the middle of the pickup seat, said, "Backfires. Cheap street equals cheap cars."

"Ah," Willi said, but the lingering ring of the four shots seemed as real as any heard in her shooting range practice.

For the third time Quannah told himself he could handle whatever happened on Fetchwin Way tonight. Rubbing the thought of Willi—with belly tattooed and a claw held close enough to rip the tattoo away, out of his mind again—he stared at his gun-happy partner, Smitty Parva. Quannah took a sip of bottled water and wished again that this stakeout night would end, that he could go home to the country farmhouse, sit on the porch for a few minutes holding hands with Willi, maybe do a little pre-bedtime smooching, and end up upstairs in her sweet arms. Ahh, yes, a good end to a frustrating day.

Smitty asked, "Why didn't you take charge?"

"Excuse me?"

"In these instances, Texas Rangers get to call the shots."

Quannah sighed. Limelight, political maneuvering, or publicity shots had never been part of his work ethic. "We *can* call the shots, if the local authorities ask us, or if our head office decides that the locals aren't able to handle the situation properly. Sheriff Tucker and his deputies are working with three other county sheriffs along with all the local police departments. Coordination doesn't seem to be a problem, so we just play a support role."

"But capturing . . . or killing . . . these three could be a real feather in your bonnet." Smitty shifted as if he'd seen movement beside the derelict house.

"I don't need to count coup, Officer Parva. Like you, I'm here to protect and serve the innocent. Right?"

"Right. So you don't care who brings them in as long as they're caught?"

"Now we're on the same page."

"Must be a weird Indian way of thinking." Smitty pulled at

the handle of his gun, caught Quannah's quick movement and reholstered.

"Yes, very weird, very Indian," Quannah said. "Mitakuye Oyasin."

"Me take-a-your-ass-in?"

Quannah sighed. "Mitakuye Oyasin. All our Relations. If you're doing good for the whole, the whole is doing good for you." Quannah sat up straight. There was an irregularity in the shadows. Someone sneaking in or out? Quannah said, "You see that?"

"Yeah, in the backyard."

"I'm going to shine the carry-all beam and jump out. You give the warning. That's all. Understand?"

"Gotcha." Smitty's voice cracked. "Shine on, Chief, shine on."

Quannah laid the heavy broad-beam flashlight on the dash. As he opened the door to get out, he flicked the beam on. A man stumbled through the underbrush.

Smitty yelled, "Police. Stop. Dammit man, stop!" With gun drawn he pounded his way through the oleanders.

Quannah ran right behind him, clicking his shoulder mike and alerting others to what was happening as he ran. "757 Fetchwin Way. In pursuit of one fleeing on foot, possibly armed. Officers on this block, head to the corners and the back alley cut-through in case he tries an out there." Almost to the rickety back fence of the property, now with only his hand-held flash for guidance, Quannah caught the scene in slow motion. The perp turned, raised his hands before him as if he held a gun and was about to shoot. Smitty, who in trained response assumed the protective return-fire stance. But instead of shooting, the perp executed a forward roll, knocking Smitty sideways and around toward Quannah just as Smitty's finger pulled the trigger, once, twice, three times and more.

A flash, a searing heat under his armpit, and Quannah landed two feet away. The pain, quick and intense, tore most of his senses from him. He couldn't speak or see. The perp, lying beside him, breathed Jack Daniel's fumes, and placed a buddy-like hand across his shoulders. "Whatcha ya'll wanna go shooting for? Shooting? Less be friends. Zat's all right, pal, less be friends."

Smitty screamed into his mike. "Officer down. Officer down. Oh, God."

The weight of the man was lifted from Quannah's back, and although he couldn't see, he heard the snap of cuffs as Smitty handled the perp. "You sorry damned excuse of an air-breather. Damn. Damn. Made me shoot my partner. Damn you. And, you're just a drunk. Not one of the killers. Just a lazy damned drunk. Oh, God."

"That sure sounded like shots," Willi said.

"Nonsense," Agatha said. "No flashing police lights are around; people aren't running out of the houses. Don't you go borrowing trouble. You've plenty to occupy your mind with your friend's problems tonight." Agatha gunned the motor and headed south on Fetchwin Way, past the 600 block, then the 500's toward the center of town, and then at the courthouse square she pulled the wheel to the left and headed toward what was once the derelict railroad station, but now was part of the soon-to-open Nickleberry Museum. With heavy foot, Agatha wound the old engine up to fifty mph—five over the limit—whizzed around corners and executed a sideways skid any stunt driver would have been proud to claim, before zooming down the dark street again. Tattoo's snake rippled in the mottled light.

Fingers tensed in a tight hold on the dashboard, Willi still managed to click off her expectations for this late-night visit. First, she'd damn well like to get to the museum alive. One of the reasons for shoving Tattoo into the middle, since Willi wasn't giving up her survival handholds or her door-side fast escape route. She glanced at the young janitress. Other than the ripples on her arms, she failed to respond to neck-breaking stops, cut corners resulting in curb tilts and speeds beyond the limits. The museum was the only place Willi had to pursue any clues that might answer why her friend lay in a coma. Secondly, find that silly butt-eating little mutt, Ludwig. Locate Anastasia Zöllmer's Rolodex of addresses along with her appointment calendar. Check on the museum's tool van.

Once the police decided that Anastasia's incident should not be in the accidental but rather the attempted homicidal category, they'd want the addresses and calendar. Willi tilted her nose in the air. Well, they should have already been on the mark, and she wasn't doing anything wrong. She, after all, had a perfect right to be on the premises on two counts. As a chairperson and as Anastasia's friend. So there. She brushed her hands, swiping from her mind any necessity of conferring with the authorities about anything she might locate, unless . . . unless she talked with Sheriff Brigham Tucker himself or Quannah and they promised to take the investigation on Anastasia's part seriously. Of course, she had to have something that might show a reason someone might have purposely run down her friend. Even great cops couldn't make a case out of supposition and want-to. Until she had something tangible, she'd just do what she did best in these situations—gather information, tidbits here and there, and get the right folks to talk to her. That's where her intuition led her to the truth. No matter that Big Chief Lassiter insisted that her sixth sense led her into trouble with a bold-type **T**. With nose in the air, she nodded. She'd do what had to be done.

As they entered the museum grounds, a van careened toward them, forcing Agatha to swerve and screech to a halt. Burnt rubber fumes swirled around the trio as they jumped out of the pickup. "Hell's bells," Willi said, "We don't want to end up wrapped around a telephone pole, too. Wasn't that the museum van? The one you drive, Tattoo?"

Tattoo twisted around to stare at the disappearing vehicle. "Yep. Yep, I just remembered. Yeah."

"Remembered what?"

"Boys from the mechanics shop. Yeah . . . uh . . . that's it. I left the keys under the floor mat, so's they could pick it up. Guess in all the excitement, I plumb forgot."

"It needs repairs?" Willi tilted her head.

"Yep. Uh . . . the hydraulic lift. That's what it is. The hydraulic lift on the back we use for heavier items. We've got a forklift in the budget. Maybe get it in another month."

At the side runway . . . uh . . . parking lot, Willi strode toward the door. "Fine. I'll give you a ride tomorrow, if you're planning on coming in on a Saturday, when Quannah returns my car since the mechanic shop obviously has the tool van." Willi frowned and considered Tattoo out of the corner of her eye. For such a no-nonsense, no-frills person, Tattoo was definitely in the confused and forgetful ozone tonight.

"Nope, no need, ma'am. Shop boys will bring it in a couple of days. Yeah, I think. I'm pretty sure."

"Tattoo?"

"Yes, Ms. Gallagher?"

"So, you'll need a ride tomorrow maybe?"

"Yeah, maybe so. You're right. What was I thinking?"

Willi stared at the young woman. "Are you okay?"

"Guess, I'm a little more upset about Ms. Zöllmer than I realized."

That sounded sincere and Willi patted Tattoo's shoulder. "Understandable."

Just as they reached the front door of the museum, a second

van zoomed past them. "So?" Agatha asked, gathering her bright skirts in a protective mass. "So, who was in *that* van?"

"Might be . . . uh . . . that professor feller. He uses one to carry them train parts and such in."

Agatha, skirts escaping from her grasp and flowing in the October breeze, which seemed to stiffen with each hour, said, "Is that one of those vans you're looking for?"

Willi paused and stared. "I suppose that first one is the one Tattoo uses—an old black thing with dents and places for ladders and tools to hang off the side. That one that just passed us, also ancient and battered, must be the professor's. The official museum vans, due to be delivered next week, are to be used to shuttle visitors from the airport or the hotels to special functions. They're planning some outings for the nursing home patients, too, I believe. They were quite expensive with wheelchair lifts and automatic steps and such. They had the Nickleberry Museum logo painted on the sides, too."

Agatha said, "Yes, indeed. I wonder if they might need a volunteer driver?"

"No. Absolutely not. Every position is filled." Willi hoped her voice came across as businesslike and matter-of-fact, not in the true panic mode indicated by the rapid pulse in her throat. This conditioned response to Agatha Kachelhoffer's driving skills brought a picture of bug-eyed patrons reaching for their Valium along with senior citizens taking double doses of heart meds. "No drivers needed," Willi added with special emphasis as she swiped the card key across the front door pad. "Come on. I want to find answers, or at least one smoke-inhaling hound."

No sooner had the door swooshed closed behind them and they'd walked toward the waterfall display than a clatter and crash of glass broke the silence. Agatha's claw-like fingers closed around Willi's arm. Willi's already quickened pulse cantered faster. She stood very still and quieted her breath to try to discern the direction of the noise. One pathetic yip reached her ears. Willi pointed at herself and then toward the noise, and indicated for Tattoo to go around. Tattoo nodded.

With each step, goose bumps ran down Willi's scalp and spine. *Please don't let that mutt be hurt, or worse.*

CHAPTER SIX

Hidden thoughts can turn to rust
Unless you find someone to trust.

—T'lanihctl
The Book of the Ancient Ones

Willi mouthed, "Be careful."

Then she yelled, "Ludwig?" Breaking from Agatha's death grip, she walked briskly around the waterfall toward the exhibits side. "LUDWIG! Here, boy, here."

With each step she took, the movement-sensitive lights flickered on. She gave cursory glances at the other exhibits, but something kept drawing her toward that pyramid scene, Chacmool and his bloody bowl. In her hurry, she tripped over some broken pottery, her shoe skittered off, and she stepped down upon a shard. Blood instantly oozed from the soft pad of her big toe. The sting made her gasp and the bit of blood made her stomach do a momentary loop-de-loop. She used the side of her foot to kick the debris away.

"Be careful, Agatha, you don't want to get hurt, too. Stay back."

Bright plumage stilled for the first time this evening, Agatha perched upon her bird legs, hands clasped in front of her. "Why can't we hear the puppy?"

"Don't know. But, he's definitely been here." The crockery from the storyteller's area lay about broken; the stage rocks Tattoo had placed were tumbled.

Tattoo said, "And we'd just cleaned up his earlier mess. Guess that dog's gonna be history, he keeps this stuff up."

"Beg pardon," Agatha said.

"Earlier, there had been blood or perhaps paint and paw prints—supposedly Ludwig's," Willi explained. "Now, what has that silly pooch gotten into?"

"Not to worry," Agatha said. "Usually, if you're in a panic, the animal will be, too. Give him a few moments to get used to our voices. He'll come out of hiding. Meantime, let's put a Band-Aid on that toe."

"Carry those in your magic bag, huh?" Tattoo asked.

Agatha stared meaningfully at Willi. "How long's it been since your last tetanus shot?"

"I hate needles. Shots." Willi shivered.

Agatha sat upon one of the toppled rocks, pointed at Willi to sit, too, and scrambled in her string bag of tie-dyed greens and blues. Willi tore her stocking away from the cut. "Don't touch it."

"Miss Willi, don't be such a baby." Agatha produced a couple of *Sesame Street* Band-Aids and covered her big toe. "Just a scratch, really, Miss Willi, nothing to be concerned about. That'll do it. Put your shoe on, and let's find Ludwig. Uh, but you might want to check out that date on your tetanus."

With a pronounced frown toward Agatha, Willi gingerly tried her footing. "I'm not getting a shot. Can't make me and that's that." She retraced their steps and paced through each display to land the three of them in front of the Aztecan home display. A loom, with a mannequin's hands entwined as if guiding the colorful fibers, sat at the forefront of an adobe-like structure. "If my toe is throbbing, that's like not a good sign, is it? And maybe a little feverish?"

Tattoo sighed, and looked at the ceiling. "Jeez, lady."

Agatha patted Willi's arm. "Give it a few moments. Maybe I just put the Band-Aid on too tight."

In the display, figurines of children played with a string of clay disks and a bird-shaped whistle. Bold geometric designs decorated mats on the floor and walls. Agatha pointed to some shards of pottery and the hay-covered floor. "Something heavy has been moved from that spot. Guess they aren't finished with this display yet."

Willi nodded. "I believe Etzli and his helper were planning on tying up loose ends on it late into tonight. But I've not seen them."

When a slight whimper reached her ears, Willi ran back to the other side of the corridor, came to a halt in front of the pyramid with Chacmool staring down at them. She and Agatha glanced up the steps. Willi said, "That pottery—that huge jar—wasn't there when the priests were making the sacrifices."

Agatha peered sideways at Willi. "Really?"

Willi swallowed. "I mean—"

"One of your visions?"

"Uh, whatever."

With one hand, Agatha fluttered the end of her waist scarf. "Pay attention to them. Sister and I've told you many times, they are given to help you solve problems in life." Agatha sniffed. "Of course, one must separate them from the . . . uh . . . plane upon which we mortals exist."

"I know that."

"So, Miss Willi, although the large jar upon the edge wasn't in your vision, was it physically there as it is now, a few feet to the right of the statue and partially off the edge of the top step?"

"No. On that side of the pyramid top, only that horrid Chacmool sat. No big vase, jar, whatever that is."

She started toward the top steps representing those last ones that prisoners would take to their deaths.

"Stop," Agatha said. "It is, I believe, a burial jar."

Willi, right foot a step higher than her left, stared upward. "Burial jar?"

"Three-foot-high, perhaps less. It's a child's burial jar."

"Oh?" Willi said, moving her right foot back down a step.

"In those times, in the desert areas, many families opted to have their dearest children who had passed over close to them. And these were sort of mummified with special death herbs and flowers that allowed them in spirit, and in bodily remains, at least, to stay with the family. Don't look that way, Miss Willi. That's no more odd than many who keep the ashes of loved ones in the living room."

"You're right, of course." She whistled. "Here, Ludwig. Come on. Make some noise and help us find you, you dang pooch." She frowned at the silence and the burial jar. "Wonder why it's there atop the pyramid rather than in the Egyptian display across from the pyramid?"

"Well, everything is not yet prepared. Perhaps a worker just decided at closing time to take it down the steps tomorrow. I love those flowing orange and green curtains at the back of the pyramid."

"Uh . . . yes, they're nice." Willi ignored the sway of the multicolored backdrop and concentrated on the jar. Perhaps Ludwig had somehow gotten in there? To Agatha she said, "You know, that jar is about the size of the area in the Aztecan village that looked as if something had been there, but moved away recently. Why would it have been taken up there?" She climbed another couple of steps. "I'll just check—"

"Watch out!" Agatha yelled.

From the corner of her eye, Willi saw the flow of orange and green, yellow and purple lift and sway as a strong draft blew down the steps. In the millisecond she glanced upward, she eyed the heavy jar tilting and finally crashing downward. Willi twisted just enough to let it pass her by. Miraculously, the jar cracked but did not break upon its descent. She ran back down the steps, Agatha dove in from the side, and they bumped heads as they bent over the foot-and-a-half-wide crockery. A snuffling and something shuffling made Willi jerk back. Maybe it wasn't Ludwig, but something else. Something more sinister?

"A snake?"

"You and your obsession with snakes," Agatha said, and put her arms upon her hips.

"Well, they do seem to come often into my life, as you know."

"Let's get this top off."

"Wait a minute," Willi said. "There were some skunks out in the train sheds today. We've had raccoons break in, could be . . ."

"I believe, after having crashed down, we would be experiencing the odiferous reaction if it were a skunk, or the yipping of an angry raccoon, don't you think?"

"Okay, Agatha. I concede. Let's get the top off." Willi struggled long enough that beads of sweat poured down into her eyes. "Maybe it's glued."

Agatha wrung her hands and leaned an ear against the jar. "Can't hear any movement now. More than likely just a cockroach, now seeking a dark corner."

"Or Ludwig." Willi took one of the construction boards, obviously left by Tattoo, who'd not finished the storyteller's area. "Stand back. I know this is a replica—albeit an expensive one—and not the real thing." Raising the board overhead, she brought it down hard on the middle of the crockery. As the creature inside rolled outward, she yelped.

Agatha said, "The poor thing."

Ludwig, eyes rolling, gasped for air, his lungs obviously straining.

Willi leaned down to him, touched his side. "I think he's been drugged. There's a strange scent."

"Chloroform?"

"Maybe. Definitely smoke, and . . . and something else."

"Let's rush him to the vet's," Agatha said, already wrapping him in one of her purple scarves.

Willi gulped. *Rush? An intentional high-speed ride with Agatha at the wheel?* Her stomach rolled over. "No."

"No? What do you mean—?"

"I mean, you rush Ludwig to care. I'm going to look around here."

"Good idea. This baby didn't jump in that two-foot-high jar by himself."

"Exactly."

Agatha hurried down the hall. "You be careful, Miss Willi. You hear? Call the police right now. I'll be back soon as I can."

"I'll be careful." Willi ignored the rest. She wasn't one-hundred percent sure she heard Agatha muttering about calling the police first anyway. Well, that'd be her story later, and she'd by daggum and Texas toadstools stick to her story.

Tattoo rushed in from the shadows to the left. "Agatha just ran past me with that mutt. Taking him to the vet?"

"Exactly." Willi stalled a moment. She wanted to search in Anastasia's office, but wanted to do it alone.

She circled around the broken pottery to give herself time to think.

Tattoo said, "Guess I'd better clean this up."

"I hope that wasn't a valuable artifact."

"Naw. Those are under lock and key, not in them open exhibitions yet. Just before the final glass is placed and sealed is when them valuable items are placed. This was probably what Ms. Zöllmer calls a space holder."

Perfect. That chore would take Tattoo a few minutes. Willi smiled. "Would you mind checking out those background curtains behind the pyramid, too? A door or something must have opened back there to send a strong draft across the top. The jar was already sitting on the edge, toppled because of that breeze. I'm sure you'd want to secure any doors or windows back there."

"Sure will do that. Right soon, we'll be a-gettin' sensors on all the doors and windows, but now we only got them in the office areas and the front foyers where the expensive art work is located. Makes sense. Probably Mrs. Oñadiz or that nephew of hers left a window back there open." Tattoo shuffled from foot to foot. "Then, if you don't mind me gone for about fifteen minutes, I need to check something out in the far warehouses. Might as well make sure all is right tight, huh? Maybe you could limp your way to Ms. Zöllmer's office and wait comfortable like 'til Agatha comes back for us."

Willi smiled. "That would suit me." For Tattoo's sake, Willi made herself favor her sore toe until she rounded the expanse of waterfall, and then she nearly ran the rest of the way to Anastasia's office.

When Willi stepped into the glassed-in room, she stood staring for a full minute at the chaos on top of Anastasia's desk. The middle drawer lay upside down on the leather desk top, partially obscuring the gold-inlaid Texas star. The crushed pair of crystal lamps dangled by cords torn from the floor sockets. Someone with a lot of anger had ripped through the room, leaving details as strangely juxtaposed as a Texas tornado. The planters filled with banana plants lay upside down on the furniture. Linen draperies were torn asunder and rolled into a heap beneath the desk. The perpetrator had ground the planter dirt into the hand-woven Native American upholstery. The cracked overhead fluorescents emitted waves milliseconds apart to cast her into an eerie Hitchcockian scene to set her heartbeat cantering. The AC kicked in. She screamed, and shivered in the blast of cold against her skin.

"Damn it to hell and back." She swallowed, her hand on her chest. "Okay, I just have to stay focused. Whoever did this is long gone. Let's see . . . let's see." A half a minute ticked away before she stilled her pulse enough to concentrate. "Okay, I can do this. Quannah would . . . uh . . . search . . . in a . . . a grid. Okay, I can do that."

Starting at the far left corner beside the French doors, she peered inside already opened bookcases, shoved debris aside on the floor, and avoided the crystal shards, evil little slithers that looked in the undulating light as if they might develop a life of their own and seek out warm skin to pierce. Willi shuddered. "Get a grip." She heaved the planters off the sofa, used the trashcan to shovel through the dirt. NoRolodex. No calendar. She had stomped through the entire room other than the side most in darkness that had Ludwig's soft leather cowled and cave-like sleeping nook. Seemed like the only place not ripped apart. Again, just like a tornado aftermath, there were pockets of normalcy within the chaos, untouched bits of life that bespoke of hope. At sight of the dog bed, a tear rolled down her cheek.

She sniffled. "Damn." Gently, she bent down. "Might as well take it to Ramblin' tomorrow." She picked it up with both hands and something crinkled. She reached into the far recesses, underneath the plaid inner pad. "Well, I'll be darned."

"If teeth marks mean anything, looks like Ludwig put up a fight for his master's calendar." A couple of pages were missing, but mostly it was intact, still wet from Ludwig's slobber. Hmmm. Willi tilted her head and tapped the end of her nose. Maybe he had a few sheets in his teeth, ran out. Yes, that just feels right. Sure, he runs out, the perp chases him down, finally catches him and throws him in the burial jar.

Willi stood for a moment, hugging the bed, decided to leave it until tomorrow and stuffed the two-inch thick daily calendar into her purse. But . . . she desperately needed the Rolodex of phone numbers. Probably, Anastasia kept those on her computer, too, but she always had the Rolodex right beside her phone. Said she liked the tactile feel of ratcheting it from card to card. The motion gave her time to think. Another tear threatened. Willi wiped her eyes and continued the search.

She'd almost given up when she realized she had not done a thorough grid by grid search. She pulled out the shreds of draperies from beneath the sofa. As she did, loose cards three-by-two inches poured from the folds. At last, the Rolodex itself landed on the floor. Willi gathered every card she could find, shook the curtains out again and retrieved another half dozen. Well, saguaro spit and bent nails, all this was not going to fit into her purse. No handy gift bags or briefcases being available, she considered Ludwig's bed again. She shoved the cards and the holder as best she could under the softer folds of the plaid inner pillow, then sort of rolled the whole thing under her arm. By now, her toe throbbed anew, her shoulders sagged and she looked sadly at her torn hose.

With what seemed like a gargantuan effort, she shuffled toward the open French doors. There, under the midnight moon, sheets of the spiral-bound calendar fluttered. She chased bits of pages until she came to the border of monkey grass which had evidently caught the last of the recalcitrant bits and pieces. She scurried out of the nippy air, rolled the pieces together and added them to the trove in Ludwig's bed.

Finally, she had a moment to think. What popped into her head was the erratic path of the van that had almost run them down. But, Tattoo had identified it as the museum van. Willi stood and her heart again picked up a canter. She stared out into the starkly lit corridors. She shook her head. No, no. That would mean someone had taken the van from the mechanics who had come to retrieve it. Oh, God. What if . . . what if . . .

one of the escaped convicts had chosen the museum as a hiding place, perhaps and had ransacked the office in hopes of finding some cash? Oh, shoot fire, and Tattoo was out there wandering around, unaware there might be more danger than finding one nicotine-deprived mutt.

With heavy handbag over her shoulder and Ludwig's soft bed rolled under her arm, Willi limped around the azure-and-blue-tiled waterfall backdrop and out into the museum proper. Now, where had Tattoo said she was going after cleaning up the pottery? Oh my gosh. Into the sheds. Into those black recesses, warrens of monster parts and rusted trains, into the very bowels of grease and . . .

"Miss Gallagher?"

A hand waved before Willi's face.

"Miss Gallagher?"

"Tattoo? You're all right?"

"I'm fair to middling. You looked like you'd done seen a ghost. You know, considering what everybody says about your . . . nervous nature—"

"Nervous nature?"

"—and your bent toward them imaginings—"

"Daydreams?"

"Yeah, them."

Willi tilted her nose in the air. "I don't have any such thing. Can't *imagine* where you heard—"

"Oh, most everybody in town knows. Don't nobody think any the less of you. Said you's like that since you were a kid, and—"

"The question is—" Willi intoned in her best sophomore English teacher voice, "—the question is whether all the pottery was cleaned up, and whether anything was amiss in the sheds."

"Amiss?"

"Anything out of the ordinary. Anything we need to call the

police about?"

Tattoo folded her arms and rubbed her talismans—the snake and the rose vine. "Naw, we don't need to be calling no police. Don't want them snooping and messing things up out in our storehouses. Every one of these here contenders would be madder than mad, if them things was touched. Naw, naw, naw. No police matter out there, no, ma'am." She looked down at her thick-soled tennis shoes, straightened her shoulders and reared back to peer at Willi.

"What about the offices? Any reason to call the police?" Tattoo pulled out her razor-thin cell phone, and flipped the lid.

Willi grasped Tattoo's hand and clicked the phone closed. "No. Ludwig had some fun playing with things in there, but I've cleaned that up." She patted the dog bedding. Then she mimicked Tattoo's action, folding her arms and rubbing some warmth into her low-life, lying bones. "No, no, no. No police needed in there. Nope." She knew good and well from past experience what she'd get from Quannah and his uncle, Sheriff Tucker. *No real evidence of wrongdoing; just looks like that mutt went goofy, and what nicotine-filled pooch wouldn't. Now, Miss Willi, when there's something truly wrong, we'll investigate, yes we will. You shouldn't be calling us off a manhunt to go traipsing after a dog.* Yeah, she'd been down that road before. She'd check out a few things before she'd get into a tizzy and tell them . . . what? Anastasia's dog went crazy when his mistress didn't return for him this evening. Well, of course, he did and had been attacked and left to die in an ancient burial urn.

She led Tattoo outside the museum to sit on Texas-lime–carved seating *bancos* in Anastasia's private office garden to await Agatha. When they heard her vehicle, they went back through the office and hallway to shut off lights and chose to go out the front door which they locked.

When Willi hauled herself into the passenger seat, Agatha

said, "Sydney Curry had to be awakened from a deep sleep. She'd been up with a German shepherd that gave birth to thirteen puppies. Hadn't had anything but naps for the last seventy-two hours."

"Sydney is the best small animal vet in three counties. That's why I use her for Charlie," Willi said.

"Charlie?" Tattoo asked.

Agatha careened around a corner, Willi grasped the dashboard and with her cheek smashed against the window pane ground out, "My miniature dachshund."

"Awww."

"Okay, so I'm dropping you both at home, right?" Agatha asked.

"Right," Tattoo said.

"Wrong," Willi countered. "Me—you're dropping at the hospital."

"Now, Willi, Sister is there seeing after Anastasia."

"Can't explain it. I just *know* . . . I *must* . . . get to the hospital. *Now.*" A muscle in her throat jittered. Was this a nervous premonition that Anastasia had taken a turn for the worse?

Agatha yelled, "Soon's I drop off Tattoo, I'll be back for you all." She burned rubber as she left the hospital portico.

When Willi jumped out of the pickup and ran through the pneumatic doors, she barreled into the arms of a bear of a man.

"Whoa there, Miss Willi, hold them horses." Sheriff Tucker pushed her back and studied her through narrowed eyes atop his bulbous nose, a nose constantly reddened from allergies and blowing. He patted her shoulder, turned his head and grabbed a blue bandana, caught the sneeze and wiped his eyes. "Excuse me, Miss Willi."

"Not a problem. Just going up to see Anastasia. Any news about her accident?"

"No, no news about *that* accident."

After two paces, she pivoted around to face him. "Pardon?"

He grasped her around the shoulders and gave her a squeeze. "Before I say more, let me tell you right off that everything's just fine. Been another . . . sort of . . . accident tonight. Down on Fetchwin Way. You probably know the whereabouts of that pretty little street with all the—"

"Sheriff Tucker."

"Guess I'm a-rambling some. I told dispatch to call you. Thought that was why you come roaring through the doors."

"Sheriff! What has happened?" The tic in her throat developed into a wild spasm like a donkey kicking up a fight. "Quannah? Is it Quannah?" The burro bucked, and she couldn't breathe. Her knees buckled as she leaned into Sheriff Tucker.

"Don't go all faint on me now, Missy. Here. Sit in this chair. He's fine. Quannah's strong. Doc says worse thing hurting him right now is his ego."

She clasped a hand to her chest to still the kicking. "I'm all right now. Lot of shocks this evening. What happened? Can I see him? Is he in surgery?"

"I'm going to go up and ask the nurses. See if he's out yet."

When he left, the lady in the hospital flower shop stuck her head out of the doorway. "Are you Ms. Gallagher? Someone calling on the store phone for you."

Willi checked her cell phone while walking inside. Dead. "Thank you." She grasped the hospital phone. "This is Willi."

"You can't ignore me, you know," her caller said. Static split across the words.

"Elba? Tattoo? Ramblin'?" She jiggled the receiver. Shoot, she couldn't tell if it were male or female. "My cell phone's dead. Sorry. Repeat what you said. This line isn't too clear, either."

"Sure, it's dead. Right. *Bitch.*"

Willi gasped. "Who? Who is this?"

119

". . . between you and me . . . you want to talk about it . . . don't." The words crackled through the line, sending shivers down Willi's spine. "Don't be whining. He could . . . again. You never know what the powers-that-be have in store. This . . . your lesson . . . not his, unless you get him involved."

"I don't even have a clue what you want, or who you are. What have I done to deserve this . . . this attack? Just explain."

"You'll figure it out. By the end of the school year, you'll be miserable, too."

"I've done something to—?"

"Have a nice evening, *bitch.*"

"Ma'am?" The flower shop attendant stood with her purse and a knitting bag along with a couple of magazines underneath one arm, her keys in hand. "I have to lock up now, hon."

"Of course." Willi set the old-fashioned receiver into the phone cradle. No hope of an ID display on the old rotary dial. "Thank you."

A comforting scent of Camelot powder drifted from the lady when Willi walked past the door. Great Coyote's balls, she'd had a weird day. *Strange, how something so benign in life as the sweet-smelling granny could be juxtaposed beside something so nasty as her stalker.* Numbness spread through every cell, zapping her strength to move or think. She was long past exhaustion, but adrenaline pumped through her, keeping her mobile and thinking, thinking so hard her temples throbbed.

A few moments later, Sheriff Tucker returned to deliver her to Quannah's room where they had to wait for two hours before he came out from under the effects of the strong anesthetics. She had left only for a few moments to check on Anastasia, but there were no changes. Sheriff Tucker had no sooner given into a need for caffeine and stepped out, than Quannah seemed to awaken with near lucidity. His back toward her, his side and hip bandage created a ridiculous hump under the covers. After the nurses prodded and talked to him for a minute, they showed her how to punch the button to give him a dose of morphine when needed, and retreated to the nurses' station.

Willi swallowed while wiping a wayward tear from her eye. She drew in a few steadying breaths before approaching his bedside. Well, he'd feel guilty and be devastated for simply doing his job, if he saw her distressed, and she'd sworn never to let him feel that way. Dang right. Guilt could turn into resentment. She squared her shoulders. A wispy lock of ebony hair escaped the thong at the nape of his neck, almost ruining her resolve. She blurted out, "So, what's up, Chief Turn-Tail? Got that cute ass of yours in the line of fire, huh?"

In a monumental heave upward and over he faced her. "Damn you, Gallagher. Keep your voice down. That's not what . . . that's all I need . . . meathead of a reporter, what's-his-name—?"

"Elliott Grimes who covers crimes?"

"Great Spirit, he'll twist the facts." He groaned.

"Need a little more meds for the pain?" She reached toward the pump.

"No . . . no. Got to get up. Get . . . going."

She withdrew her hand, but said, "I don't think so. You've told me many times about Coyote Medicine teaching through *backwards* and clownish ways, but this scenario is definitely giving new meaning to the backwards part, Chief Wounded Tush."

"Gallagher, Gallagher, Galla—" His voice drifted off, but there was, even dulled by painkillers, a twinkle in his eye. She'd hit the right note to hide her anxiety and not burden him with her fears. Now, how to keep the promise she'd made to tell him about . . . the notes, now a phone call . . . from a . . . stalker.

She leaned toward him to hear his finished statement. "Gallagher, you keep talking about my rear, I'll think you've got lascivi . . . laschiv . . . naughty designs on this poor bedridden warrior."

"Those drugs must be dream-inducing, Lassiter." At last she entwined her fingers with his, and in a softer voice added, "But soon's you're released, we'll try to make those fantasies come true."

"Uncle Brigham's here?"

"Well, sure. He went out for a cup of coffee. Anyway, he told me your partner shot you."

Quannah groaned and rolled back off his wounded side. She bolstered his back with extra pillows and walked around the bed to face him.

He said, "Wasn't his fault, though."

She brought her hands to her hips. "Don't you dare be noble and give an idiot like that an out."

"Should . . . oh, Great Spirit . . . should have had entire flack jacket. Armpit panels. I took them out. Bullet came in at my waist—not my butt. Exited in front of my armpit. No organs, no bones hit." His voice grew weaker. "Muscle and gristle wound. Be back on the job tomorrow."

"Like I said, those drugs are dream-inducers."

"Gallagher—"

"Don't Gallagher me."

"*Winyan,* now—"

"That sweet word won't work, either. By the by, your eyes are glazed and slightly crossed."

"And your point, Gallagher?"

"My point? You will come home if and when the doctors say. Then the Kachelhoffer sisters will be nurses and watchdogs to make sure *you do* follow doctor's orders."

A nurse came in to check his vitals. She wafted between them like a ghost, a comforting and unobtrusive spirit.

His eyes grew rounded. "Those two—?"

Willi wagged a finger in front of his face. "They are both trained practical nurses. Now, now. If you get agitated the nurse will have to increase the meds."

The white spirit smiled and said, "Even as you speak. Time for him to relax." She pushed the pump and sashayed out in a cloud of muted backlight from the hallway.

Willi bent closer to Quannah's less than piercing gaze. "Perhaps this is a good time to tell you about . . . uh . . . an uncomfortable situation." She bit her bottom lip. "I promised I would share with you, but I don't really want to burden you, and don't want you to remember exactly what was said so that the creep won't come after you, you see?"

"Huh? Sit . . . situ . . . a . . . tion. Good idea."

"Seems like I have a stalker. Getting nastier by the minute."

For a moment, his relaxed hooded eyelids rose. "Stalker?"

"Has a penchant for leaving me naughty notes."

He grasped her wrist, but his fingers grew lax. "Could 'splain the Jag . . . u . . ."

Willi sighed. "Well, leave it to a man to discuss either horses or cars at a crisis time."

"Don't leave . . . hospi . . . protect . . . claws . . . crazy woman."

"Don't get in a tizzy, Lassiter. I bought a gun for protection."

"You? With . . . gun? Great Spirit." He half raised his torso, groaned and flopped back down.

Willi looked over her shoulder before punching the pump one more time. "It's a small handgun. I've been practicing at the gun range."

"Jag . . . claws . . . dream."

"Yes, I guess these drugs do give you some bad dreams, sweetie. So, now, my conscience is clear, and I've not kept any secrets from you, and you know I'm capable of protecting myself what with the pistol and the practice, so you won't worry while you're recuperating from your butt booboo."

As she leaned in and drew the blanket over his humped hip and on up over his shoulders, she had to strain to catch his last words.

"Coyote shit!"

"Lassiter. Poor sweetie, you don't know what you're saying." When his snores came evenly, she kissed his cheek and left. Oh, her shoulders felt fifty pounds lighter. She shouldn't have waited so long to confide. He had seemed to understand, and if not, he'd have a day incarcerated and incapacitated to get used to the idea . . . if he remembered at all. It was the best she could do at the moment to protect him and to assuage her guilt in not confiding in him earlier. Willi shut her eyes a moment. She did not want the stalker to come after Quannah in his weakened state, which, according to the phone call, the jerk was likely to do if he thought she had told Quannah the details. It was best right now if he really didn't remember any details. When he got stronger, she'd rehash it all again, and leave nothing out.

With Willi in the passenger seat of the old pickup, Elba, who had taken over driving duties upon Agatha's return, maneuvered along Licorice Lane, taking the curves in a much smoother manner than her sister Agatha would have. Willi grinned. Sure and Agatha wanted this time to sit at the hospital since her sweetie, Sheriff Tucker, was doing the same. Hard times could bind as well as the good. Willi sighed. Her eyes, dry as a Saharan dune, gritty so she could neither shut nor keep them open, audibly popped as she lifted her lids.

In the uncanny way of close friends, Elba picked up on her thoughts and blurted out, "If you had a camel's double lids, that would take care of the pain. I heard tell they could keep out the sand, wash out the grit, and to them Arabic types be right sexy what with all them lashes. A man would have to be right horny to want to—"

"Elba! Elba, please none of your famous trio of comparisons tonight. I believe there's enough happened I'll never forget this freaky Friday. I don't need any more visuals going around in my tired brain."

Normally, the ride toward home over curving Licorice Lane offered relaxation since it ribboned through woods full of oaks, sumac and wild grapevines. Even in the nighttime October early morning, Willi imagined the shades of ambers and golds, claret and spice leaves would make a colorful canopy to embrace folks, although in the darkness, all were swallowed in shades of blacks and dusky grays. She rolled down her window to pull in the fall scents.

Elba's insistent voice broke into her reverie. "Good of Officer Parva to have already taken your car to the farm. Remember he said he pulled down the garage door, drove in and the keys were on the back porch inside the blue pot. Said he didn't lock the garage 'cause he couldn't be sure you'd have a way to get in if all your keys were on that ring. Right thoughtful young man."

"That was Quannah's set. I've got mine right here. Thoughtful isn't a word I'd use to describe that blundering idiot of a mule's behind. Good gosh almighty and Hell's bells, the man shot his partner."

"Now, Willi, he didn't mean to. Poor kid is more than likely suffering worse than old Jebanee Orfm with his ingrown toenails, worse than Angina Rattfargman what glued her yoo-hoo to the bathtub with that hair remover last week, worse than the choir director down to the Revival Church who moves so fast due to his hemorrhaging hemorrhoids. Now, I could name others like—"

"You do, and I *will* have to hurt you." Willi leaned her head out the window. "I want peace and quiet and home. Autumn scents of fireplaces and mulch are great, but I want home."

"Me, too. Need to feed Rose Pig, poor baby."

Willi grinned. Rose Pig, Elba's familiar, a two-hundred-pound sow, had saved Willi in the past from an intruder, and for her troubles retained an acid-ingrained mark on her hip in the shape of a rose, hence her name. Thinking of that brought to mind Willi's own four-legged furry friend, her dachshund, Charlie, who would be waiting for her and his nightly snack. Poor baby had probably been in and out his doggy door fifteen jillion times to check if she had driven in yet. She yawned. Yes, Quannah's insight in the world of the animals—the *Wamaskaskan*—had enriched her awareness of the four-leggeds, the winged and finned ones and their messages. With Elba now quiet beside her, Willi yawned again, relaxed against the headrest and shut her eyes to allow herself to drift, almost float into a short nap. *Ah, this was so sweet, calm . . .*

The pitter patter of Willi's heart slowed, she eased back and studied the stars. Through her gritty sight, each heavenly light star-burst like a fast-forward nighttime city traffic photo. She concentrated on the Big Dipper constellation. A soft drumbeat drew her intense focus to what Indian legends referred to as the Great Bear. Quannah's voice drifted outward from some subconscious memory of hers.

Yes, the Great Bear, that is what we prefer to call that part of the Star Nation. The stars of what the White Eyes say make up the handle of the Big Dipper, are to us, the hunters. In the autumn when the Great Bear is low to the horizon the Bear's arrow wounds drip upon Unci—Mother Earth—and her Standing People—the trees—to turn them reds and browns and blood rusts.

Willi sank farther into the contours of the seat. She had a misty recollection of a second legend concerning the constellation but as the crisp autumn scents drifted through the window, she failed to grab hold. And what would Quannah say about that?

The information you need, Winyan, will surface on a need-to-know status according to Great Spirit and the purpose within the Universe.

Willi smiled, totally relaxed now. A leaf blew across Elba and settled in Willi's hair. Without opening her eyes, she plucked it out and whispered, "Thank you—*pilamaya ye*—Great Bear, for your gift of fall colors."

Her head slammed to the right and hit the passenger window. She snapped her eyes open while grabbing for the dashboard. "Elba!"

Elba said, "Dang it, what was—?"

Thump, thump, thump sounded beneath the chassis attesting to some late-night marauding scavenger sacrificing its life for a midnight snack. Elba tried again and said, "What was that we run—?" Before she completed the question the distinctive scent surrounded the pickup. Elba snorted. "Skunk. What would Quannah say about that animal totem?"

Willi grimaced and said, "Something in life stinks to high heaven and back?"

"Or," Elba said, "might be everything in black and white ain't right. Could be watch out for what kind of stink you're sending out in the world. Phew! Lordy, that's as bad as old man Crestelman's farts in Sunday church. Don't matter where we sit, seems he sets his pooting fanny right smack dab in front of me and Sister and Brigham. Old coot must have pinto beans every living Saturday night of his life, and he ain't never heard of NoGas."

"Elba!"

"What? Lord's my witness, that's purdee truth."

"No! I mean that car."

The dark-colored car coming from the opposite direction careened into their lane. Elba whipped the wheel. Tires slid over the grass verge until she managed to swing back onto the macadam of Licorice Lane. "Some drunk, I guess."

Willi didn't think so. The only clue she had was the comment: *You'll figure it out. By the end of the school year, you'll be miserable, too.* She muttered, "I'm going to find out, you bet, but right now—"

"I know. Home. I'm getting you there fast as I can. And I wouldn't worry about a one-time incident like this. After all, seeing as how they were coming from the direction of the farms out this way and heading toward town, it ain't too likely you'll see them again tonight."

Willi said nothing, but her mind churned anew. Was there going to be some nasty little message left painted on her lawn, her mailbox or house? Super, just super. But, she'd never been one not to face her own problems. Her one drawback was she had a hard time asking for help. She supposed that was one of the many things in hers and Quannah's relationship she'd have to work on. In the meantime, if there was some ugliness awaiting her at home, she'd have to depend on her own resources to handle it. Her warrior was wounded and would be out of the battle for quite a while, and she'd had marching orders from Sheriff Tucker to go home and rest while Agatha would take the watch over Quannah for the next hours.

She glanced up again at the constellation. And Great Bear's wounds continued to bleed onto Mother Earth.

CHAPTER SEVEN

Though anger stalks the hallowed halls
Is it the true beast's threatening calls?

—Quanit'ala
The Book of the Ancient Ones

Before Elba drove off, Willi peered inside her mailbox, checked the porch and door for any ugly notes and waved to Elba that all was okay. Thank Great Spirit and all the twinkling stars, be they bloody, bears, lions or tigers, she just wanted to rest undisturbed. After a soothing shower, Willi finally eased her aching bones into bed upstairs with Charlie snoring in his basket outside her door. She sighed so deeply she was surprised the exhale hadn't moved the dog chamber a few feet. Just as she pulled up the blanket, she said, "Hell's bells and armadillo tails!" In the glow of the hall nightlight, Charlie raised his ears in question.

She dangled one leg off the bed, allowing her injured toe to touch the floor. So much for that elusive idea of undisturbed sleep. If she could just shut her mind off, these little pricks of reality would fade. But . . . she did remember that having come in the front door, she had not checked the garage, which was closed but not locked according to that dumb-goof-of-an-excuse-for-an-officer, Smitty Parva. Charlie raised his head and woofed at her expletive.

Willi grinned. "You'll warn me of anything. Good poochie."

After all, no one could get in the house itself, only the garage. Surely since the stalker had already called and possibly tried to run her off the road, she hoped there'd be nothing more tonight. She yawned and pulled her foot back under the soft blanket. Her knee-length pink T-shirt sleeper was so comfortable. *Ahh, yes. Morpheus, please, come fast.*

After about three hours' sleep her eyes opened like a little owl. Something had awakened her. She blinked, sat up on the edge of her bed and stared into the hallway at Charlie's empty spot. "Charlie, you're a cute clown, but you better not be into anything tonight." She glanced at the LCD on the clock face. "Okay, you better not be into anything at four in the a.m." Probably just went to get a midnight drink from his bowl in the kitchen. She was about to return to the still warm covers, when a decisive thump of something heavy hitting concrete rousted her just before Charlie's sharp barks catapulted her into standing and running down the stairs of thirteen steps. She'd been knocked out once on these very stairs. Don't tell her thirteen wasn't unlucky. She slowed her descent.

She rounded the baluster, swung into the dining room, hit her hip on a chair, pushed it away and continued through to the kitchen. She clicked on the light. She raced into the darkened game room. Charlie's barking, as loud as any ADT siren on the market, intensified as if to say, "I got 'em. I got 'em. Whoo-hooo! I'm gonna kill 'em. Whooo-oooooo-hooo-oooo!"

"Okay, boy, I'm here. Shush. Calm down."

Charlie faced the door to the laundry room. Light seeped around the edges of the laundry's window from the lighted garage. A car's motor revved, and from years of ears attuned to one's own territory, Willi pictured it pulling away from the garage, backing onto the gravel turn and racing out of the drive. She opened the laundry-room door, careened into her car, circled around onto the gravel, moonlit and as brightly delineated as the garage, stubbed her injured toe and yelled, "Ouch . . . ouch . . . ouch . . . dang," and managed to catch a glimpse of the green car. Charlie raced after the vehicle, and back toward Willi, and somewhat frenzied, he barked as if to say to her, "Whadda ya doing? Come on, catch 'em. Smell the gravel dust and now the asphalt. Come oooooohhh on!"

Willi gathered the wriggling mass of black and brown and rubbed him until he calmed. "Good dog, good dog. You did well." She limped back into the garage, closed the door and locked it from the inside before setting him down. Only then did she see some of her stored school boxes of materials pulled from the shelves, the spilled bottle of white shoe polish and the message on her car windows:

And Fall Break just gets better and better, right, Willi? Life for you: MISERABLE, you uppity know-it-all. Payback.

She swallowed. Her name in place of the earlier misnomer was even more frightening, making it too, too personal. This was truly happening to her, not a situation of mistaken identity, this meanness was directed at her. Okay, what would Big Chief do? Don't mess up the crime scene. Yeah, well, she wasn't driving out in public with *that* on her windows. Sheriff Tucker had trained her on those many nights she and her daddy, Phidias Gallagher, had done ride-alongs. And she'd learned a great deal from Quannah, too. So, she would compromise on the crime scene. She went into the laundry room and from one of the cubbyholes for shoes and cleansers, she pulled out a camera she kept on hand. She took photos starting with the passenger side front window and worked all the way around her car to the driver side front window. Then she cleaned up her car. So, she did destroy the scene, but she had a record of it, if needed. This was the best she could do. She wasn't about to call something this small in when Quannah was lying in bed with a gunshot wound and the sheriff's forces were frantic over the escaped convicts. Her stalker, although a frightening menace, was not public enemy number one, two and three. For a while longer, she'd take care of this herself.

"Okay, Charlie, it's someone at school, or someone who's aware that I'm off for the week. That's the only clue I've got so far. Just what I need during the break when I could use my energies to work on the committee business for the museum—this smarmy insect invading my life. Now add to that poor Anastasia, and . . . and . . . my Quannah." She wiped a tear away.

"I can't imagine anyone I've wronged. But by damned to all the mosquitoes in Texas, this is one that's going to get squished, and soon."

With the proof of the deed on film, she lay back down, truly believing she might drift into maybe another couple of hours of sleep. Nope. Every nerve end sizzled, the adrenaline rush of the race downstairs wouldn't dissipate no matter how much she tossed and turned and punched her pillow. Even the bloodcurdling yell she let loose within the shower a little bit later didn't seem to take the edge away entirely.

By 7:00 a.m. Willi had returned to the hospital, checked on Anastasia, where no changes were reported, and sat beside Quannah's hospital bed, relieving Agatha long enough to get breakfast and a couple of hours of rest.

Willi stared out at the still darkened sky and fidgeted with her purse straps. Dang, she should have brought the contents of Ludwig's bed with her to peruse. Oh, she hated to waste time. That wasn't the whole truth. She just couldn't sit here and stare at her warrior, the strength of her life, and see him so vulnerable. Unbidden tears kept threatening, she'd sniffle and wipe them away. Only way not to give in to her fear for him—which he would detest—would be to keep her mind on other things. Fine. She brushed another tear away. She'd intended to spend the morning with Quannah—who would be asleep on meds most of the day and under the experienced care of the Kachelhoffer sisters. But still she wanted to be there until he was released, get him settled in at home, and then she'd head out to get answers. The garage fiasco made her so antsy, she jumped up and paced. Maybe the stalker jerk thought she had told Quannah about the situation, perhaps would attack him at home while he was weak, maybe . . .

"Miss Willi. Miss Willi."

"Huh?" It was Sheriff Tucker, not Quannah's voice, she heard speaking to her.

"Despite that pretty pink sweater and right nice slacks, can't say as what color—"

"—burgundy—"

"You don't say. Well, despite that nice outfit, you look like you're on the warpath," he said, laying his Stetson hat on the chair. "Mayhap you got to talk to that ornery nephew of mine. Guess he got you worried about that dream . . . vision . . . whatever he had."

Sheriff Tucker had never been comfortable with his nephew's "Indian" ways, as he called them. He had kidded Willi about her daydreams since she was no higher than a cricket's hind legs, and was at ease with that, not equating it to any Native American mysticism, despite his nephew's insistence to the contrary.

"Vision?"

"About that there Jag sports car attacking your . . . your . . . navel."

"He may have muttered something, but no, I'm not worried about any drug-induced paranoia." *Dang right. She had enough of the real thing to worry about.* "No, I'm waiting to hear if they'll let him go home, but it might be better to keep him here safe in the hospital another day and night."

"My very thoughts, too. Yep, more'n likely he'll prove less trouble to these no-nonsense nurses than he'd be a-bellerin' at home. I just met the doc coming out of another emergency operation, and said that very thing to him. He agrees."

"Good, good. Then I'll just stay right by his side here, where no one can—"

"Whoa, li'l warrioress, whoa there a spell. Ain't nobody after his ornery hide, right? Smitty Parva's so torn up he's gonna be here beside him most of the day waiting on him hand and foot. Give the sisters a break until Quannah goes home."

"What?"

Sheriff Tucker held up his hands, palms outward. "Now, I okayed that. Smitty's a good man. He was caught in a bad situation not of his making, and left feeling like it was. Man needs to be needed and trusted by his . . . his partner, right now. Quannah'd be the first to admit that." Sheriff Tucker squinched up his eyes and pulled out his blue bandana in the nick of time to catch the sneeze. " 'Scuse me."

With head held high and an implacable set to her chin, Willi said, "I definitely will stay. I'm not about to leave Quannah alone with some gun-happy—"

"He's doing this off-duty, and don't have no gun until the official investigation is finished. 'Course, small as our force is, that might have to be today or tomorrow, but I won't 'low him to bring his gun here, okay?" Sheriff Tucker scrutinized her face. "Mayhap there's some other reason you got for worrying so? You ain't snooping into things you ain't supposed to be, or—?"

Willi twirled away so he couldn't see the hot spots no doubt coloring her cheeks as pink as her sweater. "Now, Brigham Tucker, what would I be involved in? Neither you nor Quannah need to occupy yourselves about me right now." She patted his broad chest, so much like his nephew's. "You've got more worry wrinkles than a hound dog's muzzle. I know what you're dealing with, and what with Quannah not able to help, I know that's extra worry. You take care of the Huntsville escapees, and I promise to be very careful in everything I do the next couple of days."

"Any particular thing you might need to be special careful about, like that stalker Agatha mentioned?"

Willi frowned. "Agatha's got it wrong. Nothing serious. Some silly prankster from school, I'm thinking. I've gathered what information I could and—"

"Snooping always causes you problems, Miss Willi, and I don't need no—"

"There aren't any crimes locally, are there, now, for me to be concerned with . . . other than one pistol-packing, chocolate-imbibing, overly zealous deputy, right?" asked Willi with what she hoped was a reassuring smile.

"You know about his love for them peanut butter and chocolate things, do you? But about you getting mixed up in any ongoing case . . ."

"It's not as if I'm going to head out to the wheat and corn fields and track down those three escaped convicts. That's the only crime Nickleberry and the county are concerned with at the moment, I believe. And hopefully, finding out who the hit-and-run culprit was in Anastasia's accident. You do have men on that?"

Sheriff Tucker waved placating palms at her. "Yep, if it's a hit-and-run, you got the right of that, but—"

"But what?"

"You got that gleam in your eyes, Miss Willi, just like when you'se a kiddo. Yep, them little wheels just a-turning."

"If my little wheels are turning at all, I'm lucky, after having so few hours' sleep." Dang. She clamped her lips tightly together. Her heart skittered as she smiled brightly at him.

"Elba took you home at a decent time; you should have managed a couple hours of beauty sleep. What were you a-doing?"

Cleaning up shoe-polish indictments? Calming a dog bent on eating all marauders in green getaway cars? Planning on an agenda to discover who ransacked Anastasia's office and who was stalking yours truly?

She said, "Worrying. Yes, worrying about—lots of things—and especially—" She managed a sniffle and glanced toward her warrior, mouth opened wide, snores reverberating strongly. She gently eased him over on his side. The snores quieted.

"Aww, now, he's gonna be fine, but I sure don't want to be the one to face him with the news."

"What news?"

"That he's got another day and night here, and I surely do not want him awake seeing you so tired and asking questions to get whatever he might think you're not a-tellin' him, even though—*even though*—we both know there's nothing but a bit of worry on your part for his wounded butt-end. Right?"

Willi's eyes opened wide. Yeah, Big-Chief-Who-Could-See-Through-Her could on occasion read her mind. She straightened her sweater over the hips of the burgundy slacks and nodded. And, she certainly had a fair-sized collection of unresolved items she didn't care for him needling her about at the moment. She said, "Right, but he can't be alone—"

Sheriff Tucker pocketed his blue bandana and checked his watch. "Quarter hour and Smitty Parva will show. You want to be here to greet him?"

Good grief and fried baloney. Guess Parva would at least be some deterrent to her stalker bothering Quannah, and if she were elsewhere, the nasty note-sender might assume she'd not confided in Quannah. Yeah, she'd make like a mama bird protecting her fledgling, and fly elsewhere to take the predator's attention away from her vulnerable loved one.

"Did you say you wanted to welcome him in?" Sheriff Tucker

asked with a wicked twinkle in his eye.

With hands on her hips, she sighed. "I think not." She brushed Quannah's hair off his forehead and kissed his cheek. "I'll tell Agatha that Smitty Parva will take over, and she can rest today for the big homecoming tomorrow."

"You're going home, yourself, to get some real sleep?"

"Home? Me? Sleep? Now there's a good idea. As soon as I see the nurse about a tetanus shot."

"Now, Missy—"

"Due to a cut on my toe." With a quick look to Quannah, she hurried out the door so fast and into the elevator that the end of another question she had no intention of answering drifted out of hearing. "Now, explain why would you be needing a—?" Willi shook her head. She couldn't get into it with Tucker now.

She did stop by the outpatient clinic and got a shot. She thought of home and sleep and what a good idea that was. Obviously, an idea before its time, since she rushed out of the hospital to her newly washed car and toward one place she might get some answers.

She glanced into the back seat of her car where she'd placed Ludwig's treasure trove to peruse at a quiet lunch later. She had dug out the calendar already to see what appointments had been lined up. Luckily, for the morning there'd been none but general museum business and a brunch which she asked Agatha to call and cancel when she reached home and phone. Nothing else was listed until later this afternoon. Before then, Willi could make calls at lunchtime and decide who to meet herself, who to cancel and who to shuffle over to someone else's shoulders. She felt this obligation on two counts. One. She was the committee chair for choosing the permanent curator. Two. Anastasia was a good friend. Friends stepped in when needed. *It was the law of the West.* How many times had she heard that in her life? Also part of *the law of the West* was bad varmints didn't get away with nefarious deeds. She pulled in her bottom lip. Okay, she had to prioritize. She could concern herself this morning with one of three things.

Anastasia in a coma, neither her parents nor Ramblin' having yet arrived.

Quannah, practically in a medicated coma . . . but he had folks constantly checking on him that he knew, even if one of them was that idiot Smitty Parva.

The stalker from school. Nasty notes, cryptic phone calls, and shoe polish messages were almost juvenile compared to the first two situations. Of course, being run off the road, was not to be taken lightly. But, she couldn't prove that was this stalker. That could have just been one of the late-night drinkers on the road or someone who had nodded off, but wasn't brave enough to stop and apologize.

So, instead of driving east out of the hospital parking lot and toward the home of the Nickleberry Mustangs in all their blue, white and gold glory, she made a right toward the shared home of Anastasia Zöllmer and Ramblin' Anders. After all, it was Saturday and the likelihood of finding teachers there was a minimal hope—although, as crazy as the stalker seemed to be—he might very well be there.

As the outskirts of Nickleberry gave way to open land similar to that near Willi's own home, she ticked off what she wanted to clarify with this visit. In this direction she maneuvered around horse farms rather than dairy farms, past rich grazing pastures rather than small farm allotments. Okay, first, she wanted to know why in blazes Ramblin' wasn't at the hospital. Had he and Anastasia been fighting? That certainly wasn't the feeling Willi got when she and the acting curator had walked arm in arm on the verge of girl talk yesterday before the interviews began. Had Ramblin' just been gone on business and not yet returned? He'd certainly not answered any of her frantic attempts to reach him by his cell phone number.

The newly renovated Tuscany style single-story awaited her at the end of a curving drive of oaks clutching arms overhead to form an October canopy of orange and brown. The house was revealed gradually and as deliciously as a fancy chocolate in its gold-embossed wrap. So absolutely Anastasia's style. Elegant and rich and earthy. Willi swallowed. At the curved park in front of the arched opening to the front courtyard, she simultaneously shut the door and checked the time. 9:17 a.m. Surely, he'd be up by now. She rapped with the lion's-head knocker.

He came to the door in black slacks, midnight turtleneck and huaraches. The unexpected pallor of his skin contrasted with the attire. Purple shadows swallowed his eyes.

The expanse of lime-green glass along with the chrome furniture shone in the seven shellacked layers of the pumpkin-colored floor. Her eye followed what seemed like a basketball court length of expanse to the modern double doors leading to the outdoor kitchen-entertainment area. She knew that tidbit about the floors because she had helped the couple apply three of those coats. The early morning sun flooded through the closed doors, bringing the more Italian outside in for a very comfortable mix—just like she had thought of the couple—a very comfortable mix. "Ramblin'," she said, stepping briskly past him and into the interior—not so Tuscany—but rather ultra modern—so like Ramblin' Anders.

"Willi." He shoved his hands in his slacks' pockets, followed her through the living room, past the dining room delineated with a funky stainless steel chandelier made by Ramblin' and into the gigantic kitchen set into a 180-degree curved wall of glass, all cabinets being below counter so as not to obstruct the view of the trio of indoor parrots' cages in the atrium. Cawing, talking and singing, the parrots, obviously not sensing that their mistress and pooch were in dire straits, were themselves in fine feathery fettle this morning. Ramblin' and Anastasia had designed this unique space, and it bespoke of their attention to detail. He swallowed and waved his hand in invitation to the area and again said, "Willi, help yourself."

Not a stranger to their kitchen, Willi grabbed a cup and helped herself to a latte from the machine.

"Croissants and grapes on the table," Ramblin' said, refilling his own tall cup. "What brings you out so early?"

Willi took a deep breath. A tremor coursed through her. She wanted answers, but at the same time, feared them. Seated to his left at the table with the mosaic glass top—another Ramblin' creation—she said, "Ramblin', I need to know—"

"—You and me both," he interrupted. "I guessed your visit means she didn't show up for her Saturday morning stint at the museum."

"Excuse me?" Willi pushed her cup aside. "What are you talking about?"

"Look. You don't have to pretend. I know."

"You know? Then why aren't you—?"

He slammed his cup down. "Yes, I know. I know about her seeing someone else."

Willi blinked and pulled her sweater sleeve down to give herself a moment to think. She croaked out, "Huh?"

"I saw 'Tasia last night," Ramblin' said.

Another thing that had endeared Ramblin' to Willi was his sweet shortened version of Anastasia's name. Willi shoved the croissant beside the abandoned latte. Oh my gosh. Last night? So, so . . . it was Ramblin' who ran Anastasia off the road and into the pole. Oh dear Lord, she couldn't believe it. She shook her head and stood to stare out the window toward the ancient trees grappling for overhead space with their gnarled October arms. A shiver ran down her spine. Her bottom lip trembled until she caught it between her teeth. She sniffed, squared her shoulders and faced him, albeit with a heavy heart about what kind of answers she would now receive.

"Explain, Ramblin'. Have you not been attending your anger-management classes? I want to know *why*."

"Hey, you're out of line. I've never missed a one. That was an agreement between 'Tasia and me since—"

"—since the last time you sent her to the emergency room?"

"The one and only time. It's never happened again. Ever. Not even after . . . after last night. You want to know things? I'm the one who needs answers. Crazy. Going crazy since last night. Got the last Friday flight out, drove like a mad man from DFW Airport, just to meet—" he swallowed and took three deep breaths—"to meet 'Tasia."

Willi did a mental backstep. Perhaps she'd jumped to the wrong conclusion. She asked, "You saw her last night? Where?"

"The museum. Where else? The hallowed ground of her life."

Willi sat down in the black lacquered and chrome chair. She crushed her napkin and held it to her chest. "Then . . . you all—what?—had a fight?"

"Would have."

"If—?"

"If I'd stayed after seeing—" With hands on the table top, he waved his head back and forth like a lion trying to loosen the grasp of an adversary. He slammed his fist down on the glass top, creating a fault line in the mosaic. He reared back his head and roared in anguish.

Willi pushed her chair away, and opted for a really quiet and steady teacher-voice, one used to de-escalate cafeteria fights. "So, you were angry for whatever reason, followed her, got more enraged, and . . . and what ran her down?"

With another roar, Ramblin' Anders slammed his own chair back. "What the hell are you talking about, Miss High and Mighty Gallagher?"

With every ounce of self-control she could muster, she remained seated, licked her lips and said, "Maybe you didn't realize what the end result was. Perhaps you drove away before you saw—"

"What planet are you on today, bitch? Where do you get off accusing me . . . what the hell *are* you accusing me of?" He walked over to the sink and splashed cold water on his face. "I . . . was . . . out . . . of . . . line. Sorry. Old knee-jerk reactions die hard."

Willi let the calmer mode settle a minute. He broke the silence. "I sure as hell didn't run her down on foot. In those cavernous sheds at the back? I don't think so. She was too busy to see me."

Willi said, "In her car."

"Car?"

Willi faced him, her mind doing a mental gerbil-wheel run, a thin layer of nervous perspiration forming on her forehead, which she wiped with her napkin. "You . . . you really . . . don't know, do you?"

He grabbed a paper towel to dry his hardened features, stepped into her intimate space, an inch only between his nose and hers, and managed to ground out in a more civil volume, "What are you talking about?"

"She's in the hospital."

" 'Tasia?"

"She wrapped her car around the HEB grocery parking lot pole." Willi didn't add her own idea about a hit-and-run driver leaving the scene.

"My God. Is she—?" Tears shown in his eyes and he turned away.

Willi reached out a tentative hand but withdrew it. He was either the consummate actor or had had no inkling. "I tried your cell phone many times."

142

"After I saw her last night, I turned it off." Again, he bent over, flattened his palms on the table, head down between his hunched shoulders and said, "Ohmygod, I should have stayed and faced the son of a sorry excuse for a—" He swung his head in that leonine gesture again. He drew out his cell phone, flipped the lid and checked his call list. "Your numerous calls and . . . the hospital twice." He shoved the cell phone in his pocket and came out with his keys. "I've got to get to her. I thought . . . I thought . . . what an idiot I was. Damn, damn, damn it to hell. I'll kill that bastard." This time the roar and both double fists smashed into the table top sending fissures throughout the art piece.

Willi jumped back, stood and grabbed his arm. "Who? Who was with Anastasia in the outer sheds?"

He shoved Willi's fingers off and headed for the door. "Had his hands all over 'Tasia. She didn't seem to be fighting back. Dark Lothario in a loose-fitting floppy jacket or serape or something. Get out of the way, Willi."

"You didn't know him?"

"Just saw her in his arms. You know . . . it pushed my buttons. I saw red. Oh my God, I've got to get to her. Now, get the hell out of the way, Willi."

"How about I drive you? You're in no condition to—"

She was speaking to dead air in the wake of his rush out the door. "—or not. I'll just clean up this breakfast mess, and see myself out." And, like a good friend she did that, freshened up in the powder room, made a last perusal and frowned. The glass doors leading out from the living room to a Tuscany-styled outdoor grill and shaded oasis were open. Sure as roadrunners fanned their tail feathers, she knew that the doors had not been open when she'd entered. She remembered looking over the long expanse of pumpkin floor and to the outside. Ramblin' had not opened them, either. Wind was negligible with the stonework surrounding the backyard area, so that could not have caused them to open.

Goose bumps traveled from scalp down back, and over her arms. She peered closely at the wide-open expanse of living room, dining room and kitchen. No place existed among the chrome and steel and glass for anyone to hide. She glided across the pumpkin acreage, quietly shut and locked the paired doors, before she decided to search out the more private sections of the home down the long hallway. Where the public part of the house was open, the bedroom suites and offices were separated and on three different levels.

Willi had the feeling of entering caves—very regal and well appointed, but quiet, muted with that underground sensation of stillness and age. Here the Tuscany influence took over in nooks and crannies, bathrooms that seemed to wrap around Willi in absolutely decadent luxury. Nothing seemed amiss in the suites. She peered into Anastasia's home office with skylight, carved wooden desk and file cabinets, and in the corner a cowled dog bed, no doubt Ludwig's home base. His chew toys brought a lump to her throat and a mental reminder to call Dr. Sydney Curry.

She eased out of Anastasia's domain, down three steps across the hall and into Ramblin' Anders's office—a work of modern mosaics in steel frames, all geometrically shaped, but still pleasing and muted. The air seemed different, heavier somehow. Neck hairs rose on Willi and she stood very still, not flicking on a light although this room needed illumination, as there were no outside windows. Giving herself a moment to get used to the gray tones of the gloom, she inched around the room with her back to the wall. No place to hide at all. Ramblin's desk—a glass-topped rectangle—had metal legs, no drawers. No one could scuttle under there. No closet to duck into, yet the feeling persisted that someone was, or had just been there. The top of

Ramblin's desk held a phone, a notebook computer, and one slip of paper, creased and upright. She peered back over her shoulder to check the doorway, inched to the table, quickly turned to keep her eye on the hallway outside, and grasped the sheet.

*ShOu**LD** HavE MINDed ur* **business.** HOW *do U like me* **IN** *yours?*

The goose bumps crawled all over her this time, and she shivered. Her mouth, drier than a Saguaro's landscape, couldn't work up enough spit to swallow. Okay, she had to stay calm. The stalker loved this sick game, obviously. So, he'd waited outside the hospital and followed her out here. Damn it, she'd never seen the Green Monster in her rearview mirror. Maybe it was someone who knew her well enough to know who her friends were, perhaps only had to see the general direction she'd taken. He could have arrived minutes afterwards, obviously parking out of sight of the long drive and oaks, verify if her car was present and sneaked into the house while she and Ramblin' were handling an emotional crisis.

Hell's bells. She narrowed her eyes, and finally managed to lick her lips. By dang, come Monday, she'd go to school and figure out what lamebrain coward was doing this to her, and he was a coward, to run in, leave a nasty note, make a frightening call, never revealing or confronting. With that idea in mind, Willi breathed easier. He'd probably gone out the way he'd come in, and she'd missed him when she searched the four bedroom suites. Monday was two days away, but meantime, she figured out someone else who might know about what happened in the sheds in the early evening yesterday.

For just one millisecond, the idea of Ramblin' being her stalker surfaced, but she clamped down tightly on that paranoid idea. Probably just what the jerk wanted her to think. Sickly bile rose in her throat at the thought that he had overheard her intimate conversation with a friend. Perhaps he was the one who had been with Anastasia in the warehouse. Willi grabbed the sides of her head and pushed. No, no. Two separate incidents—the stalker and Anastasia's situation. That was one of those inner knowings Willi had learned to trust. Ramblin' might be a skunk, but he wasn't this particular tail-swinging stink of a jerk.

Willi rushed back into Anastasia's office. "Forgive me for snooping, but I'm not sure all the pages are there on your museum papers." She grabbed the zippered address book in the top drawer of the carved desk, hightailed it out of the Anders-Zöllmer home, and headed toward an entirely different side of town. By darn, she'd get somebody's story today, come Hell or high water.

CHAPTER EIGHT

Secrets woven like a veil
Are fabrics of the gypsy's tale.

—Chi'ichimi
The Book of the Ancient Ones

Willi smiled as she parked just inside the gates before a double-wide mobile home with a sign proclaiming *OFFICE* alongside the blue and white *ADT* security picket. She would, she would, she would get answers here. By dang, she'd get into her no-nonsense teacher mode, and neither high water, Texas tornados, nor droughts would stop her. This determination and hope came from the fact that finally, her brain cells had kicked in to give her one more possible lead, to allow her to find another person who might have some answers about what happened in the museum last night. Anastasia's home address book had given her the address but no phone number, hence her travels to the trailer park.

Pea gravel, known more commonly in Texas as caliche, rolled under her feet when she crunched her way toward the prefab concrete steps. Three pink plastic flamingos, no doubt escapees from some Florida yard, watched her knock on the door. Despite the dark roots, the woman who toed open the door had probably broken hearts from Nickleberry all the way to the Texas Panhandle.

Willi said, "Hi there. I'm Willi Gallagher. I need some info."

She said, "What can I do for you?"

Willi raised an eyebrow at the woman's white, tight shorts and the spandex band across her 38 B's above the ruby in her navel. Willi introduced herself and added, "I'm here to see an employee of the museum, but I forgot the lot number." Okay, perhaps *forgot* was a stretch of the truth seeing as how it wasn't exactly listed alongside the address.

"I'm Corylee. Come in. Take a load off, and I'll check the book. We got over two-hundred lots, you know."

A hodgepodge of piles of clothes, stacks of CD's, mountains of designer western boots, and toppled hills of fashion magazines greeted Willi. "Two hundred? That must keep you and your husband busy."

"Husband? Not me. I'm hooked up with my best friend's hubby for odd jobs need doing. Of course, it drives her crazy thinking we might be having nooky on the side."

"And she's your *best* friend?"

"But me and him been friends longer, you know what I mean, and nothing's gonna stop that. Where the hell is that book?" She shoveled trash off the side of a desk, found a pack of cigarettes and lit one. As she jabbed the air with the smoke, she said, "I love going in and climbing up in bed between them to watch T.V."

"Uh . . . between your . . . uh . . . friend and your *best* friend?" The tone of Willi's voice evidently passed right over the dark roots and peroxided head.

"Yeah." Corylee bent to give Willi a picture of her white tight shorts rising over her buttocks. Willi looked away and tightened her lips. Corylee said, "Pisses her right off, you know."

"Do tell."

"Hey, you know, she don't really love him. Told me so herself. And he sure don't love her if he lets me do that. Dissing her, his wife, right? Hell, he even takes care of part of my bills, especially if I fill a couple tissues with tears. Bare-assed skin and tears gets to a man, you know."

"I guess so. Ought to be a country western song titled 'Tissues and Tears.' " Willi wanted to be angry at this man-mangler, but she had to admit all women—including herself—sometimes used their feminine wiles in one way or another to get their way. She personally tried hard not to do so, but there had been times. She offered a weak grin. Maybe that was part of the feminine *law of the West.* She had to give Corylee credit for integrity— honesty with oneself.

"Ah, here's the book. Now what'd you say the employee's name was?"

Willi turned to face Corylee, who was thankfully seated behind the desk and its debris. "Drianina Manauia."

"Damned weird name."

"I believe it has roots in the Aztecan language."

"Whatever." Corylee shuffled through pages of the loose-leaf notebook. "Ah, yeah."

"Yes?"

"She's got trailer site number 196. Practically in the woods." Corylee placed a finger on a yellowed laminated map. "Nine streets down. Turn to your left at Coyote Tail. The hot top winds around, peters out onto a gravel road. We're just getting those lots set up back there."

"Back in the woods, but it's still part of the trailer park?"

"Last sections—K through J—will be finished in 2012. You wanna book a lot now, you get better rates. Usually, I just offer the best rates to good friends, but you look like a nice lady. You got a boyfriend?" Corylee took a strong drag from her cigarette and blew the smoke toward the window unit, the better to allow it to disperse throughout the home. "He good-looking?"

Willi scrutinized the map, ignored the personal questions—as if she would ever reveal to this crotch-hunting creature the love of her life, Quannah Lassiter—and posed one of her own. "Lot number 198, right?"

"196. But there's seven or eight vacant spots between the last trailer on Coyote Tail and that lot. Her choice. Spooky out in those woods, but she's a strange woman. She don't have many visitors, especially no men friends, far as I can tell." As if that marked Drianina Manauia as dead and useless, Corylee slammed the book and knocked the ash off her cigarette.

Five minutes later Willi drove down Coyote Tail Drive. She squared her shoulders. Well, seeing the owner solidified one thing for Willi. She was *not* the type to want to share her man, and she knew Quannah wasn't the type to share his lady. So, she was finally going to meet someone who could help her answer such things as: who was in the back lots with Anastasia last night? What kind of vehicle did they have? Did they leave in anger chasing down Anastasia and running her into the HEB grocery parking lot pole?

Two more minutes and her tires slid off the macadam and crunched over the gravel road. The lots with the requisite concrete pad had numerous live oaks and sprouts of wild onions mixed in with the golden cannas. Around two more curves and the gravel gave way to mere dirt ruts. *Thank you, Corylee, for that warning.* To the left a single-wide mobile home peeked from a copse of thick cottonwood trees. Beside it sat a blue minivan with double yellow stripes down the side, a car more likely owned by a youth or someone in their eighties going on their second childhood. A young Hispanic woman pushed a lawn mower over the last patch of a quarter-acre area, obviously used as an extension of the small lot. Ah. Perhaps the car belonged to her. When Willi walked toward her, the young woman killed the mower's engine and narrowed her eyes.

"Hello. I'm looking for Drianina Manauia."

"Okay." The woman wiped sweat off her forehead with the

end of her T-shirt.

"Are you—?"

"No. I'm Día. Día Muñoz. Do yard work for lots of those in the park. You need your grass mowed?"

"Sorry, no. I don't live here. Do you know when she'll be back?"

A black and white long-haired dog approached Willi and licked her hand. "Hey, poochie. How you doing?" She rubbed between his ears, and he wagged his tail, turned and backed up so she could get to just the perfect spot on the right-side ear. "Is that better, boy?"

"Pancho. Get over here. Leave the lady alone." Día said, "Sorry."

Two horses neighed back and forth. Willi peered around.

Día said, "Behind the mobile home."

"Really," Willi stepped past the end of the trailer.

"I don't know that . . . uh . . . Mrs. Manauia would want—"

"Oh," Willi said, and pulled up short as she viewed the two animals. "That's not what I expected."

"Most don't."

"Clydesdales?"

"Yeah." Día pointed to a wooden gypsy caravan in bright reds and turquoise. "To pull that in local parades and fairs."

"Hmmm. I guess the Aztecan hieroglyphics painted on the sides aren't the typical gypsy stereotype, and certainly not that frightening jaguar, fangs bearing down?"

Día glared at her, and turned toward the front of the yard. "Guess we'd better—"

Willi traced the soft nose of one of the great horses. He snorted out hot air by way of greeting. Pancho wiggled near to get another ear rub. Willi complied. "Don't be jealous, boy. Here you go, here you go. Is that all better?"

"Like I said, she's not here."

"Do you know where—?"

"Maybe late tonight. She likes people to call *before* they visit."

Willi grinned, pulled out her pen and paper from her purse and said, "Lovely. You'd make a great secretary, too. What's the number?"

No mistaking the look of disapproval this time, but Willi kept her smile in place and pen at the ready. Through clenched teeth, Día ground out the numbers and pulled the starter on the mower, effectively drowning out Willi's *thank you*.

She drove down the ruts then along the gravel road and onto the macadam. "Well, shoot fire. I turned the wrong way."

By the time she'd maneuvered around and got herself oriented correctly, the blue minivan with the yellow stripes pulled out and turned in front of her. Odd. Willi slowed to stay out of the gravel dust, but when the small vehicle swung onto the macadam, she moved in closer. Día Muñoz was not behind the wheel. No way. Willi followed the car to the freeway, all the time wondering how anyone else could have gotten past her down the macadam to the car in the two minutes it took her to leave the mobile home and turn back around. *Impossible.* So whoever was in the car had been at the mobile home during the time of her visit. Willi frowned. Perhaps she had been mistaken, and it was the young girl driving. Willi waited until traffic stalled and inched up beside the minivan where she plainly viewed the occupant.

The woman had high cheekbones similar to Día Muñoz, however her jowls puffed out, and a wart hovered near the left side of her bottom lip. Wiry salt-and-pepper hair hung down to stocky shoulders. Her left-hand fingers, covered with turquoise, coral and silver rings, beat a tattoo upon the steering wheel. A manly watch of proportions needed for the severely myopic rested between two wide silver and turquoise clasp bracelets. When the woman turned her head and saw Willi, she smiled and the matching clunkers of earrings peeked out from the tangle of hair. Her eyes opened wide. Her smile disappeared as she inched forward while pulling her front visor to the left and down, partially obscuring her features. When traffic moved at a regular pace, she zipped right and onto the off ramp.

Miffed, Willi tromped on the gas and drove two exits down before she could swerve into the right lane and exit. By then, the blue car and its cowardly yellow stripes were out of sight. Damn the old biddy. Why couldn't she have come out of the mobile home and at least introduced herself instead of making her yard girl lie for her? Some people. Maybe Tattoo had the right of it, and Drianina Manauia *was* that horrible old Mexican woman. Oh well, it was a silly incident, and she'd been silly to pursue the car for no good reason other than her curiosity. And the result had been a silly waste of time and energy, serving no purpose but to get her farther afield from her goal of the moment which was to locate someone who could tell her what happened at the museum last night.

Well, Mrs. Manauia, you may run, by daggum, but I'll catch up with you eventually, and will figure out some way for you to answer my questions. Of course, to be fair, Willi may have arrived at an inopportune time, and Mrs. Manauia, unless she peeked out a window, might not have known she was glaring on the highway at her earlier visitor. Willi was inclined to be gracious since another epiphany had struck as quickly and as brightly as the Texas sun struck her almost blind, hitting against the chrome lights of a pickup in front of her. Someone else was at the museum at that time.

Willi twisted the wheel to return to Nickleberry proper and a Fetchwin Way address, 279 Fetchwin Way, to be exact.

When Willi reached the Dalrymples' home, she parked in front, and walked down the tree-lined drive toward the guest house. She wanted to visit with Yaotle, Dr. Etzli's helper. He'd been at the museum all yesterday afternoon and in the evening. He'd been there when she received the call from Quannah about Anastasia's accident. He might have seen who had accosted the acting curator or perhaps had seen a car leaving directly after she did. Anything at this point would be helpful. Yaotle—the Warrior—might very well hold the info needed to convince the police to look into the incident as more than an accidental hit-and-run.

The Dalrymples' landscaping leaned toward lots of shady foliage with nooks and crannies of hidden garden rooms. No one would see her from the main house until she came in view in front of the French-door windows, and no one from the guest house would see her until she actually stood at the door entryway. Some three car lengths away from that entry she stood in disbelief, then slunk into the shadows formed by a giant oak protecting leafy palms. The blue minivan with yellow stripes sat beside Dr. Etzli's red Jag.

Willi rubbed her eyes. Nope. No play of shadows and light there. Blue. Yellow stripes. Minivan. How many of those were likely to show up in a burg the size of Nickleberry, Texas? That would be a resounding *uno*, one, and *no más*.

Okay, she had to get a grip. Really, it made sense. Etzli worked on the Aztecan pyramid display as part of his résumé for the job posting, and Drianina Manauia was the storyteller who had set up in front of the pyramid in order to entice children of all ages to enjoy the legends of the old Mexica gods, the ancient tales and myths of her unique heritage. Made perfect sense that she might consult with Etzli about details. Now, whether that got Willi any closer to info about the actual accident, she'd have to see. Ah well, *poco a poco, paso a paso*—little by little and step by step. Anyway, she felt she was doing something and that was good. Good. With that clear in her mind, Willi figured there was no reason not to see Yaotle and Mrs. Manauia at the same time.

Ah, finally, something working out well for her quest. About dang time.

As she stepped out from the palm fronds, the guest-house door opened and out walked a beautiful Hispanic woman. The spitting image of the photo on Etzli's bedside table. Long, tiny, curled black tresses bounced as she fairly danced out the door. Wearing custom-tailored red slacks with a waist-length jacket accented in black, she was obviously going out for a power-dressed workday. Willi took one more step out from the shadows. The woman did not head toward the red Jag, but slid into the minivan.

Willi muttered, "That can't be right," and eased farther into the shadows. The woman backed out so fast, there was no way she could have seen Willi's car in front, since the lady in red headed in the opposite direction. Big deal. So Mrs. Manauia had loaned her the car. So, Willi's plan would still work. She'd talk with Yaotle and the storyteller as she'd planned. Dr. Etzli greeted her at the door. "I wondered," she said, "if I might talk to your aide and Mrs. Manauia for a moment."

"Mrs. Manauia?"

"Yes, that was her blue minivan that just left, correct, but with some other lady driving it."

Etzli frowned, ushered her in and before answering asked if she'd like iced tea. Inwardly, she groaned, but knew that like Texas hospitality traditions, the Hispanic traditions were similar. No business before the amenities of weather and refreshment. While he got ice and lemon, she peered around the quarters. "I'll just freshen up." She headed down the hallway to the bedroom and bath. She washed her hands, but felt like throwing the soap rosettes set out for guests. No Yaotle here. Nor Mrs. Manauia.

Seated in the main room, she barely managed a smile and a few sips of the tea. She asked, "Mrs. Manauia?"

"You must be mistaken. That was not Mrs. Manauia."

"I *know* that." Infuriating man. "Do you know where she is?"

"The lady who left?"

Men could be so dense at times. "Mrs. Manauia?"

"I've no idea, Miss Gallagher. She's the storyteller at the museum, is she not?"

Willi was almost sure he could see the green sparks from her eyes. She certainly pictured them bursting out, landing volleys of crisp flames against his hard head. "Yes, the lady who owns the blue minivan with yellow stripes."

"That's Nina's car. Nina Ricardo. You may have seen her photo in my bedroom the other night."

"Nina Ricardo's? Not Mrs. Manauia's vehicle?"

He frowned again and raised his hands in denial. "I've no idea what she drives. I've yet to meet her."

"I suppose," Willi said, "it surprised me when she didn't leave in the red car."

"Ah, she does borrow it now and again, loves to drive it, in fact."

"Who wouldn't? A sleek sports car like that?"

He shook his head. "Oh, Nina doesn't care so much for my wheels for that reason but because it is a sports car that's a representation of the ancient clan of shape-shifters. She is a granddaughter many times removed from one of the men who believed that the great beast of the jungle, the jaguar, could shape shift into other forms, even human, when needed. Nina says she can understand how her ancestors felt when she's behind the wheel. Makes her feel like she could become anyone she wanted to, anytime she wanted. She, in fact, gifted me with an old jaguar headdress with attached torso and front paws with claws. You must forgive we curators. Such things are fascinating to us." He reached into a box set on the floor and drew forth a fearful cat's head including the sharp teeth, yellowed in some areas, chipped in others.

"Impressive how large the head of one of those animals really is."

"Indeed. Ah, and besides the historical significance there's another plus. I won't have to look any further for a Halloween costume."

"How true." Willi wrinkled her nose at the raw scent mingled with old dust emitted by the headdress. Unwilling to give up on the minivan enigma, she tried another tack. "Does . . . Nina— did you say?—does Nina Ricardo have a mother, aunt, older sister with salt-and-pepper hair, dangly earrings . . . uh—?"

"Not that I know of, and I think she would tell me. Nina is my girlfriend. She is an overseas purchasing agent for a textile retailer. We only get to see each other about once every six weeks and during vacation. She will be back in a few hours. I'd love for you to meet her."

"Has she always driven that car?"

"The minivan?"

She added bombs to the fire flames, letting them target him right between the eyes. Bam! "Yes. Rather a distinctive car."

"Yes, as far as I can remember."

Willi raised a finger in thought. "Uh . . . where does she leave the car when she's overseas?"

"I really don't see for what reason you would—" He replaced his frown with a more pleasant demeanor, obviously recalling that she might have great influence upon the future of his career. "She leaves it with some girlfriend in Dallas, which is near the DFW Airport. Now, if you've more questions in that vein, please come for drinks tonight about 6:30 and meet her yourself."

"I may very well do that. I'll give you a call if I can make it. I suppose I might catch your assistant, Yaotle, at the museum since he's not here."

"I assure you, Ms. Gallagher, I can answer any questions

about the display and about my acquisitions, but if you insist upon conversing with Yaotle, he will be in our office at the museum processing some orders for small figurines we hope to add to the display before the final judging. I myself am going as soon as it gets—uh . . . as soon as I finish up with some phone calls."

She managed one more gulp of the iced tea, rose and said, "Thank you for your time."

As she wandered down the thickly vegetated outdoors to her car, her cell phone rang. She answered, and heard a very anxious man's voice. She said, "Professor Stöhr, calm down."

On the other end of the line, he said, "I tell you after my visit to the hospital when I came around midnight to pick up some papers, I saw most clearly lights on out in the number seventeen work shed. My office, you realize, is an old one nearby. Yes, me. This is what I saw. Lights moving. No vehicle went in. I would have heard it. No vehicle went out."

"Okay, did you call the police?"

"Of course not. First I go to inspect the area. And what do you know, Madam Chair?"

"You tell me, Professor."

"The trash is all cleaned up. Floor swept. I ask myself, how did this happen so quickly? Me? I did not have time as you suggested to tell Ms. Zöllmer before her unfortunate accident. Now, I ask. Did you inform someone yesterday?"

"No, my time was a blur of activity after our luncheon."

"Most interesting."

"Yes, I agree. So, perhaps, Professor, you might go ahead and call the police?"

"Ah, to what purpose? To report that housekeeping elves have done their good deed of the week? You see?"

"You have a point, sir. There may be another explanation. Perhaps Tattoo found it on her own rounds and cleaned it up."

Silence met her on the other end of the phone for a moment. "Maybe so. That would make sense. I feel much relieved, Madame Chair." There was a pause and he said, "A second matter."

"What?" She closed her eyes a moment and tried for a less abrasive tone. "What might that be, Professor?"

"Some items have been removed from my train display."

"For cleaning? Appraisal?"

"For example, in the dining car, sets of crystal salt and pepper shakers are on each of the elegantly set tables. One set is missing. A small thing, and I thought perhaps I had just not unpacked and placed them, but, no, that is not so. Me? I had taken a picture of that very setting when I added finishing touches. I referred to the photo and table number three had all its accoutrements."

"Nothing else is missing?"

"No, and many other things are most expensive. It is an odd item, you see."

Willi asked him to write a report and include the photo for the committee and clicked the phone lid. Well, Hell's bells and bats' tails, she didn't really need to have to search out a petty thief at the museum, nor the "elves" referred to by the professor. She knew for a fact what time Tattoo had gotten home, and she also knew the Jackie-of-all-trades didn't have wheels for the rest of the evening. So, who did clean up the mess? She shrugged. In the big schematic on the universal chart, did it really matter that much? Maybe Professor had a little old lady syndrome and worried about molehills. Yeah. *Forget it, and move on for now. Like Scarlett O'Hara, she could only handle so many crisis situations at once. Tomorrow. Tomorrow she'd deal with this one.*

Her cell jangled again as she drove away from the curb. She glanced at the ID. "Yes, Professor Stöhr?"

"Madam Chair, I apologize for ringing again. I'm so sorry about the demise of the little Ludwig."

"What?"

"Evidently earlier your cell phone was out of range, I was in the museum when a Ms. Kachelhoffer—"

"Agatha?"

"Yes, when she called to let you know. She said something about your phone giving an out-of-range message. I'm sure she will try again, but she did mention the importance of calling the vet. Also, I just learned Ms. Zöllmer is able to speak, and know you were most anxious about your friend."

"Thank you. I'll go right now." Willi cut her wheel sharply, made a U-turn to take her away from her visit with Yaotle, and toward the hospital. Her heart practically sang. Anastasia was improved; Willi would also get to see Quannah. Even if he was snoring under the effects of morphine or Demerol, just to touch him would give her some comfort. But if he were awake, lucid and remembered her confession about her license-to-carry, her .357 Magnum and the stalker, it might turn out to be another very different conversation. She felt tears well in her eyes at the thought of Ludwig, blinked, and sniffed. She would not, absolutely would not be the bearer of this news to Anastasia's bedside. At least, not until she'd talked with Dr. Sydney Curry.

When she reached the hospital, Quannah was not in his room, and the nursing station informed her that he had been wheeled out for about an hour for X rays and blood work. He was doing fine and would be able to go home tomorrow, but was to have bed rest for a week.

She headed for Anastasia's room, found that she'd been moved from ICU to a private room on the same floor as Quannah, and waited outside the room until the staff had finished bathing their patient. Now, where in Blue Blazes was Ramblin'? Shouldn't he be here after all his histrionics? By 11:00 a.m.

Willi finally walked in.

"Willi." Anastasia's voice was weak to the point of trembling, but clear. "Nurses ran Ramblin' and my parents off to the cafeteria for coffee. Have a seat."

Mollified, Willi took a chair beside the bed and patted Anastasia's arm. "How are you?"

"Lost blood . . . deep cuts . . . neck and shoulders. Throat hurts." She touched the bandage surrounding her neck and chest. "Big cut on my head. Doing fair. Just weak."

"You gave us such a scare. The police think you had some kind of attack and ran off the road by yourself without any provocation."

Anastasia frowned, seeming to concentrate.

"But someone called in, and whoever the anonymous person was thought there was another car involved." Willi leaned in closer. "Like it was more of a hit-and-run, than a single-car accident."

"Another car? Don't know."

Willi sighed, letting out a long breath, not realizing until that moment how much she'd set store in the belief that Anastasia would recall all the needed answers. "What is the last thing you recollect?"

"Moments before the accident. Went out to Tattoo's office. Left a note tacked to her door." Anastasia closed her eyes. She stayed quiet and immobile so long Willi leaned in even closer to discern if the bed covers rose and fell with her respirations. Anastasia coughed, and her eyelids fluttered. Willi jumped backwards in the chair.

Anastasia said, "Somebody grabbed me and . . . and held me so tightly, I couldn't even turn my head." She shivered. "Recall that."

"Who was it?"

"Thought at first . . ."

"Yes?"

"Ramblin' . . . but . . . no . . . I don't know. Likes to surprise me, but . . . he wouldn't . . ."

"I bet Ludwig was throwing a barking fit," Willi said.

"No."

"No? Why not?"

"Left him in the museum office."

"Oh, okay. Then what happened? After the man grabbed you?" Willi whispered.

Anastasia swallowed. "Remember starting the car. Heart beating so fast."

"Running away from him?"

"I guess." Anastasia groaned and rubbed her temple.

"Do you think you could describe anything about the man? Clothes? Eyes? Scent?"

"Dark clothes. Bandana, something . . . flowing in front of his face. Hat? I don't know. So fast. Happened so fast."

Anastasia's eyes closed again and Willi grabbed her wrist. "Wait. Don't drift off yet. Did he hit you? Is the injury to your head from that or the car?"

"Don't know. Can't remember. Oh, God, it hurts."

"Just one more thing. After the attack when he grabbed and mauled you, what happened after that?"

"Then I recall—oh, let's see. Three men strapping me down."

Willi nodded. "Probably when the EMT trio put you in the CareFlight helicopter."

"Maybe. Hard to breathe. Lots of lights and so much noise. Willi? I should have checked . . . on them sooner."

"On what? Who?" Willi asked. "Tasks at the museum? Don't worry about that. You concentrate on getting well for Ramblin' and . . . Lud—. . . all of us."

Anastasia's eyes closed, and this time she emitted a tiny nose wheeze which Willi took as a snore.

Great. Ludwig was dead. Anastasia still in a sleeping stupor and unable to answer comprehensibly. But, she's alive, and she's better. She is. Willi held on to that thought. Okay, since she couldn't talk with her friend, she'd take this opportunity to visit Quannah. She just had to be careful. The one thing she did not want to do would be to reveal anything that would worry him about her, certainly not while he was incapacitated here in the hospital. So, she'd tell him about Anastasia's coming around. She'd even tell him about Ludwig. Those two subjects couldn't possibly get her into any trouble.

She walked into Quannah's room. The warrior had returned to his borrowed teepee, and was sitting up eating a lunch of gelatin, brilliantly dyed green beans, questionable meatloaf and watery mashed potatoes. He grinned between mouthfuls. "This is really good. I'll share. Would you like a taste?"

"Not so much." Willi declined further by waving his offer of the cherry dessert away. "You seem better." She leaned over and gave him a quick kiss. "Or maybe not, if you're enjoying *that* food."

"It's the greatest." He leaned his head to one side and lowered his voice. "They don't let you go home until you've eaten a couple of solid meals. I'm eating and asking for extras."

"Think that'll work, huh?"

"You bet, Gallagher." He hid a belch behind his hand. "Excuse me. Now, tell me what's going on."

"Going on?" She smiled sweetly and plumped up his pillow. When she got him safely behind home doors with friends guarding him, then she'd let him know about the stalker. Until then, she'd hold her counsel on that one. "I have news. Good and not so good."

"When do you not, *Winyan?*" He pushed back the empty tray, buzzed the nurses' station and asked for more dessert and another two rolls. "Good news first, please."

"Anastasia is out of the coma, but still mentally sketchy."

"See? I told you she'd be fine. And the bad news?"

"Ludwig is dead."

"Anastasia's dog?"

"Yes."

"What happened?" He leaned forward, his hooded eyes intently alert today, the lawman in him ready for the hunt. Only a small grimace escaped him as he shifted his arm and hip.

Since Ludwig had nothing to do with the stalker, she said, "When we—Tattoo, Agatha and I—went to the museum to get Anastasia's calendar—"

"Took all three of you to do that, huh?"

She squirmed and said, "Is it time for more meds?" She reached for the pump. His fingers stayed her, and she added, "My, you have your strength back."

"Almost. Third day is the worst, but I'm determined to do without the painkiller today. Now, about the three of you going to get one little calendar."

"Well, you had my car, hence Agatha drove. We got the entry keys from Tattoo who tagged along to retrieve them when we finished. Simple, really." Feeling better, she straightened her shoulders.

"And the dog was lying dead upon the said calendar?"

Damn his hooded eyes. His look could pierce right through steel, much less the mush of her brain today. She cleared her throat. "He fell down the pyramid steps, Agatha rushed him to the hospital, and Sydney Curry—you know, the small pet vet—called and said he had died."

Quannah narrowed his eyes. She made preliminary moves to leave, retrieving her purse, putting the straps over her shoulder, and had leaned over to give him a parting smooch, when he quietly said, "Why was he on top of the pyramid, rather than with Anastasia? Some reason he couldn't get down the steps by himself and get to her side?"

"My, my, the questions you ask."

"Gallagher."

"I'll check with you later, hon." She turned to leave and took two steps.

He grabbed her purse, reeled her in, around and tightly held her to his chest. He soundly kissed her, taking her breath away. She was sure she might be a little giddy and cross-eyed. Intoxicating lip locks after three days of kiss deprivation could do that to a lady. With his lips near her ear, she expected to hear sweet nothings. He whispered, "Was Ludwig incapacitated at the top? Hmm?"

She tried to rear back, but he was ready, and his clasp tightened. Nose to nose, chest to chest, her breathing became strained. She managed, "Child's death jar."

"Ludwig was in the jar?"

"Yes. Now let—"

"Dimensions?"

"Two feet around. I can't breathe, now—"

"Height, Gallagher?"

"I'm about five-foot-three give or take an inch or two."

"Gallagher." She tensed at the rumble in his chest.

"Three feet high."

"How did you discover the dog in there?"

"The jar may have fallen over and down the steps."

"With you underneath? Great Coyote's balls."

"Oh, it missed me by miles . . . ouch . . . a foot . . . ow . . . half a foot at least."

He kissed her again, and gently pushed her away, his amorous maneuvers obviously depleting his strength. His eyes closed, he took a couple of steadying breaths, but despite that, the color seemed to drain from his face. "Who put him there?"

Ignoring his question, she straightened her sweater and said, "I'm not sure I like your third-degree tactics, Special Investigator Lassiter."

A lopsided grin greeted her statement, and he said, "I'm sure you didn't. You loved it, Gallagher."

She tilted her nose in the air and was about to retort when the nurse walked in, took one look at Quannah's washed out features and pushed the medication pump.

"No, don't—" Quannah said.

"Don't you *no* me, officer. You look like you've been tangling with a wild cat and just got tail slapped. The third day is the most difficult, and you're not doing it without lots of the happy juice. Doctor's orders. You'll have tomorrow at home to face the agony. Enjoy the Demerol today." The nurse walked out, and they were once again alone together.

"*Winyan*," he said, grabbing her hand. "Don't stick your nose into anything else. Go to Uncle Brigham with this. Promise me."

"Of course, Lassiter, if that's what you want."

He narrowed one eye, as if not quite believing what he heard, but he nodded as the Demerol relaxed his muscles. She leaned down to kiss his brow and whispered, "Sheriff Tucker is out of town today for a regional meeting with other West Texas sheriffs. Soon as he's back in town, I'll go visit him."

"One last thing," he said, while his eyelids betrayed him and blinked downward.

"Yes, my heartmate, yes?"

"Beware, Gallagher, of the jaguars—all of them."

"Jaguars?"

"Yes, all . . . of . . ."

"Wait, wait. Lassiter, is this from a dream, a vision? An all-points bulletin? What jaguars? How many? As in the jungle type? As in cars?" A vision of the blue minivan with its yellow stripes hovered before her. "Are you sure it's not minivans? Lassiter? Don't you dare drift off now. Damn you, Lassiter."

CHAPTER NINE

The smallest deed can often blind
When one desires the truth to find.

—Go'ik'kimi
The Book of the Ancient Ones

Willi sat at a corner table of the Kachelhoffer sisters' tea room. She lounged back in one of the comfortable leather roller arm chairs used for the diners. Dark green walls, wood paneling and a crackling fire warmed her body and spirit. Her emotions had needed warming ever since she'd heard about Ludwig's demise. But she'd dismissed the importance of his passing in the rush from Anastasia's bedside and then to Quannah's, but now she paused. She had to confront the fact that murder had been done, and possible attempted murder. No way had Ludwig gotten into the three-foot high burial jar by himself. Both Agatha and Quannah had pointed that fact out to her. Ludwig had purposefully been placed there and left to die. Poor baby.

Murdered.

Willi tilted her head in thought. Probably, Anastasia's two attacks—the first at the train sheds, the second in what could now only be construed as a hit-and-run at HEB—failed. What had Anastasia done to get the attention of a killer? Willi peered down beside the table at the bag containing poor Ludwig's bed and what was left of Anastasia's appointment calendar. She must find time to peruse the information before a murderer found out his victim was out of her coma. Then she'd try again to interview Yaotle—Tommy Balboa—and talk with Ramblin' a second time. She breathed a bit easier with a plan in mind, being as there was nothing worse for her than to sit and twiddle her thumbs when danger threatened loved ones.

Willi's stomach growled attesting to an immediate need for food. Agatha waited tables today, and Elba cooked behind the scenes since their third partner, Viola Fiona, had taken a month to visit Ireland and friends there. Setting a cup of hot apple cider in front of Willi, Agatha frowned.

"What?" Willi said.

"Oh, nothing, dear. Guess I looked like a scowling old witch. We're missing some of our spotted blue bowls. Half a dozen gone." She wiped her hands on her green apron. "When you have no big mysteries to solve you can put your thinking around that problem."

Willi smiled. "Ah, the mystery of the blue bowls."

"*Spotted* blue bowls. Quite expensive." Agatha pointed to an antique sideboard where linens were kept. "Some weeks ago, we had six place mats taken. All the same pattern. Blue and black stripes with white roses intertwined. Quite distinct. Viola Fiona will be most upset when she finds out."

"Uh-oh. Were those some she'd brought from the old country?"

"Right you are. Why would anyone do such silly filching?"

"Selling small items to get money for their drug fix of the day? Setting up their own housekeeping? Who knows? Folks do the dangest dumb things."

"That's true. We're not the only place to suffer."

"What do you mean?"

"You know sister and I've joined Games for Fun."

Willi nodded. "The group that gets together bi-monthly to play Scrabble, Clue, and other old board games?"

"Right you are, Willi. Well, Emmett and Ilene Hawley hosted Games for Fun last week. They own the new gift shop two blocks down. They've had small items taken, too. A set of designer sheets, nice flannel winter set, and I believe a bath set. The kind with a trash basket, tooth caddy, soap dish and dispenser that all match. Things like that."

"Some kleptomaniac in our midst, perhaps," Willi said.

"Rasco Coontz has also had problems."

"Someone's nabbing books from his used book store, too?" Willi sighed. "Good grief."

"No," Agatha said, shaking the brilliant hued skirt free of crumbs from the freshly baked breads. "Rasco's Readery also sells reading tables, lamps, inlaid chess boards and the like. He's missed some candle holders and a lamp. Just really odd, don't you think?"

"Yes, but—"

"But you have more serious concerns right now, I know, dear. Sister and I are both glad to hear Quannah and Anastasia are doing better. Now help yourself to the appetizers." On a side stove—vintage 1800's look, modern gas in usage—some items were always kept bubbling and warm for quickies. Today's was broccoli and cheese soup and sausage balls, both of which Willi devoured while waiting for her chicken salad and homemade rolls. Just as she relaxed, three other patrons strolled in, and pulled out chairs to join her.

With her mouth full of sausage balls, she could only nod and wave a hand in polite welcome as a number of the museum folks walked in. Professor Stöhr, Dr. Etzli, and the woman who Willi had chased in the minivan sat down. At sight of her, Willi almost choked on her sausage ball.

Dr. Etzli, after removing his black hat, sunglasses and cape, introduced her as "our storyteller, Mrs. Manauia." "We are all so glad to finally meet her."

Willi swallowed and said, "You're Mrs. Manauia? Uh . . . We almost met. Out on the highway? This morning?"

"I'm sorry, *querida*. I do not have an idea of what you're talking about," Drianina Manauia said.

"You drive a blue minivan with yellow stripes, right?"

Dr. Etzli raised an eyebrow at Willi as if to say, what is your problem with minivans?

Mrs. Manauia, heavy jowls and earrings in movement, patted Willi's arm. "No, *querida,* no. I drive an old pickup. Better for the storytelling props and the hay for the horses, you know."

"But—" Willi looked into the intensely dark eyes of the woman and decided she would get nowhere through further protestations. Maybe she was wrong, but no. Impossible. No two women could look so much alike. Two other customers walked in, pedal pushers and striped shirts on, canvas slip-ons and hair dyed similar colors of blonde. Somewhere in their sixties, both were small-town clones. They ordered and used the same deep Texas drawl and east Texas twang. Willi sighed. Okay. Okay. Best to use this opportunity to find out what Mrs. Manauia might know about happenings last night at the museum. She allowed the three to order before leaning in to ask her questions.

Professor Stöhr halted her. "I beg your pardon, Madam Chair, although this is a serendipitous and unexpected meeting, we would like to air some concerns. First, Mrs. Manauia is missing one of her props from her storytelling area."

"Really?"

Drianina Manauia nodded her head. "Yes, *queridos,* it is so. I tell an old ghost story of a child in the Aztecan burial urn. Yesterday evening I brought the urn to the museum and sat it beside an area where uh . . . the worker who calls herself Tattoo was going to build me a tri-fold background. This morning, there is no sign of it anywhere."

"I'm so sorry, Mrs. Manauaia, but—"

"Drianina, please, *querida.* Drianina."

"Drianina. There was an accident at the museum last night." Willi explained about the toppling burial jar and locating Ludwig inside. "What time did you bring the jar?"

"I suppose near eight in the evening. Yes, that is so. I had to drive afterwards to get hay and home in time to feed the Clydesdales."

"Why did you leave it on top of the pyramid steps?"

Drianina pushed her salt-and-pepper tangle of hair behind her ears. "*Querida,* why would I do that? Up all those steps?" She shook her head. "No, no, no. All I could manage was to use the dolly with rollers to move it from pickup to the left hand corner at the bottom of the pyramid. I will bring a jungle's worth of trees and bushes to surround my area, too."

"Well, someone did," Willi said.

Professor Stöhr wiped his mouth with his napkin, not one of the blue and black with white roses, but rather a soft green with muted yellow day lilies. "And the small hound was inside? Odd, don't you find that odd, Dr. Etzli?"

"Truly, yes, most strange."

Agatha opened the blinds of the window on the far side of the room where sun streamed into the space. Etzli cringed, "Do you mind?"

"Oh, sir, I'm so sorry."

He swallowed and offered a thin-lipped smile. "Your tea room offers a wonderful respite from the searing heat of the Texas sun. So lovely, as it is."

Parker Nolan strode through the door, removed his hat and offered a bow to the ladies at the table. He placed his hat on one corner and hooked his jaguar-tipped cane on the other knob of the chair back. "I came as soon as I heard," he said. "Dreadful business. So sorry, Dr. Etzli."

"What's going on?" Willi asked, confused.

Etzli took a sip of his hot tea before setting the cup down carefully. With his hands in a prayerful motif, he said, "Yaotle."

"Your aide?" Willi asked.

"Yes. He has gone missing." As if the news were more than he could face even in the dimmed interior of the tea room, he replaced his sunglasses.

Parker Nolan took up the tale. "We all, of course, must keep hoping that he'll turn up. I believe it might be simply a night on the town, a tryst with a lovely lady, a hangover, perhaps."

Professor Stöhr pushed back his broccoli soup. "Oh, then perhaps you have not heard all the news, Mr. Nolan."

Parker Nolan tilted his head to one side. "I saw the note tacked to my office door this morning about him missing, and that we were all to meet here. We must insist on installation of computers immediately so we can get emails. Our communications at the moment are slower than the Pony Express. Have there been more developments?"

"Unfortunately, yes." Etzli removed his glasses. Agatha opened the door to the kitchen, causing light to stream across the group's table, and he replaced them yet again. "Something really horrible has occurred," he said, and swallowed.

Mrs. Manauia laid down her soup spoon and buttered a sausage ball. "Yaotle's pickup—his sparkling old vehicle he's so proud of—was found."

"Really? Where?" asked Willi. "That should give the authorities a place to start looking."

Mrs. Manauia smiled. "Indeed, that is the positive outlook, and the sheriff's department is searching now the land and domicile where it sits." She waited to deliver her final announcement after she popped the sausage ball in her mouth and chewed. "Right at the driveway of our acting curator's home."

Willi slapped her napkin on the table. "In front of Anastasia's and Ramblin's home?" She started to add that it hadn't been anywhere in sight when she left the area earlier.

"Yes, *querida,* perhaps there is a connection between Yaotle and Ms. Zöllmer, for that is where the sheriff's deputy located the vehicle."

"Indeed?" asked Parker Nolan, a frown creasing his smooth baby face. "Indeed?"

"And even worse," added Professor Stöhr as he patted his vest lapels. "Yes, I say it is even worse news—the condition in which they found the vehicle."

"And what," asked Parker Nolan, "would that be?"

"They found—" began the professor, but was interrupted by Mrs. Manauia, who obviously wasn't going to be upstaged in telling a story. She raised a dramatic finger for attention and lifted her chin high so as to look down her nose at those around the table. Willi gasped at her rude behavior. Professor Stöhr turned red in the face. Etzli leaned in and removed his sunglasses while Parker Nolan in an age-old habit of all humans, reached for his own comfortable talisman, his silver-tipped cane.

Mrs. Manauia's earrings jingled as she moved her head around to stare at each one, bringing them closer to the storyteller's circle. "The truck bed was soaked. Soaked in blood. Lots of blood. Too much." She shook her head in a dire prediction that no one needed to give voice to. "Too much blood." And the tintinnabulation of her earrings sounded more like Poe's heavy metal bells of death.

Willi glared at Mrs. Manauia. "How do you know all of this? Usually the law is circumspect about divulging such information."

Mrs. Manauia smiled. "*Querida,* do not be upset. I have not usurped your place as Miss Marple of the Range. It was merely my luck to be tootling along when they placed a road block up around the pickup. My curiosity, and the fact that I recognized and told an officer that I knew the driver, allowed me some ten feet away into the inner circle. Yes, the wise and knowing inner circle, as I should be as a descendent of the Jaguar clan. It is time ancient lineages are recognized."

Parker Nolan guffawed. "Don't for a moment think that the general folks recognize any such thing, Mrs. Manauia. Perhaps in time, when they've had a decade of the richness offered by a finely run museum with your storytelling included. Sorry if that disappoints you, ma'am."

Mrs. Manauia ignored him and turned her attention to Willi. "Yaotle was a warrior, you know, of the old beliefs. He understood the grandeur and the power of the ancient tenets. If his blood has been shed, I'm sure the gods will look upon it as a great and brave one sacrificed."

Willi raised an eyebrow. "Okay." Hmm. Maybe Tattoo had the right of it when she described the storyteller as one who *just gets an evil delight, a real evil delight out of scaring the bejesus out of folks.* "Surely, you aren't suggesting someone uh . . . sacrificed . . . Yaotle for some ancient Aztecan divinity."

Mrs. Manauia raised her hands while shrugging her shoulders. "*Queridos,* some sacrifice *themselves* upon the altar of Chacmool, the red tiger—a Jaguar kinsman. Chacmool is often found in the Temple of the Warriors, and of course, Yaotle translates as *warrior.* Certainly, he might give himself for the glory, you understand, for the ability to be used for a higher good."

Parker Nolan caressed his cane and scowled. "In that case, we'd have found his blood in the bowl of Chacmool, not in his pickup seat."

Willi, looking from one to the other of her open palms, said, "Pickup? Chacmool? Pickup? Chacmool? Hmm. I'm inclined to agree with you, Parker." She peered at Etzli's stricken face. "I'm so sorry, again. What thoughts do you have to offer about what happened? When did you see Yaotle last, Dr. Etzli?"

"I left him at the museum last night around midnight. He said he might just sleep on the couch in our office as he had to get to ordering early this morning."

Some thought niggled away at Willi. Maybe a few more questions would bring it to the forefront. "I saw you and him last night at the HEB store parking lot, but I can't quite place him or what he wore."

Professor Stöhr spoke. "Dresses much like his mentor in all black. Even those puffy sleeved flowing shirts of his are black instead of Dr. Etzli's white buccaneer look."

"Everyone," Etzli said, "should develop a unique style, especially those of us in the public eye."

"Black, black . . . black." Willi whispered to herself. Dr. Etzli dressed almost in all black other than his shirt. Ramblin' Anders chose that color, too, although in a more modern style of turtle neck and sleek slacks with black huaraches.

"Madam Chair, yes?"

"Oh, just wondering about something Anastasia said this morning."

All leaned into the center of the table. As she stared at each in turn she swallowed. Etzli's dark eyes, etched with redness, could have been the model for a Count Dracula revival poster. Parker Nolan's British blues narrowed in cold appraisal.

Willi placed her fingers to both cheeks to calm the heat rising. *Why in Blue Blazes did I open my mouth? Now I've got to tell the waiting vultures something.* Mrs. Manauia's calculating brown eyes, strangely devoid of surrounding wrinkles despite her advanced age, regarded Willi, while the professor pulled out his watch and considered the time. At that moment, Quannah's voice seared through her thoughts: *Beware, Gallagher, of the jaguars—all of them.*

Willi blinked away the idea and opted for a version of the

truth. "Anastasia said it was too dark in the shadows to see her attacker."

"Attacker, Madam Chair?" Now the professor's eyes did regard her warily. "You mean in another car which ran her into the pole?"

"No, not exactly. It seems she was attacked before she left the museum by a rather brutal beast who bruised her and had intentions of more. But she can only recall an impression of flowing black cloth."

"Ah, *querida*," said Mrs. Manauia with a negating wave of her bare fingers, sans all the rings Willi thought she'd seen through the speeding minivan's windshield. "Don't for a moment believe that the person was Yaotle. No, no, no. He would be far more likely to protect, not harm, unless the perpetrators were dishonoring the ancient ones."

"What would a true follower do in that case, Mrs. Manauia?" It was Willi's turn to lean over, open her green eyes and nail the storyteller.

"A true follower would invoke the ancient ones to come to aide, to advise, to lead." Mrs. Manauia raised her finger and tilted her chin high. "If it were the olden times, the entire Jaguar clan would demand a blood sacrifice for disrespect. And that," she said, "is obviously not this modern day scenario since Yaotle is the slain one." She took a quick breath and continued. "Where is this Ms. Tattoo? Was not everyone informed to join us here? Absence may speak of a guilty nature. She works in the far sheds all the time. Perhaps she is responsible for the attack or attacks, now that there have been two."

"Actually, one murder, two other attacks," Willi reminded the group.

"Don't jump to conclusions, Mrs. Manauia," Dr. Etzli said. "Perhaps there is more to come to light. Yaotle is missing. There could be other reasons for the blood in his pickup. Until he is found, until the sheriff's department tests the blood, until Yaotle returns, we will not know. I refuse to believe the worst at this point. Yaotle is fine."

For some reason all that black still bothered her. Ramblin' not only dressed in black, he had a black nature at times, hence his need for rage management classes. Dr. Etzli—the Shadow personified—certainly had a mysterious dark persona depicted in his choice of dress. Now, Yaotle—the warrior—seemed to share this somber penchant. And, of course, she couldn't stop Quannah's foreboding and unbidden warning from reaching out its dark meanings to her again: *Beware, Gallagher, of the jaguars—all of them.*

As everyone began to make peremptory moves towards leaving—folding napkins, shoving back drinks, setting tips on the table—Parker Nolan issued an all-inclusive invitation. "As you all know, I've been lucky enough to find a house for lease, and have a barbecue supper planned. Just a chance to relax together on the back veranda before the weather gets really cold, and certainly before we all have to go our separate ways." He handed each a business card with a clear map on the back. "About sevenish."

Professor Stöhr shoved the card into an inside vest pocket. "Good that you're just renting. After they've chosen the curator, perhaps I can take it over." The twinkle in his eye and the cuff to Parker's shoulder indicated he was in jest.

Parker took it as such. "Ah, now, as these Texans say, don't count your chickens until they hatch. I believe we've all got a good chance at the honor."

The professor nodded, his double chin showing as he lowered his head. "Right you are, Mr. Nolan. Me? I must say it's been an honor to be pitched in battle against such outstanding adversaries as you and Dr. Etzli."

Willi frowned, and then allowed a smirk to cross her face.

They had obviously all marked Anastasia Zöllmer off the course. Those three *amigos* had better watch out. Willi knew the stuff Anastasia was made of, and as soon as she got a second wind, she'd be back to wheeling and dealing, pulling at her blonde spikes and taking charge. She'd give those three a run for their money.

When they all left, except Willi, the remaining air immediately chilled. Through the space around the window blinds, she could see that the sun had been clouded over by the October sky, and the temperature of the entire room had plummeted. Agatha pulled the heavy brocaded curtains around the corner table. "I can tell you have things to think about. Matters to peruse." She glanced down at the bag hidden by the long tablecloth. "It's rush hour now, but our other helpers have arrived. Sister and I will take a break in a while, so if you need us, call." She cleared the table of all the luncheon debris and set a steaming pot of herbal tea—one of Elba's especially relaxing blends—and a fresh cup and saucer on the table, which allowed plenty of room for Willi to spread out the paperwork, and in a whirl of rainbow skirts, flashing jewelry and silk blouse Agatha withdrew. One of the tea's ingredients, sweet cinnamon, smelled so delicious.

A moment later, Elba appeared. "Aggie forgot to tell you."

"What?"

"She sweet-talked Brigham."

"Sheriff Tucker, yes." Willi grinned. "And she found out what?"

"That the caller, the Spanish-speaking lady, who called in about the accident?"

"What about her, Elba, not that my patience is growing thin or anything."

"Now ain't you hotter than a rabbit being chased, more jittery than a girl on a first date, hepped up more than an old hippy on bad pot."

"Whatever." Willi glared at the old woman. "The caller? Could she ID the hit-and-run driver?"

"Wasn't no such thing. A hit-and-run driver, I mean. Seems she got flustered when she first called. There was a car right beside Anastasia's car, but it didn't run her off the road. The witness said smoke was billowing in front of Anastasia, and she was swatting at it, not paying attention to the road, and then got scared about something in the dang fool car, stomped on the pedal and the rest is what you saw at the parking lot. Maybe a bee or wasp. It's happened."

"Must have been . . . I guess . . . but the smoke. Well, that was simply her cigarette smoke, I imagine."

"Could be. Could be. We'll know when she gets her memory all total and together."

"Yes, I hope so," Willi said.

Elba turned to leave her to the relaxing tea, and said, "Aggie also said, don't forget to call the vet."

"I will, I will. She's just not first on my list right now."

Willi drank another half a cup of the blend, and topped off her second cup from the pot. Great horned owls and rats. Willi grimaced at one of her versions of cursing. She wasn't quite to the damn-it-all-to-Hell-and-back versions, but mighty close. Her stomach roiled at the idea that someone out there might have attacked both Anastasia and Yaotle—Tommy Balboa—and that *someone* was still on the loose. Any lowlife who could willfully leave a small helpless four-legged creature to die had to be the scum-dragging butt-end of society.

She faced her dilemma squarely: She *could* go to Sheriff Tucker, Quannah's uncle and certainly one of her dearest friends, as Quannah had asked. She *could* lay out the few crumbs of info before him. Or . . . she *could* blindly go forward and try to glean more facts. JiminyJeez, either way was going to lead to confrontations. From past experiences she knew she'd be questioned ad nauseam by Sheriff Tucker, not to mention being told a hundred times in a thousand ways not to get involved.

She cupped her face between her hands and groaned. If she moved forward by herself, she didn't know that she'd do more than irritate the killer inadvertently, thereby placing herself in jeopardy. No, that was silly. She didn't know anything really. Could she tell the sheriff at this point who had put Ludwig in the urn? No. Would she be able to describe Anastasia's late-night assailant? Hardly. Did she even have a guess as to Yaotle's part in this? Absolutely not. So . . . she knew nothing. She was in far more danger from her stalker who she suspected had nothing to do with the attacks upon Anastasia or Ludwig.

Well, that took care of that dilemma. She would not go to Sheriff Tucker and 'fess up about gathering evidence—the calendar—and cleaning up other evidence—the shattered urn—unless she had some solid information to give him. Decision made, she lifted her chin from her cupped hands and straightened her shoulders. She gulped down the entire cup of the relaxing tea and sat for a moment, letting it do its magic, attested to by the ease in her tightened shoulder muscles, the tenseness leaving her jaw line, the anxiety abdicating its tight hold upon her emotions.

Now, down to business.

She had planned to go through the bag's info. That was okay, but then she had wanted to interview Yaotle, Etzli's aide, after her early lunch and perhaps talk with Ramblin' again. She was too late to get to Yaotle. She shut her eyes. No, she shouldn't think that way—*just getting a real evil delight* in believing the worst. Right. So, for the moment—until Yaotle could be located—she would move ahead with what she had. First and foremost, there just had to be a clue, a minute lead in the papers through which she now shuffled and straightened upon a cleared spot on the table. Yes, there had to be, just had to be something . . .

   . . . something caught her eye atop the pyramid, a shadow that moved out from one pillar in the grouping of three. Willi looked down at her woven skirt, quetzal feathers covering it and the halter top. Heavy loops of purest gold adorned her ears, neck, upper arms and ankles above her bare feet. Her father, a feather crafter, had sent her for instruction from the priests, for she had been disobedient.

   She hung her head for a moment in shame, but then raised her head and walked forward with confidence. She had a right to question; she had a right to answers. She was not some weak-willed little village weaver. A smoky haze surrounded her; she coughed and waved it aside.

   The shadowy figure beckoned to her, first with one hand, beringed and bangled, then with another hand in a black glove. As a member of an elite landlord's family, she was due all respect. With head held high she advanced to the inside recesses of the temple decorated with carvings of jaguars in many postures, both benign and deadly. There she bowed in obeisance to the obsidian god of the Great Pyramid of Tenochtitlán, Tezcatlipoca. This Tezcatlipoca held a gold-rimmed mirror of the blackest obsidian, indicating he saw everything that happened. His stone hand reached for her, forcing her to look deeply into the mirror of knowledge. She frowned only momentarily at the ability of the stone to shape shift into human mobility. After all, it was common knowledge that Tezcatlipoca, the deceiver and sower of discord, could appear as a monkey, a coyote, or a skunk, as well as the divine Jaguar.

   Willi whispered, "Nahaual."

   "Yes, daughter," the obsidian visage replied. "Yes, that refers to our secret ability to shift shapes from human to animal—tomal—form."

   Willi sighed, feeling drowsy as if she'd been drugged but in a restful way. The smoke fog surrounded her again, tendrils closing around her neck, snaking down her throat. She coughed and hacked until she cleared the passageway to fresh air.

Her instructor continued. "Look into the dark mirror and learn of all the shape-shifters in your life."

When she peered deeply, she saw herself in the mirror in battle with . . . with a monkey who grasped her necklace and raced away to hide it, only to turn tail and grab at a few quetzal feathers. Willi chased the monkey to a high tree hideaway where strange things lay about, including a half dozen napkins of blue and black with white roses. Shiny trinkets and magical lamps lit up the tree house. The monkey grinned, pulling back repulsive lips and baring teeth at her. Willi grabbed the monkey by the tail, swung it around and around until she grew dizzy and let go. The creature sailed higher and higher and higher until it flew out of sight.

"That is one, daughter. Easy to take care of. Now, the next is not so easy."

"Oh, no." With one hand Willi pinched her nostrils together. "I've tangled with this shape-shifter before."

A skunk wandered up to her, turned tail to let loose perfume unholy, but before the scent reached Willi, she jumped into a pristine clean pickup and roared away.

"Yaotle?" she asked. "Yaotle, is this yours? There's no blood inside." Now, a vile odor came with the foggy miasma encircling her head and inching down her nostrils. She blinked it away as her mentor spoke.

"No, child, he's not there. He's not the skunk. Concentrate. Focus."

The skunk appeared again, in a form as large as a bear. This shape-shifter's stench was overpowering, but worse was the word coming out of its mouth, an accolade referring to Willi. She grasped the first things she could see—books—and threw them. "Chaucer in the eye, Poe to the head, you beast. Now, try Dean Koontz to the midriff, a whack on the hind side with Agatha Christie."

"Ah, well done, daughter. Now peer deeply, deeply into the black void, for the most dangerous still awaits you."

Three coyotes and a jaguar—the prince of discord stood before her. Suddenly she and they were caught in a veritable whirlpool. At one moment the coyotes wore bright orange bandanas, in the next they drove a van which careened wildly past the very pyramid she now stood upon. One made a lascivious lunge toward her, tried to copulate, was slapped away by another. Before long, the three fought against each other. In the crescendo of battle, one finally emerged a moment, before disappearing into the watery depths. But in that moment, she viewed his entire body covered in tattoos, sinister depictions of gore and rape and plunder.

She grabbed hold of something to keep from being sucked down into the vortex of water. She pulled at the jaguar's skin, but only a black cape and hat caught in her hands, then Aztecan jewelry poured off the animal's paws and ears. She blinked, and the jaguar raced away in a blue minivan, changed to a green-tentacled monster with wheels, and finally jumped into a country pickup.

Almost out of reach now, the jaguar pounced on solid land, the whirlpool dried up and Willi faced the wild creature, fanged teeth bared in their yellowed glory, gums bloodied with a past kill, talons reaching out toward the bare skin around Willi's navel. Eyes—darkest black, deepest brown, coldest blues—bore into her soul, waiting to devour and make an example of one of the elite daughters of Tenochtitlán who had not lived a life revering the gods of her father and grandfather before.

The obsidian one said, "Yes, it's time to do battle. Get ready. Be prepared. Only one will win. Will it be you, daughter? Will it be the shape-shifter? Will you have to learn to be the shape-shifter to defeat your enemy?"

Before Willi could answer, a red-eyed bat, wingspan at three feet, flew out from the obsidian mirror, around her head, and chased her from the pyramid, into the dank undergrowth of palm fronds and down, down into the sand and grit and mud of earth.

"Earth to Miss Willi. Earth to Miss Willi."

She blinked and stared into Elba's and Agatha's concerned eyes. Elba said, "Beam her back down, Scotty. Her brain cells, too, please."

"Very funny," Willi said, shoving the powerful concoction of tea away from her. "I was merely relaxing for a few minutes."

"And what did you learn in your meanderings on the other side, and don't try to fool with us. We know you too well," Elba said.

Agatha nodded. "Tell us all, and let's see what we can interpret. You know, we elders are better interpreters than you youngsters."

"You call thirty-two a youngster?"

"Indeed. And being a Capricorn, you'll live many, many years, so you are in a very astrological sense, a child," Agatha responded.

"On the other hand," Elba said, shifting her ample bosom into a more comfortable position, "Capricorns are born old in some ways. For example—"

"Ladies," Willi said, rubbing her temples. "Do you want to hear about—"

"—the daydream?" they asked in unison.

"—the vision," she insisted, nose tilted in the air. She glanced at her watch. "Oh, my gosh. Have I sat here that long?"

"Pooh," Agatha said, "two o'clock is early afternoon. Now, do tell us all the details."

She was about to when the tea shop phone rang. "Don't say a word until I get back," Agatha said.

When she returned, Agatha's face was ashen; even the peacock colors she wore seemed muted; certainly her fluttery characteristics had vanished. "Two murders now for sure."

Willi, eyes wider than an owl's, asked, "They found Yaotle's body?"

Agatha patted her arm. "You must be strong, Miss Willi, you

must be strong. We'll both close up and go to the hospital with you."

CHAPTER TEN

Obsidian eyes that watch from afar
Know things aren't really what they are.

> —Canat'quatl
> The Book of the Ancient Ones

Willi ran into Quannah's hospital room. A pristinely made bed, freshly mopped floor and emptiness met her. Her knees would no longer hold her up, and she sat down on the crisp sheets where she allowed her tears to flow. The news had left her numb on the ride with Elba and Agatha. Not until she'd gotten through the consoling of Anastasia's parents and given sympathy to Ramblin' did she finally succumb to any real emotion.

Anastasia gone?

Willi had been blessed through the years not to have lost any of her contemporaries, her high-school chums, her best friends. Her parents' passing had left a huge hole in her life, and certainly a few of her former students had lost their lives to drugs and childbirth and even the military, but never one of her peers. This up-close near-to-her-age look at mortality wasn't pleasant. And the loss of forthright, intelligent, cheerful, fun Anastasia—well, it was more than she could fathom in an hour's time.

She placed fingers to her cheeks to meet a coldness that went deeper than the October chill in the air. Since Sheriff Tucker was out of town, Smitty Parva had done the honors of delivering Quannah home a few hours ago. Evidently, his meal strategy had worked since they released him earlier than she expected. She had called to let them know about Anastasia, but had had to leave a message on the machine. She licked dry lips. Must have called while they were in transit. Knowing her warrior as she did, she'd lay big odds that he had bullied Officer Parva into stopping by the office before going on home.

Agatha had zoomed off to the farm to take over nursing duties from Smitty Parva after she had dropped Elba off at the tea shop to bring Willi's car to the hospital.

Willi slumped with her hands between her knees. All the daily dalliances of life continued, all the mundane maneuvers of mind marched onward, and yet something truly nasty threatened the town of Nickleberry. No doubt now.

Murder.

Clear and simple cold-blooded murder.

A big-eyed petite black nurse, her nametag with Benita Dubois askew, had spoken to Elba and Willi. "I'm so sorry about your friend. Nurse Nayland and I came in to take Ms. Zöllmer down for X rays. We told the officers what we found."

"And that was?" Willi asked.

"The officer in charge said we weren't to discuss it, Ms. Gallagher." Benita Dubois's dark eyes, pools of kindness, relented, and she drew Willi aside and whispered, "I know you'll find out soon, and maybe it's best you find out here. Sit down." She led Willi into another room and knelt beside the chair as Willi obeyed and sat.

Willi's heart skittered like a catfish on the hook. She gulped. "Just tell me, please."

"Ms. Zöllmer passed away."

Tears sprang to Willi's eyes and overflowed. She didn't even reach up to wipe at the flow. "Complications from her injuries? Just too . . . too horrific for her to survive? But she looked fine when I visited earlier."

Benita grabbed tissues from the metal box affixed to the wall and pressed a handful at Willi. "No, ma'am. Not exactly. There was a pillow beside her, not under her head."

"Are . . . what are you saying?"

"I'm not saying anything. The police bagged that pillow, and I know for a fact since I was standing right there beside them, that they ordered forensics to test it. They think . . . they seemed pretty sure, in fact, that someone might have . . ."

"Smothered?"

"—smothered her—"

"With the pillow?" Willi kept repeating the details as if that repetition would make the horror diminish, make the news less terrible. "With the pillow."

"Yes, ma'am. I'm so sorry. I can get you a couple of aspirin, a cold compress. You sit here a moment. I'll be right back."

While she waited, Willi made a few phone calls, finally reached one of the officers who knew her and her connection to Anastasia. He cautiously confirmed that they were considering the situation as a possible homicide. Benita Dubois offered a small cup with two extra strength capsules and a drink. Then she pressed a cold compress against Willi's cheeks and neck. "Thank you, thank you."

"Not a problem. Is there someone I could call for you?"

Willi shook her head and said, "And that's it . . . the end of a beautiful friend? What . . . what else can you tell me?"

"Someone had lit a cigarette for her," Nurse Dubois said. "She'd been asking, but . . ."

"I know," Willi said, reaching for more tissues. "Not allowed inside the hospital. So, maybe she didn't, but rather her visitor—"

"She smoked it." Nurse Dubois said. "I'd helped her with her makeup this morning. Her lipstick was on the half burned-out stub. It had fallen from her hand."

Willi shut her eyes and swallowed back bile. Damn-it-to-Hell-and-back, Anastasia would have been weak, helpless against his strong hands pushing downward. "Where were her parents? Ramblin'?"

"Her parents had just stepped out to have a bite to eat. I don't know this Ramblin'."

"Her boyfriend. You didn't see him? Black slacks, black turtleneck?"

Nurse Dubois shook her head and said, "One last thing. Maybe I shouldn't tell you, but I know you sometimes work on such cases, sort of unofficially. You are the one the papers refer to as Miss Marple of the Range, right?"

At Willi's nod, Nurse Dubois continued. "This person . . . horrible person . . . shoved so hard he cracked her cheek bone. Again, I'm so sorry." Benita Dubois's eyes glistened with tears when she went back on duty.

My dear Lord. Guess now the authorities would believe the anonymous caller and Willi. Hit-and-run murderer, perhaps not, since she had survived the crash. But someone had returned to finish the job, possibly the same someone who had attacked Anastasia in the train yard at the museum. Well, sure, *now* the authorities had probably taken Ramblin' Anders in for questioning. Naturally, they would suspect him first and foremost. He was at the museum during the attack, also in the hospital at the crucial time, and they only had his word that he was not the one responsible for Anastasia's wreck.

Willi sighed. She had gleaned a few hints from Anastasia's appointment calendar before she had fallen into the . . . uh . . . vision of the jaguars. Somehow, Willi had managed to jot down a few items to consider. She took a deep breath and tried to focus on what she could do, not to help Anastasia now, but to bring some rightness back into a world gone horribly wrong the last few days.

Yesterday, Friday 9:00 a.m. at the Nickleberry Museum. That's when all this horror started, and yet it seemed eons ago. She glanced at her watch. *Saturday, 3:00 p.m.* Impossible. But there it was. Tears threatened again with the overwhelming amount of visuals suddenly flooding her mind.

Images of Shelton sculptures, green and blue tiles behind the waterfall, and jaguar-tipped walking canes mixed with visions of shredded orange cloths, curtains of the same hues flowing behind the pyramid, burial urns, smoke and the great cat's talons, yellowed with age. These mingled with TV images of three killers' mug shots, Quannah with warrior's paint on cheeks and bared chest, Tattoo's snake and rose writhing together.

"Ahhhh!" With both hands she pulled at the hair on her temples. "Brain, stop!"

She reached into her purse for her crumpled notes. Words blurred. What in Hades was wrong with her? Why couldn't she focus on anything? Deep breaths. Deep breaths. What would Quannah say or the Kachelhoffer sisters or Sheriff Tucker, all who always had her interests uppermost, dearest ones that they were?

"Don't do no good to tear around without figuring out where you're going and why first off." She smiled. That would be Sheriff Brigham Tucker.

"You're as confused as a snail in a dog race, as mixed up as a five-year-old in a poker game, as puzzled as a 'possum caught in the headlights." She wiped away the last tears from her eyes and whispered, "Yes, Elba. Tell me something I don't know."

Quannah's face came before her, his grin in place, his hooded eyes seeming to see through her, and he winked. *"Do things in order to help you find peace. When you're at peace and calm, you can think, Winyan."*

Willi stood up. "About time I heard from you." Looking

toward the door to make sure nurses had not heard her talking aloud to the people in her head, she drew forth her cell phone. Okay. "I need to know that you, my stubborn-headed and Hell-bent-for-leather warrior, aren't out getting shot up by your partner." This time the home phone was answered by Agatha.

"Stop your worrying, Miss Willi. Sure, he made Officer Parva take him to work for a few minutes. Best thing could have happened. Wore him out. He didn't even fuss about taking his meds when he got home. Tucked into bed and out like a light. You go ahead and do what you need to do."

"Thanks, Agatha. I feel like a burden has been lifted from my shoulders. I can breathe again, knowing he's okay."

"By the by, did Sister tell you we consulted the crystal pyramid on your behalf?"

"Pyramid? Like a crystal ball?"

"Yes, but even more ancient. And it's actually two pyramids, the age old balance between male and female since one is inverted, you see."

"Considering all the bad things which have come to center around a pyramid and Chacmool, I'm not sure I want to know what you discovered."

"Only two strong messages came through," Agatha said.

Without enthusiasm, Willi said, "Okay. What?"

"All that is black is not dark."

"Is that anything like all that glitters is not gold?"

"Now, now. Don't scoff at help one receives from the universe. Do you want the other message?"

"Would it matter?"

"Inked warriors can clear one path. So, there you have it. I hope you find those helpful in some way. Please let us know. You know Sister and I always like to get confirmation back that we've been in touch with a higher knowledge than we mortals." Agatha paused and added, "Perhaps the messages will help you

figure out where you're going and why."

Willi gasped, and goose bumps rose as she heard in reality the words her mind had placed in the sheriff's verbal venue moments ago. "You've been going out with Brigham Tucker too long."

This off-the-subject change didn't daunt Agatha at all. "Sometimes we must be hit with the same message a number of ways, a number of times before our stubbornness gives in and acts upon them, hum?"

"You think? I'm a slow learner and a trial and tribulation to my friends, sometimes. Thanks, Agatha." With that Willi said goodbye and replaced her cell phone while she straightened her list for the second time. On this perusal the words were clear, although where they might lead her was still a bit cloudy.

Anastasia had written some cryptic notes beside one person she was to meet with yesterday afternoon: Tattoo.

Receipt forms? Broken? Missing? Stolen? Check on costume, too.

Willi could make no sense of it, but perhaps Tattoo knew since Anastasia had noted that she had advised Tattoo of the meeting. Willi also noted that Anastasia had a late afternoon appointment with Mrs. Manauia. She'd scribbled beside the storyteller's name a few items also: *Social??? Last job? Letters of rec. inc. ??? Charge for item from Mexico to us? Error? What's going on here?* Stapled to the page was a plane ticket receipt. Was it concerned with a trip Mrs. Manauia had made for the museum and was due reimbursement? At any rate, there seemed many questions she needed to answer.

Willi tried the phone number listed beside the storyteller's name, but received no answer, not even a generic answering machine voice. Perhaps she was outside feeding her Clydesdales. Willi let it ring a dozen times before giving up. Okay, so she would try to get in touch with Tattoo and get answers from her. She hated to let Agatha and Elba believe that the two messages: *"All that is black is not dark"* and *"Inked warriors can clear one path"* were not responsible for her deciding where to go and why. Perhaps the thoughts were, like everything else seemed to be today, just generic ramblings. She'd keep them in the back of her mind simply because her neighbors' uncanny gifts had proven beneficial and lifesaving in past times.

When she reached Tattoo at home, the janitress seemed pleased she'd called. "Be happy to chat if you don't mind giving me a ride to a doctor's appointment. You did mention an offer of a ride the other night. I was about to have to call and cancel, and it's really tough to reset for an appointment on a day off. Uh . . . I forgot this was the weekend, and I won't get the van back until Monday. We could talk on the way to Fort Worth—that's where the appointment is. I'd pay for gas."

"Don't worry about that," Willi said, and rushed out of the hospital. Good gosh, what was the matter with Tattoo? And even though Willi had been requested as driver, she couldn't be so uncivilized as to out and out ask that question. She'd have to wait and see if Tattoo volunteered the vital clues about her health condition, or if the doctor's office was a specialty, she might be able to glean from the surroundings what problems such a vibrant young woman could suffer.

After getting settled in the car, Willi said, "I've got some important questions."

Tattoo leaned back and closed her eyes. She gave directions and then said, "If you don't mind, I'll have to get really quiet and centered in preparation. Could we save the chat until after the procedure?"

"Of . . . of course. Procedure?"

The open-ended question received no response from Tattoo, whose bare arms rippled with vine and viper, as she seemed to settle into a meditative state. Willi's heart pitter-pattered. Was another person in her life in questionable health, in danger of . . . being . . .—that word she'd come to dread—. . . mortal? Willi shook her hands to instill more flow to her suddenly useless fingers upon the steering wheel. Well, by Texas tornadoes and horned toads, if this young woman could bravely face her medical crisis with reserved calm, then the least Willi could do would be to try for the same stoicism and offer strength during Tattoo's time of need.

As per Tattoo's instructions, Willi drove directly toward the hospital district near Rosedale in Fort Worth. When she reached the red bricks of Rosedale, Tattoo pointed to a turn to the right, then left and after about ten other such twists, Willi had driven past all the hospitals, clinics, medical supply houses and therapy rooms to a rather seedy side of town. "Are you sure we're at the right place?"

"Yes, turn into the parking lot to the side of this building here."

Willi did, and as she locked up the car, she asked again, "Are you sure?"

In answer Tattoo walked toward the front of a three-story building, the lower third of which had aged and blackened bricks. When Willi faced the front of the edifice, a fanciful scroll painted across the black picture window proclaimed the facility as SKINWIZARDRY, body art for the mind and soul. "Huh?"

"Come on. I'm a few minutes late for my procedure."

Inside, ethereal flute music as well as the scent of black cherry candles lit throughout the open foyer met them. The room was open, meaning there was only a two-foot-wide, three-foot-tall reception desk behind which a bad boy sat on a high stool. With a red, white and blue cap on backwards—the better to show off his flourish of thirteen earrings—and an open leather vest—the better to show off his chest tattoos, he welcomed them in a pleasant voice. If it weren't for the sounds of ink machines, slight moans and groans from the patrons lying supine or sitting with hands resting on the backs of tufted chairs so as to leave back and spine to inky ministrations, it appeared as if it was a high-class hair salon.

"Hey, Wizard, how's it shakin'?" Tattoo asked.

The receptionist answered by way of pulling back his vest to reveal his left side pecs with a hula girl sans top going through hip gyrations as he used his muscles to good effect. "Is that not cool, Tattoo girl?"

"Awesome."

Wizard came from behind his perch, gave Tattoo a hug, while he took in every inch of Willi. She turned her head to the right, intending to ignore his rudeness. Mistake number one. There out in public for God and everybody to see was a pictorial grouping of various painted posteriors, rosy rear-ends and baleful butts depicting the advertised glorious art for one part of the body, if not for the soul. She gasped. Mistake number two. Wizard immediately put a colorful and hairy arm around her shoulders, surely meant as a comfort, but Willi felt her eyes getting large in shock. Too much input, too fast.

Wizard said, "You're a virgin, aren't you?"

"I beg your—"

"Tch, tch, tch, sweet thing, just put yourself in my hands. I know what you need. A little rose—no, too soft. I see fire in those eyes."

Damned right, and you'd feel some of that fire across your face if I didn't have an aversion to swatting red scorpions and cheek hieroglyphics.

Quite obviously not able to read her mind and what the fire in her look truly signified, he continued closer to the abyss. "Yes, sweet thing, something with a kick, an inking of mystery and spirit. Ah, ah, I have it." He pointed to one particularly round buttock and its . . . uh . . . displayed art. "Yes, sweet thing, a tiger in the tank, so to speak. We can make it a striped, or a leopard or . . . a red jaguar." Without waiting for a response, which probably added to the life and health of his inner ear, he twisted her around and put both hands on her buttocks. "Hmmm. Firm, round, ahh, nice. Perfect. Which one do you shake most wicked? That's the side to place it on. Come on back to the private lair, and we'll get you disrobed and prepped. I will do you myself."

She turned faster than a Tasmanian devil going in for a blood kill and soundly slapped Wizard. The crack of palm against scorpion resounded throughout the premises. Patrons lying supine tried to rise to see the excitement, ink artists grinned and made unintelligible grunts of "yo," "man," "dude?," "real cat woman," "whoa."

Wizard raised both hands, palms outward, and shrugged in a nonplussed way as if being slapped were not a biggie to him. Go figure.

"Wizard," Tattoo said to the receptionist-owner-artist, "she's my wheels today, okay? A friend, you know? You're bound to have had one or two of those in your life. I'm here for my baby. You inking or PootiePie?"

Willi shut her eyes. She didn't want to meet anyone named PootiePie. And what in burning Hades was Tattoo talking about now? Surely, she was not here for some back room procedure— something to do with a *baby?* Not in these times, not when only three or twelve blocks away—she lost track of the turns—there was an abortion clinic. She refused to open her eyes again until Tattoo shook her arm.

"This here's PootiePie. He's going to do my procedure. PootiePie, this here's Ms. Gallagher. The one with the .357 Magnum."

This statement certainly made Willi open her eyes and glare at Tattoo. It seemed to have sealed her fate with the artisans and patrons of SKINWIZARDRY, too as they all made comments such as "cool mama," "shake a wicked hip, baby," "yo, you duh lady." She turned to greet PootiePie. Sure enough, she was right, she didn't want to meet anyone with that name, but there he stood in all his glory. Willi realized her jaw hung open, but try as she might she couldn't seem to get the dang thing to close.

PootiePie was beefy. Oh, yeah. Somewhere around four-fifty, maybe.

PootiePie was tall. Yep, about six-foot-six. *Holy Guacamole.*

PootiePie was a walking circus of body art from his bald head to his giant-sized toes.

PootiePie was naked other than the . . . uh . . . nut huggers . . . which were revealing enough that Willi's mind again stated in bold Times New Roman 12-point font: **For all intents and purposes PootiePie was naked.** Well, she'd not be judgmental, but his physical presentation did take a moment or two to register.

Willi finally managed to unhinge her jaw and close her mouth. Her eyes wandered from his chest honoring of "MOM" to various ribbons with names such as GINGER-ANGEL-BAMBI-LORI-SWEET THING #3 and SWEET THANG #4. His spelling skills had obviously declined between partners. Just above his deeply entrenched belly button was a wooden ship in a frothy sea going down, down, down . . .

She averted her eyes from PootiePie's marginal covering. Heaven knows, she would be the first to admire the most pleasurable anatomical features of a man, but for gosh sakes, there was a proper time and place. Like when she was alone with Quannah. Invoking his visage and the idea of revealing parts made her tingle with pleasure, but again eyeing PootiePie, her rosiness diminished considerably. She closed her mouth tightly, praying that she might locate a bathroom soon wherein to divulge in a bit of well . . . divulging. She would get control of her snooty response and treat him as any person deserved to be treated—with respect and courtesy. PootiePie turned tail and told them to follow.

Willi prayed silently. *Dear Lord, if there is any value to this carpet, do not let him be wearing a thong, please, please, please.* Fully covered buttocks, awesomely muscled, but *fully* covered ambled toward a back room, which proved once again to Willi that the strangest prayers can be answered if the hope and need is fervently sent upward. Her mind could not grasp hold of anything pertaining to what she had planned to do with this afternoon.

At the moment, she just didn't want to hurl as she passed the man whose back was bleeding even as the Christ upon the cross bled upon his spine. She truly needed to calm down the quakes of her stomach, not an easy feat when she glanced at a broad-chested man in the final throes of a fight with a python wrapped around his waist, across his chest and writhing over his throat in search of his prey—a colorful depiction of a voluptuous siren who believed in the same dress code as PootiePie.

As the trio passed by all the front room patrons, Willi finally tore her eyes away from the close-up views of art dreams and glanced out a side window. A blue minivan with yellow stripes pulled up and parked. She ran over to the window. So? Who would be getting out? Drianina Manauia, who claimed she'd never been in such a car? Or would Nina Ricardo, the sharply dressed girlfriend of Dr. Etzli come into the tattoo parlor? Or maybe neither would since the metroplex would have far more of the cars than would Nickleberry proper.

Some man or woman—Willi couldn't tell—got out with a hood pulled over the head to thwart the escalating wind and chill. Willi shrugged and moved away. Not often did she wish for such things as extra-strength aspirin, or mind-numbing Valium, but this day was bringing her close to asking for them.

As if reading her mind, PootiePie pointed to a pristine glass cabinet behind him, which was locked. He keyed it open and raised a brow. When he pointed to the possibilities, Willi chose aspirin. "Thanks."

He insisted Tattoo take two Motrin in preparation. Gee, just like at the dentist's office. This back room was quieter and muted in color and décor. A three-hundred-gallon fish tank burbled in a location easily viewed by patrons lying on the reclining table or in the chairs. PootiePie disappeared into a washroom, reappeared in hospital scrubs—pants, top, hat and mask. He said, "Girl, there's a tube top waiting for you."

Tattoo disappeared to put it on, sat on the chair with a padded arm- and headrest. If it were a normal chair, she'd be sitting backwards, but, evidently this was the proper position for a . . . *procedure* . . . of the type she was about to experience. PootiePie washed his hands in that orange medicinal soap, dried and put on gloves. He cleaned Tattoo's right shoulder with alcohol, pulled out a new disposable razor, soaped up the area and again cleaned it, this time with the soap and the alcohol.

"I'm glad," Willi said, "you take sanitary precautions."

PootiePie, seemingly transformed by his scrubs, was all business. "Most dangerous thing about getting inked is not proper cleansing." With his elbow, he nudged Tattoo on her elbow. "You know, right?"

"After three, I've got it down. You already got the stencil ready?"

"Yep, I do. You just relax now."

Tattoo nodded. "Ms. Gallagher, what was it you wanted to ask me? Talking will keep my mind off the pain."

"Oh my gosh, will there be a lot?"

"No, but another dose of that painkiller would insure that."

PootiePie raised his gloved hands. "Would you mind?"

Willi grabbed the bottle, emptied two into one of the little pleated cups. It really was like the doctor's office. She offered the tablets and water to Tattoo.

"Thanks. So what's cooking, Ms. Gallagher?"

Willi pulled up a roller chair, wondering if she would be destined throughout this investigation with trying to get answers from either the emotionally ranting and out of control, or those medicated and near oblivion.

"A couple of things." She pulled out the sheet with her questions, or rather the cryptic ones Anastasia had. *Receipt forms? Broken? Missing? Stolen? Check on costume, too.*

"Yesterday when you called me around two in the afternoon, you did that because you had an appointment then with Ms. Zöllmer, didn't you? You were concerned that she had missed the appointment."

"Sorta. Maybe."

"A missed appointment happens now and again," Willi mused aloud. "You'd just call each other and reset. Why the panic about yesterday's missed date?"

PootiePie rubbed Tattoo's shoulder with stick deodorant. At Willi's look, he explained. "Makes the design transfer better and darker onto the skin. When I pull the paper away, it'll leave a purple likeness of the tattoo for me to work with."

"Right," Willi said, and repeated her question to Tattoo. "Why the panic yesterday?"

"Uh . . . well, after you and that professor left, I checked out the sheds, found where vandals had been roosting out there."

"So you were the one who cleaned up the vandalism. We didn't have time to warn you of the exact spot. How did you discover it so soon?"

Tattoo grabbed a small towel and wiped perspiration from her forehead.

PootiePie said, "Shouldn't be sweatin' yet, girl. Just now getting the ink caps, needles and tubes ready. Smoothing on the

Vaseline now." He caught Willi's concern, and added, "Makes the needles glide more easily over the skin."

"I . . . uh . . . found the mess quick like," Tattoo said. "Hey, I saw you and the professor racing away from that train shed. Andretti's got nothing on you, Ms. Gallagher."

Okay. Willi raised an eyebrow. "Was your meeting about something special?"

"Special?"

The low buzz of the tattoo machine offered an unnerving backdrop to the conversation. PootiePie, behind his sterile face mask, said, "I'm going to start the line drawing now, girl. Remember the first minute or so is the roughest. After that your skin will kind of get used to it, and the pain will begin to subside."

Willi covered her eyes with one hand, but opened her fingers at the last moment to see him start moving the needle along the purple line. She gulped, and gave Tattoo a few minutes to become used to the procedure. As she seemed to relax with it, Willi continued. "I mean was there something important you all were to discuss?"

"Such as?"

Willi sighed and looked at her notes. "Such as the costume?"

"She told you about that?"

Crossing her fingers, Willi said in her matter-of-fact English teacher's voice, "As much as she knew. You fill in the blanks, please."

"Stupid old ratty thing went missing, and she thought I misplaced it."

"Why would she think that?"

Here Tattoo wiped her forehead again. "I dunno. People always blame me first."

"What kind of costume?"

"Had an animal head with teeth—yellowed things. Let's see.

Oh yeah, it was a panther's skin, leopard, I dunno. Draped over the shoulders. Had these scary looking claws. Guess they were real and all, or she wouldn't have been so upset about it missing."

"With which display did it go?"

"Pyramid . . . or maybe the Aztecan family life one. I dunno. It was checked off the delivery list signed by me and placed in the storage room in the bin noted on the paperwork. After that, I never saw it again."

Willi eyed the bloody trickles on Tattoo's shoulder, got up and got herself a cup of water. Maybe Tattoo was doing fine, but Willi's knees felt like noodles sliding out of the Italian Chef's can. She peeked at her notes: *Receipt forms? Broken? Missing? Stolen? Check on costume, too.* She needed to word her next question in a way that Tattoo would believe Anastasia had already told Willi the important pieces. "So what about the items that *were* broken and those that *were* stolen? How were you two going to handle those?"

"Items were fill-ins."

"Fill-ins?"

"Things our buyer got at specialty stores, or had handmade to look like artifacts. Items needed for vresi . . . virisimili . . . for making the details right in the display. Things the museum hasn't acquired in the real format, you know?"

"Like small bowls, plates, décor pieces?"

"Uh . . . yeah, I guess."

Willi's skin had a goose bump dance at that admission, but why? She frowned in concentration to bring the elusive idea to the forefront, but merely added an extra ache to her headache despite the aspirin.

PootiePie said, "Great. All the line work is done. Gonna let you rest a minute while I get the mags out."

Willi asked, "Mags?"

"Magnums are the particular needles we use for coloring and shading. Talk about shifting into a whole new dimension, these colors will do it. Black upon shades of black inkwork are super, but when we use the tints, it lets the tigers, and lions and bears come alive."

"Oh my," Willi said. She shut her eyes and her earlier vision of creatures and smoke, whirlpools along with obsidian, shape-shifters and tricksters mixed with all the data she'd gleaned from Tattoo, from the three contenders for the museum post, from the storyteller and from Ramblin'. One of them was a true shape-shifter, someone hiding behind a cloak of evil. That, she would bet on. Too many signs, too many weird happenings to discount that basic truth. At least worry about the museum had relegated her stalker problem to a far corner of her mind. What she needed was an hour or two to mentally sift without benefit of relaxing tea visions, without interruptions so that her thoughts could coagulate into meaningful ideas upon which she could act. She addressed PootiePie. "How long will the . . . uh . . . coloring part take?"

"Maybe fifteen minutes. Then I'll want her to just sit another ten minutes before we let her go. We're particular about our special patrons."

"Tattoo, if you'll be okay, I think I'll search out someplace to have a coffee . . . or . . . something."

"Sure thing."

PootiePie pointed behind the building. "You'll wanna walk. Not much parking except right in front of lots of these old places, and you could circle for an hour before someone gave up a space. Most everyone parks right here beside us or the next block up in the welder's lot. Go out the front door, through the side parking lot and two blocks to the back. Take a left and there's two spots to choose from. On the left side is a quick-order café. Joe's. Across the street on the right is a bar and grill."

Tattoo spoke up quickly, raising her head. "She wouldn't like that place."

"Got decent grilled chicken fajitas and coldest beers in town." He pointed to a female compatriot inking the back of a man with the Eiffel Tower. "Eleanor often goes over and gets take-out for us."

"But, Ms. Gallagher won't like that place," Tattoo said vehemently.

"Relax, relax. Just giving her choices. Name of the place is Wild Thangs."

"Okay. Be back in about a half hour, Tattoo."

"Ms. Gallagher, you be careful, now, hear?"

She got so tired of folks assuming that no matter what their age was, she was fifteen years younger, less smart, less sophisticated. My gosh. At thirty-two, she'd seen a thing or two in life and could take care of herself, thank you very much. And she could almost smell the roasting peppers on the fajitas, and feel the trickle of that first cold, cold sip of light beer. *Just one since she was the driver. Come to mama, baby.*

CHAPTER ELEVEN

Shadows—good and evil—slithering in and out
Attest to genders changing all about.

—Canat'quatl
The Book of the Ancient Ones

Willi sauntered around to the parking lot. There she saw the hooded person approaching the blue minivan with yellow stripes. "Excuse me," Willi yelled. "Are you by any chance—?"

The shadowed face surveyed her, turned and rushed down the street.

"—Nina Ricardo?"

Willi gave chase. "By dang, I'll solve one mystery." She ran two blocks and hooked a left and sure enough she registered Joe's on that side. But the spooked driver sprinted into Wild Thangs down and on the right. Willi burst through the doorway to come up against a wall of darkness and heavy smoke. Her hearing clicked in first as a raunchy song by Madonna bleated out verse about hot loins and mutual needs. Great.

The clatter of pinball machines, the crisp connections of pool balls, and the yelps of glee over a ball in the far pocket drew her attention to a back room. Under the miasma of smoke, the neon signs read "Ladies" and "Gents." She headed in that direction. She peeked under each cubicle door, but located no sweats-clad legs. Okay. Could have been a man. No way to tell with that slim body and the hood. Maybe the person was in one of the warren of rooms that seemed to make up Wild Thangs. Willi decided on a table in the shadows—not a difficult feat since none was illuminated enough to see any of the occupants. Fine. Not a problem. With back to the far wall, she could keep a lookout for anyone leaving. From her vantage point she could see the mutely lit circle of dance floor to the left, the front door to the right and the other entryways to the farthest rooms, including those with pool tables and a bar. By dang, she'd find out who drove that damned minivan, and learn why they refused to reveal themselves.

A waitress slapped a menu in front of her. "I'm Dayneen. Cold beer? Coke?"

"A light beer please."

Dayneen, antiseptic wipe in a thickly veined hand with age spots the size of a Dalmatian's markings, cleaned the table. Her blush applied over thick pancake makeup rippled off into the crevices and cracks of her dry skin. She asked, "Bottle? Glass?"

"Glass, thanks, and I'll take an order of chicken fajitas. Uh . . . Dayneen, did you see a man with gray sweats on, hood up over his head, run in here a few minutes ago? It could have been a woman. I followed her through, and she didn't go to the bathrooms."

"Mighty desperate, ain't ya? Naw, no one like that run by me. I don't 'low no one past me into Mz. Everett's kitchen. She'd have my hide. Now, you want to mix it up with the girls, ya kin go try the pool tables or wait 'bout five minutes and the jukebox crowd will start to dancin'. Ya kin grab ya a girl, then, honey."

Willi frowned at the implication, but figured maybe Dayneen had misunderstood her question. She took the first sip of frosty brew just as the jukebox clicked over onto a Shania Twain CD selection. Partners pranced onto the floor to a boot stompin', leg-lifting, toe-tapping fast one. Partners. Hmm. Willi blinked and took another large gulp of the beer. Ohmygosh. Okay, everything was fine. Maybe the . . . uh . . . couples would change from all females to mixed couples on a slow song. She searched the bar, the poolroom, the dining tables around her, but no hairy brutes came into her line of vision unless the muscled-up one with a cut off top and a back awash with tattoos was a male. The dancer turned around. Uh-oh. She winked at Willi, grabbed a chair from the table, turned it around to straddle it and face Willi.

"I'm Lorina."

"Okay."

Dayneen, by placing the plate of steaming fajitas down, saved her from having to come up with anything intelligible. Dayneen said, "Now, Lorina, don't be breaking nothing else this week. You gonna owe me your whole paycheck come next Friday."

Willi thought it prudent to at least be civil. "I'm Willi."

Lorina stared. Hard. Into her eyes, and started bobbing her head up and down. Up and down like the bulldogs some retro '50's rednecks keep on their back window. This movement having obviously brought to the forefront of her brain what she wanted to say, Lorina cleared her throat. "Don't want you chasing my girl."

"I beg your pardon. Your daughter?" Willi looked around for a younger and hopefully more feminine version of Lorina.

"Día Muñoz." The head bobbing ensued and a glint shone in Lorina's eyes, a glint that told Willi she was dealing with someone who always had a grudge to bear, an anger to assuage.

"I don't think I know a—"

"Chased her down where she works. Yep. That's what you did." Lorina had to increase the head bobs to keep pace with the fast thought processes. "Then come chasing her here."

"Where does she work?"

"Over to Nickleberry. The trailer park."

"Ah."

"Damn right. She's my girl. Ah. Ah. Ah." That witty ending sped up the head gyrations, and furious blinking was a special unattractive addition, plus the grimace probably meant as a smile, but somehow ruined by the blackened and missing teeth.

"I see . . . well, I think I . . . she's the lady who mows the yards?"

"Now you're getting it through your thick head. Chasing her down the highway, that wasn't cool. She don't like it. I don't like it."

Willi took a cold and long pull on the beer to avoid explaining thick heads.

Lorina sniffed, stretched her behemoth muscled arms above her head and hollered, "Dayneen!"

Dayneen, behind the bar, gave her a wait-a-minute signal.

Lorina said, "She's real pretty."

"Dayneen?"

"Something wrong in your head, lady? Día. I'm talking about Día."

"Of course. She's your daughter?"

"Hell, you are slow, lady. She's my better half, and I don't want you messing with her. Come from two different worlds. Can't you see that?"

"I think we have a failure to communicate. I'm not interested in Día as—"

"You calling me a liar?" Lorina stood up, crashing the chair to the floor. "Dayneen, bring a doggy bag. She's leaving." Dayneen did, forking Willi's as yet untouched fajitas into the Styrofoam container.

Willi stood up, too, and unintentionally also knocked her chair over. "I'll say when I'm ready to go, thank you very much, and all I wanted was to ask Día Muñoz a few questions about one of her employers. So, I'll go when I'm ready."

The jukebox offered a fluke of a silent moment, and Willi heard three distinct cracks. Around her a female trio—one in biker leather, another in jeans and bangles, the third in T-shirt and hair in a buzz—with pool cues broken at dangerously sharp angles circling her.

Willi placed her bag straps over her shoulder, left a generous tip and the payment on the table, picked up her box and said in as calm a voice as she could muster, "And whether you ladies like it or not, I believe I'm ready to leave now." With head high, knees trembling, she walked quickly out the door of Wild Thangs. When she got to her car, the minivan had disappeared. Her hands shook when she placed the fajitas in the back seat.

Tattoo rounded the corner to hop in the passenger side and said, "I'm starved."

"Help yourself to the fajitas," Willi said. "How'd the final . . . uh . . . procedure turn out?"

"Great. Just a minute and I'll show you. Squint and imagine there's no swelling." Tattoo shoved some papers into the space between the seat and console and grabbed the box from the back. "Just PootiePie's instructions and such. Like I don't know how to take care of my tattoos by now. Give me a break. Got a trash sack, I'll put them there."

"Not to worry. We'll trash it when we stop."

Tattoo turned so Willi could see her new artwork. Willi squinted and said, "Wow."

"Pretty awesome, huh? But, it's gotten chilly. Wish I'd brought a jacket."

Willi bobbed her head as stupidly as Lorina had. She was pretty damned sure she recognized the Aztecan hieroglyphic from Anastasia's notes. A hieroglyphic standing for something the storyteller had mentioned, or was it one simply remembered from her . . . vision? *Tezcatlipoca, the deceiver and sower of discord.* Now, which one was Tattoo? Which shape-shifter in this mystery was the young plumber cum repair person—the monkey, coyote, skunk or . . . or the deadly jaguar? She pushed the thoughts around for a moment, noticed the goose bumps on Tattoo's skin, and finally offered, "Oh, yeah, chilly. On the floorboard behind you in that basket I keep extra things. Grab a sweater or jacket, whatever."

"Thanks." Tattoo put on an L.L.Bean flannel shirt with an Indian motif. "Oh, this feels good."

As Willi drove back to Nickleberry her mind churned with the as yet unanswered questions revolving as fast as the whirlpool of her vision. But one niggling idea she could put to rest with just a teeny tiny bit of . . . snooping. All it would require would be a quick look inside Tattoo's living room a second time, and perhaps her kitchen. When she reached Tattoo's she jumped out and said, "I can't go another minute without a bathroom. May I use yours very quickly?"

With key in the door, Tattoo said, "Well, I guess . . . no . . . uh . . . no. Sorry. Plumbing's backed up; gonna have to go rent a Roto-Rooter. Thanks for the ride and the fajitas." Tattoo slipped inside and locked and bolted the door.

Humph. Guess the bathroom ruse didn't work, so on to plan B. She knew as sure as puppies had tails, that something important might be discovered from Tattoo . . . or maybe just that peek inside would do. Maybe. Willi looked around at this decrepit block of Fetchwin Way. Clouds scudded through a gray five-o'clock sky. Folks would be coming home from work soon. Well, those that worked. She'd have to manage to come back a different way.

She drove down to the renovated end, turned left and drove on Logan's Lane until she thought she was behind Tattoo's rental. Getting out of the car in the quickly forming shadows of the setting sun, Willi pulled her pink sweater over her hips and edged her way down an alley connecting Logan's Lane to Fetchwin Way. There were enough bushes and trees that to have taken a vehicle down the alleyway would have added a life's worth of scratches. Rotted privacy fences with jagged holes allowed no privacy at all. She eased inside such a natural opening, only snagging her sweater once. Certainly, she had no intention of violating the law, not like an actual breaking and entering. A simple saunter by the duplex, a peek in a window or two. No big deal, for heaven's sake. Having convinced herself, she strode more purposefully.

The semi-enclosed back area was ten car lengths long, with only enough side yard to squeeze in a car . . . or the museum van, which roared to life. Willi slunk behind a ramshackle shed. "Dang. The same one." A branch scraped down her arm, drawing blood. "Oh, fits and starts, that . . . hurts." The van backed out. Guess the mechanics *did* deliver on Saturdays. Great. If Tattoo had left to go buy or rent a Roto-Rooter, Willi would have time to find out a few things. The coast was clear. She did a stiff-legged Charlie Chaplin step-along through the tall dried grass, around the debris of an abandoned washing machine, broken yard furniture and various machine parts whose names and usage she couldn't begin to guess. She eased open the door to the back screened porch and was about to try the kitchen door handle when a light went on.

Hell's bells, and damn.

She bent over and on hands and knees worked her way to the shadowy corner where she could peer through the low window. Tattoo *would* have to have a visitor. Some surveillance partner Willi'd be, not even waiting and checking to see if anyone else were there, just assuming Tattoo had roared off in the van.

Chairs shuffled, silverware clinked. "Vittles on, girl . . . starving . . ."

Willi had to concentrate to catch phrases, but as her ears became more attuned to the nuances of the two voices, she understood more.

"You've got to get out of here, for good," Tattoo said.

"I decide when, girl. Me, not you."

That deadly voice sent shivers down Willi's spine, but obviously it was a friend or relative of Tattoo's. More than likely one of those less desirable relatives we all have but would rather not parade out in public unless necessary. Tattoo had mentioned them the other day in the museum. Poor kid. That explained why Tattoo had offered the plumbing problems. Going back in the home and playing hostess to such familial cousins was one thing, but having to introduce them to her co-workers an entirely different thing. The kindest thing Willi could do for now would be not to force her way inside Tattoo's home on some flimsy pretext. Maybe the best course was to leave and find out answers another day. All she wanted was to ease her way off the porch, across the yard, through the alley and back to the safety of her car. She couldn't think of any reasonable excuse she could offer if caught on the back porch. Wait, she could say she'd come back for the L.L.Bean shirt Tattoo had borrowed. Willi glanced around her. Right. Sure. And she had to come around to the back door as opposed to the front for . . . duh-uh . . . what reason? She shifted her weight to stand up, and one of the weathered planks creaked.

"Sumabitch, Tat', you hear that?" A chair shifted and footsteps approached the back door. Willi scrunched down underneath the window with back against the house siding, where she was beneath two ratty aluminum chairs. A trashcan, just outside the door, sat at the end of the two chairs, making for a decent hidey hole. At the moment she was completely enclosed in darkness as the sun had said its last *adiós*.

The back door opened and heavy boots with steel toes stomped onto the porch, the screen door flew open, and the booted man stepped out into the yard. Willi's heart beat so fast, she placed a hand over it to keep it in place. Oh, jeez. She could peer through the screen and make out the mid-section of a hefty figure. He yelled, "Tat', turn on the porch light."

Willi's head grew light and she was sure when he had illumination he'd only see the whites of her eyes as her irises were rapidly rolling backwards. *Oh, Great Spirit.*

Tattoo leaned out the kitchen door. "Ain't got that electric breaker yet. No porch light."

Willi's eyes fluttered back down to their natural location, but her heartbeat hadn't slowed one rpm.

Tattoo's guest said, "One of them damned things you got to have the time and inclination for, right?"

"Stop yelling and get in here. You want all the neighbors to start looking out their windows? That what you want?" She went back in, he stepped on the porch and just before following her through to the kitchen, kicked the metal trashcan.

When the ringing in her ears stopped, Willi ever so carefully worm-crawled from underneath the chairs, and peeked again through the low window. Tattoo served chili over French fries, some dish using the most delicious smelling apples spiced with cinnamon, and chips and salsa. Willi's stomach growled and she froze. Surely, the people four streets away at the HEB grocery could have heard those rumbles.

Tattoo said, "You all gotta go. I can't do this anymore. I got a job—a decent job. Don't wanna mess my life up. You hear?"

"Going soon. But, family is family, you know?"

"Yeah, right. But—"

"Hand me some more fries. You cook good, just like your mama. How's she doing?"

"Same ol', same ol'. Waiting on tables somewheres over in Itasca. She'll die on her feet. But you and—"

"I know. I know. Gotta get soon. Not a problem, sweetie, not a problem."

Willi, her nose resting on the windowsill, squinted and searched the kitchen for what she sought. There was a beautiful southwestern tureen on the table, obviously containing the chili. Willi peered toward the door to the living room, but could not see into the room itself. Focusing closer to hand, she had to admire the silver filigree stands holding Tattoo's cookbooks. And, there right on the table next to the man's hand was another item—blue and black with white roses. Oh, she couldn't wait to tell the Kachelhoffer sisters. Just proved they couldn't see everything in their crystal balls or crystal inverted pyramids, either. Hah! Well, one mystery was solved, but . . . no. No, nothing was solved if you didn't know the reason behind the actions. Okay, but she had an idea. Daggum it, if only he'd turn around, Willi could see if there was a familial likeness, but his broad shoulders bent over his meal hid his facial features. He threw down his napkin and shoved his chair back. Willi scooched down.

As he left the room he said, "Where in hell is that boy? More trouble than any of us, and he's gonna cause problems if he's out doing what I think he's doing." He turned on some loud Van Halen old rock and shut the door to the living room. Willi could feel the vibrations through the porch wood.

Tattoo ignored him, and cleared the table. Underneath the clatter of pots and pans and Van Halen howls, Willi eased off the porch none too soon. She had no more than cleared the back bushes and climbed through the broken fence slats, than the lights of the van illuminated the dry grass behind her. She peeked back through the opening, but could only see a man's figure outlined in the kitchen door. Even at her distance, she heard him yell, "Don't put the *comida* away, baby. I wanna eat, too. You got some jalapeños to go with that chili, huh?" His accent carried clearly over the Van Halen beat. Willi shrugged. Just another typical multilingual cross-cut Texas family at staggered eating schedules. Sad, but so often true.

Willi shook her head. Poor Tattoo. Trying to dig herself out of a certain lifestyle, and yet, so many things were against her—especially the thefts. Damn. Willi's eyes teared up. Daggum it, answering some of the questions, getting a few of the chaotic items in place, was supposed to make her feel a certain pride of accomplishment. So why in Hades were her shoulders slumping inward almost to her chin, and why was she ashamed she'd snooped, and why did she feel so awful about having to do her civic duty? Damn it. Damn. Damn. Damn. Life—as the students said—sometimes sucked sump water. Backwards, even.

When she reached home, she was glad Quannah was asleep and could not see her disheveled appearance—hair six ways to nothing, sweater ripped and slacks covered in grass burrs. The last thing she wanted to do was upset him while he was recuperating. After thanking Agatha for her nursing duties and watching her drive away, she cuddled a moment with Charlie. His muzzle sought out the same crevice of her neck that Quannah often did, resting there, taking in her smell.

"Yes, you are my snookums sweetie, yes you are." She set her purse down on the kitchen table along with the trash she'd gathered from the car's front seat. "I'll take care of it later. Right now my furry one needs some loving, yes he does."

A little baby talk went a long way in releasing the tension built through her illegal entry onto Tattoo's back porch. Dang, since it was illegal, she couldn't turn the museum worker in for what Willi had seen during a trespass. Maybe she could convince Tattoo to make restitution and not have to be turned in to the law . . . unless . . . unless . . . those relatives of hers had already led her into more avarice and unlawful avenues. "What to do, Charlie? What to do, huh? Well, whatever I do, I won't involve Quannah until he's one-hundred percent, and I mean all the way well."

After she combed her hair and changed her slacks and sweater, Charlie woofed and snuggled in for a good nap on her shoulder. Willi turned on the TV, but kept it low so as not to disturb Quannah's rest. The three mug shots of L.T. Nadge, Edwin Heberly, and Iago Rios came on the nine and ten o'clock news. The announcer said, "It's now believed the dangerous trio has left for more southern regions. The good folks of Nickleberry can sleep better tonight."

Hmph. She'd sleep better about those three when Quannah said so. "Isn't that right, you doggy mess, you." She kissed Charlie on his nose.

"I'd take one of those," Quannah said from behind her chair. Willi yelped, jumped up from the chair and stood with her hands on her hips.

"Woman-With-Tweety-Bird-Medicine is easily frightened. Something on your conscience, Gallagher?"

"Absolutely not, and it's Hummingbird Medicine, thank you very much. And you, my special *hombre* are looking so good, and your lady is so glad you're home." She was in his arms by the end of her sentence with her head on his broad chest. "How are you feeling?"

"Much better, *Winyan,* much better." He kissed her and stroked her hair. "Now, tell me what you've been up to."

She told him an edited version of what had occurred concerning Anastasia. Despite many pauses to strangle the threatening tears, he never interrupted.

At the end he said, "It is hard, *Winyan,* to lose a good friend. I know you will carry her spirit with you in an honorable way for the coming year."

She peered into his dark hooded eyes, still a bit unfocused from medications, and decided to err on the side of her warrior. He needn't be worried with her foray into the tattoo shop, Wild Thangs bar and eatery, and certainly he shouldn't have to be concerned about a tiny little misdemeanor of the porch scenario. After all, she may have uncovered a small Nickleberry crime. It wasn't as if she were involved in anything dangerous. She hadn't been anywhere near the three murderers he was looking for nor had her stalker been present much today, and that was plenty for him to take on for the moment. After another minute of kissing and hugging, she went upstairs for her bath while he traipsed into the kitchen for a snack.

Beneath the water pelting her skin, she sighed. Strange, now that she had time to think about it. Her nasty note-writer and stalker hadn't bothered her much today, Saturday. And, if it were someone from school as Willi figured, she would have bet they'd use the weekends for even more skullduggery. Hmm. Well, thank goodness they hadn't. Monday was the first day off for the October break, but she was going to cruise around the high school and see if she didn't spot some anal-retentive teacher working during his vacation. Especially one in a green car.

Later snuggled in beside Quannah, Willi was at slumber's soft release, when his deep voice and the light from a bedside lamp half roused her. She opened one eye. "Whut?"

"Where did this come from?" he asked, holding up a receipt printed with the SKINWIZARDRY logo.

"It's Tattoo's, I'll . . . tell . . . morning."

"Tattoo?"

"Hm-huh. Get the light, sweetie."

"As in the girl who works at the museum."

"Yeah, yep." Willi yawned and turned over. She reached back to pat his rear. "Sweet dreams."

Quannah rose up on an elbow and leaned over her shoulder. "Last question. You know where she lives, what street?"

"Uh-huh."

"Gallagher, Gallagher, wake up."

"Whut?" She pulled the blanket over her head.

"What street?"

"Fetchwin Way."

"Ah," Quannah said. He pulled down the blanket and kissed her earlobe while he whispered, "Just what have you been do-ing? I wonder. Can't let you out of my sight for a moment."

"Dat's sweet. Okay." After that Morpheus worked his miracle, and she slept deeply with the knowledge she was safe, he was safe, and all was right with the world as long as they were side by side. "Dat's sweet," she mumbled to her pillow. "So sweet."

Chapter Twelve

The calm of morning will be dispelled
When clouds of doom in the noon have swelled.

—P'o'lo'tle
The Book of the Ancient Ones

"That's not a dang bit sweet," she said when she bit into the strawberries Quannah had cut up for their Sunday morning pancake topper.

"A little syrup and it'll be fine." He offered the dark maple to her, but she shook her head and tried the Karo instead. "Suit yourself, stubborn one."

"Stubborn? Me? Never. That adjective is all yours, Big Chief. Me? I'm challenged by remembering phone numbers, addresses—"

"—of your best friends," he kidded her. "Even my cell number you sometimes forget."

"Well, none of us is perfect. That's why day planners, calendars and Post-it notes were invented—for us who are numerically challenged." Great, he was in a lucid, good mood. She really needed to ask him about some of the Indian things going around in her head, but she didn't want to do it in such a way as to clue him into the museum happenings. She asked, "What are you going to do this beautiful Sunday?"

"You haven't looked outside yet, have you?" He got up and pulled up the kitchen shades.

"Uck. Dark, brooding, weepy rain. I'd prefer a whale of an exciting storm—lightning flashes, high winds—thank you very much."

"Gallagher, I'd have to agree."

"So," she said sweetly, "what are your plans for the day?" She raised an eyebrow along with a forkful of strawberries and pancake. He might have thought he was going to get away with answering her question with a question, but over time, she'd figured out that particular strategy. "Hmm?"

He said, "Was there something particular you had in mind? Anyplace you wanted to go?"

Dang him. He was really good at that ploy. She glared at him and chomped on her food. No, she didn't want to go anywhere except for a short trip through his mind . . . not hers . . . his . . . for particulars about some of the legends. He was a storehouse about so many native races. She shoved another forkful in and chewed, still with a decided twist to her mouth.

"What did I say?" He raised his hands, palms out. He picked up the Startlegram—*The Star Telegram*— out of Fort Worth and with a great fanfare of paper rustling and folding, he disappeared behind the comics. She was simply grateful he wasn't one of those Sunday football couch potatoes. If he'd been in top shape—as opposed to having his hiney shot off—he would be out chopping wood, mending fence around the farmhouse, doing odd jobs after his morning read. From behind the paper, he said, "I'll get back to all that when the side, *not* my *rear,* is well again."

"Dang you."

He merely chuckled. She knew he no more understood his ability to be in mind sync with her than she did. But at odd times it happened, and she was as open and clear as a Sunday school bell. Well, she had wanted a trip through his thought processes. *Watch what you wish for, huh?* When he flipped to the next section, she pulled down the middle of the paper. "Got a question, Big Chief."

"Got an answer, Woman-With-Tweetybird-Medicine."

"When you warned me about the jaguars, what did you mean?"

He leaned his head to one side and looked at her from the corners of his eyes. "I did? Don't recall that. Guess the drugs had a hold on me." He set the paper down and shoved his chair back. "In fact, I recall you pushing the meds button, as if—"

"Stay focused, Lassiter, stay focused here."

He crossed his arms in his chief's stance. "What have you been keeping from me, Gallagher? Other than your trip to SKIN-WIZARDRY?"

"How did you—? Oh, yes, I vaguely remember you shaking that receipt out of me when I was so comfortably on the edge of sleep. That was for Tattoo's new body art." Trying to get him back on the subject she wanted, she added, "It was a red jaguar on her shoulder. One of the reasons I was wondering if you knew—"

"What did you say her real name was?" He interrupted and turned to the front page to peruse the big stories.

"Don't know. Never asked, I guess. Is it important?"

"No, no, just curious. Strange moniker for a young girl."

"I suppose it is." She busied herself clearing off the table; he immediately rose up to help. "No, you don't. Give yourself a few more days. I know you aren't a slacker even with so-called women's work, but let me wait on my warrior today, okay?"

With a gasp as a slice of pain went through him, he nodded and sat back down.

If he'd just give her some tidbits about the Aztecan beliefs, she'd gladly do his chores for a month. "In the hospital you said something about shape-shifters," she reminded him.

"Guess I was concentrating on the old tales—really ancient ones if they had to do with the Jaguar clan of shape-shifters."

"Why is that?" She put the utensils into the dishwasher.

"Because they were Aztecan, perhaps also in the Incan mythology. Not sure, but I know they weren't in my Native American, mostly Comanche tales. But I've read about them."

"Tell me."

"According to old legends many of the Aztec gods had the ability to appear in animal, human, or any other form—wind or rain, for example." He eased back into the chair, and she finished with the dishes and turned on the machine. She pulled her chair closer to him. "Each month," he said, "had a deity, and each month the priests sacrificed victims to that particular god. And that was a lot of folks."

"What do you mean?"

"The Aztecan calendar has twenty months."

"So at least twenty died each year."

"At least," he concurred. "One of the gods often roamed the earth as a jaguar. Clans that grew up around that belief therefore wore jaguar skins, heads with teeth, paws with the claws still intact. Very fearsome shows I bet they put on before a sacrifice." Quannah rubbed his smooth Indian-skin chin, and she leaned in to caress it, too.

"Go on," she said.

"This jaguar god—don't know why I can't think of his name—anyway, he could also take the form of a coyote. He was sometimes called the Lord of the Smoking Mirror."

Willi gasped and sat up straight. "Tezcatlipoca."

"Yes, I think you're right." Quannah frowned but went on. "He carried a sacrificial knife made of obsidian. The knife symbolized a black wind—a whirlwind devoid of life. Kind of a contrast to the bright wind which brought the breath of life."

Willi shivered and pulled her soft housecoat tighter.

Quannah stared out at the bleak October sky. "He also had the weird name—and I do remember this one—Yaotle—when

223

he chose to preside over warring factions, deciding which warriors would succeed, which were to fall in bloody death."

"Not a nice deity," Willi offered. Hmm. Wonder if Tommy Balboa knew about that bad side of his namesake, or if he just wanted the name because it meant *warrior?*

Quannah pointed out the window at a bright cardinal. "See him?"

"Yes," Willi said, scooting her chair even closer so they could use the armrests to cross arms one over the other and hold hands while watching the winter soldier. "He's beautiful."

"True, *Winyan*, like you—bright and a little flighty."

She playfully punched him on the shoulder. "Yeah, well, thanks, I think."

Evidently not ready to let the subject go, Quannah said, "He had a bright side, too."

Still in sync with him, Willi said, "Tezcatlipoca?"

"He was revered because of fear, but he was also honored as one of the gods who helped guide the México-Aztecs on their journey to settle down in what is today Mexico. Youths, who were dispatched in his honor in a yearly festival, considered themselves as demigods." Quannah raised an eyebrow. "Some story also told of him changing an unfaithful man and his wife into scorpions."

"Seems kind of unfair that she had to suffer because of him."

"I agree. Remember, they're only myths, right, Gallagher? Any particular reason you were interested?" His dark eyes bore into hers as he tilted her chin with one finger to study her reaction. "Anything happening at the museum other than the situation with Anastasia? I'm truly sorry about her, but I don't want you worrying about it. At the moment, the officer in charge of the case feels certain the two incidents—her running off the road, and the pillow suffocation—are two separate things. In fact, seems this is the second such death the hospital has had in three weeks. We may be looking at a worker on staff as the culprit, no one to do with the museum, if that's what you might be worrying about. Ramblin' Anders seems to be cleared, too. So, is there something else at the museum I need to let the case officer know?"

She considered the strain around his eyes, the tiredness seeping back into his face, the toll the last week had taken on him, and hugged him. "Certainly not. In fact, things that had seemed horrific before, seem rather insignificant beside other events."

"Other events?"

She sighed heavily and gave him a watered-down version of her stalker situation, acting as if there were no serious ramifications beyond the notes.

"I know," he said, "you aren't telling me everything, but I trust you, Winyan, and know you'll confide when the time is right. However—"

"—I knew there'd be an however."

"However," he continued, "if it does turn truly dangerous—a personal approach of any kind—call me immediately. You haven't been approached other than the notes and the phone calls, right?"

She thought about the encounter in her garage with the shoe polish, but that wasn't a true meeting with *the perp*. "No, no actual meeting. Otherwise, I'd know who."

He said once more before his hooded eyes encased her in an intense stare, "Nothing else at the museum I need to know?"

She offered him a dazzling smile. "I simply want to be able to talk knowledgeably to those concerned with the pyramid and Aztecan family life displays in the museum. You've given me some wonderful ideas that I can ask them about. Thank you, Lassiter. You're as handy as a string tie in a one-handed grip."

"Hmm. Thanks, I think." He poured a fresh glass of orange juice.

"You've got strain marks around your eyes. Why don't you go take a snooze? Got your tummy as full as Charlie's, you ought to go right off to sleep."

"I'll do that, but first I need to make a phone call or two. I'll use the library nook." He balanced himself on the kitchen cabinet and turned his head to smile at her. "How about later we listen to that CD of old C&W songs Parva bought us?"

"Sounds like an after-lunch plan even if . . . the gift did come from that hyper little idiot."

"He's doing everything he can to get back into your good graces. It has some Margo Smith yodeling songs on it." He winked.

She leaned up close to him. He whispered in her ear, "It has Merle Haggard's slow version of 'When My Blue Moon Turns to Gold Again.' The one you like to slow dance to. Hmm?"

"Well, seeing as how C&W is *your* favorite."

"Next time he shoots me, I'll have him purchase a golden oldies rock and roll CD."

"He shoots you again, I'll be rocking and rolling all over his backside with a barbed-wire broom." Willi opened two medicine bottles, held out four capsules on the palm of her hand and nodded toward his orange juice. "Take them, or you'll get no phone—*work*—time, warrior or not."

"Those dang things put me into sound sleep. For four or five hours. I'll hardly get any calls made."

She squinted her eyes in that no-nonsense-from-you-sophomore look, and he capitulated. She knew any calls he had to do in "the library nook" were ones probably to do with his latest case. Of course, it didn't sit well with him that he couldn't be right on the hot trail. Maybe the calls would help him cope with that need. She sighed, put chicken and seasonings into the Crock-Pot, set out the garlic bread to thaw, and went upstairs to bathe.

Dressed in well-worn jeans, a soft cotton turtleneck, and a patchwork vest gathered at the waist, all in the muted blues of the jeans, she opted for soft leather moccasins dyed to match. Hair in a ponytail, she bounced down the thirteen steps. As she passed by the library nook, Quannah's deep voice startled her a moment, and then a rush of comforting warmth enveloped her. Just seven months into a mutual living arrangement, she was still pleasantly surprised at times by his presence. She leaned against the door frame, out of his sight but where she could admire the raven hair, the strong neck, with just enough weathering and wrinkles to attest to his outdoor nature.

Into the phone he said, "Fetchwin Way?"

He listened for a moment and said, "609A, you sure?"

She stepped past the door, did a double take and stood again against the frame. 609A? Now that sounded familiar for some reason. She shrugged and walked away as Quannah said into the receiver, "Nadge? We've got to be sure this time."

Willi sighed. Ah, one of the three escapees. Did they think he had some connection to Fetchwin Way? 609A in particular. Or maybe he said 906. Why couldn't she keep numbers straight?

Oh, well, she needed to get a salad tossed so it could be nicely crisped and seasoned by the time the chicken was finished. She busied herself with homey chores, and grinned. Washing clothes, doing the dishes, vacuuming had much more appeal since she did it for two as opposed to her alone. As she emptied the dishwasher she hummed. Since it had just finished, steam billowed up and out like smoke when she popped open the door. She let it dissipate while she bagged and tied the trash to take it to the bin, a job Quannah insisted was his, but she wasn't about to let him lift more than a fork for a while. At lunchtime, she went to get him away from the business calls.

In the library nook, she found nothing but a note beside the phone for her. Without looking at it, she crumpled it in her hand. Her heart pitter-pattered. Surely, he wouldn't leave on an errand without telling her. She ran around the corner to the stairway, but stopped with one foot on the first step, swung back down and into the living room.

Ah, there he was. On the couch, he lay under a yellow, red, black and white striped afghan made by Hortense Horsenettle, the school librarian. Willi smiled. Home. Made up of all kinds of memories, all kinds of friends—even the day-a-word librarian. She glanced around her living room and noted the paintings by other friends, a pottery bowl thrown by another co-worker, an Indian dream catcher given to them by Quannah's uncle, Brigham Tucker. A coaster set made by one of Willi's former students in the same Indian colors as the afghan.

Wasn't that what Tattoo was trying to do? Get a new life with decent things in her home, a better group of friends, pleasant co-workers. She said she'd come from a tough background, but was working hard to better herself. She was trying to make a home for herself instead of just having a house.

Willi sighed. Maybe she could talk her into making restitution to Emmett and Ilene Hawley, Rasco Coontz, and the Kachelhoffer sisters. Willi would try to convince the young woman to take the fake artifacts back to the museum. After seeing the items in Tattoo's kitchen last night, and remembering the things seen in the first visit to her living room, Willi put two and two together. Dang it. She hated that. Well, by daggum, everyone deserved a second chance. Something about the rough-edged Tattoo touched Willi, and she couldn't—wouldn't—turn her in for the petty thievery if the girl could make it right on her own. Willi understood she just wanted a place that looked like home, but was going about it the wrong way.

Willi offered a small prayer to Great Spirit for all her own blessings and smiled at the best one snoring on her—*their*—couch. She opted to let him snooze for a few more minutes while she straightened the nook. She flattened out the crumpled note which was in Quannah's sparse print. *Sydney Curry, vet called. Return her call.* Oh, she'd forgotten to do that yesterday after . . . after the horror of Anastasia's passing. Murder. Maybe not to do with all the museum rivalries, but murder just the same.

Willi sat down to place the call and spotted the receipt from SKINWIZARDRY. Why had Quannah saved it rather than throwing it away after she explained about Tattoo's new body art? Just as she crumpled it up, a name at the bottom caught her attention. Rhonda Nadge.

Nadge? Willi frowned. Where had she heard—? Oh my gosh.

L.T. Nadge from El Paso. The bank robber who killed a guard. He and his girlfriend were going to be this generation's Bonnie and Clyde. Isn't that what the news had been saying? Willi rubbed her temples. Why hadn't she been paying attention?

Was that why Quannah was checking out the receipt— because the name *Nadge* was on it? Could that be one of the ink artists at the salon? Or? Willi ran upstairs and scrabbled in her huge over-the-shoulder bag, pulled out Anastasia's address book and thumbed through it. Nothing under Nadge. Thank goodness. For a moment, she'd thought that maybe Tattoo—

She flipped through the pages to the T's just to make sure. Yeah, there it was. Tattoo's phone number—well, cell phone, and her address and her *full name. Rhonda Faye Nadge. 609A Fetchwin Way.*

Oh, Great Coyote's chin whiskers. Willi tapped the address. Why hadn't she known that? Because Agatha had taken the directions over the phone that night and she'd driven there. Willi had merely recognized the place by landmarks, never once noting the actual address.

Heavy boots with steel toes. Probably just what a modern day countrified version of Clyde Barrow would wear to his—what did he call Tattoo?—*sweetie's* home. Willi's knees bent and she folded back onto the bed. And she'd been not a trashcan—one boot kick away—from those killers last night.

Her heart picked up tempo. She swallowed back sour phlegm. No, now wait a minute. Something just did not mesh. Really did not mesh. So what if her name was Nadge? That hardly meant she was kin to the killer, or was his girlfriend. And the lout in her house last night might just be some relative—obviously one who had overstayed his welcome, but not necessarily one of the escaped convicts. Of course, Quannah had an over suspicious mind being a lawman. Sure the surname caught his attention what with the manhunt in full swing. It made sense for him to check out every angle in order to catch a bad guy.

Willi tapped the end of her retroussé nose with her forefinger while contemplating Tattoo's or rather Rhonda Faye Nadge's personality. No, there was something better about Tattoo than what Quannah's possible scenario might have pictured.

Wait a minute. Miss Marple of the Range was going off half-cocked. Willi slapped her forehead as she walked back around to view her sleeping warrior, a man who would not be snoozing if he thought his killer were within spitting distance of the farm, which Fetchwin Way certainly was. So, makes sense that he called and checked the name and the address out, but he must have discovered the innocence attached to the name with that particular street address, and headed for a Sunday siesta, perhaps helped along by the doctor's prescribed regimen. Of course.

He was right. Those meds would knock out a good-sized horse for half a day. Certainly, the chicken would be put on hold along with the CD listening until tonight. No sense in her wasting the time though. What better opportunity, while he rested, than for her to walk her talk. Which meant, go see Tattoo. Sit down for a heart to heart as friends, and get her to see the light about the petty thefts.

Willi raised her chin. She would be a friend and help her take things back, and stand beside Tattoo to help her truly get on the track she wanted. Taking half the chicken in a casserole dish, some of the tossed salad and a loaf of the garlic bread, she made up a wonderful dinner offering. She grabbed a batch of her brownies from the freezer, too. All of this she placed in an over-the-shoulder thermal bag. Just in case Tattoo still had visitors.

This time she wouldn't have to worry about old heavy boots. She'd be going in the front door, thank you very much. On her way out, she threw the receipt for the body art into the trash where it belonged. Halfway down Licorice Lane heading into town, she sighed. "Daggum, I forgot to leave Quannah a note on the board." She flicked on her favorite KCLE rock and roll golden oldies station. "I'll be back long before he wakes up."

Quannah awoke to pitch dark, forgot where he was, rolled over and landed with a crash onto the living room rug. "Next project. New padding." He rubbed his side, surprised the fall hadn't sent a slice of pain through him. The meds Willi made him swallow were still doing their work.

He read his digital watch. 7:00 p.m. Great Coyote's tail, it couldn't be that late. A steady rain pattered upon the roof, punctuated with an occasional thunder boom. Lightning offered a momentary glimpse of the living room.

"Willi? *Winyan*, you upstairs?" Maybe in the shower. He'd give her a few minutes, maybe check up on the progress of his questions about Rhonda Faye Nadge—alias Tattoo, residing at 609A Fetchwin Way.

Rubbing his eyes, he snapped on the lights in the dining room and kitchen, pulled out the orange juice and drank down a big glass. He lifted the Crock-Top top. "Now, that smells great. You usually make enough for an army, though." He had chided her about cooking so much, but had finally gotten in sync with her culinary philosophy that she preferred to prepare a really nice meal but only two or three times a week, hence the big portions for leftover meals. Seeing as how her leftovers were fit for a royal's table, he never complained. They had learned to take turns with her two preps to his one each week. He noted the covered basket of garlic bread, and peeked in the fridge at the crisp salad. He stumbled over Charlie and grumped to the dog, "She always does those up like a pro. Usually makes a big one to last two or three meals, though. Hmm."

He walked around the corner to the bottom of the stairs and yelled up. "Come on down. Your fault we missed the after-lunch CD . . . and lunch. I'm awake and hungry now. We'll put the CD on after we eat, okay? Willi?" There was no telltale sound of shower water flowing through the pipes, and no lights on at the head of the stairs. He didn't bound up the twelve steps which Willi always insisted were thirteen—she counted the step down onto the foyer floor; he didn't—but struggled as fast as his side would allow.

All quiet, no lights. Hairs rose on his arms, he turned his head in every direction listening, feeling for her presence, trying to catch her scent before he flipped the light switch. He scrambled into the master bath, checked the other second-story rooms and guest bath. Sweat broke out on his brow. Where the hell was she?

He caught his breath, and calmed down. She'd never leave without a note of some kind. Well, that wasn't true always. Willi was a free spirit, and if she felt something needed doing and right then, off she'd go faster than eagles' tail feathers could fan out. But one of their concessions as a couple had been to improve their communication. Ah, yes, the message board. He inched his way back down to the kitchen where he checked the white board, where she usually left him cute hearts, sometimes a drawing of a hummingbird or an Indian chief with a silly grin with conversation bubbles over their heads, reading: *Be back by 3:30. Had to check on the Kachelhoffers. See you about 5:30. Luv you, Big Chief . . . your goofy lady—Winyan.*

But only a white board faced him. Pristine, freshly scrubbed. No writing. A wonderful and sickening duo of sensations hit him at the same time. He'd come to rely on her little messages which was the wonderful part and he smiled, but . . . the pit of his stomach attested to the horror of her not following through on that habit. Now sweat trickled between his shoulder blades, and his hair was almost ringing wet. Partly the meds working their way out of his system, partly pure-dee tenseness about Willi not being where he thought her to be. The fact that she hadn't, for once, left a message on the board, was not in and of itself what worried him. And it was not a matter of trust. She had his full and undivided trust. It was their history together which often translated into her wonderful heart answering calls of family and friends before thinking of all the consequences. She was spontaneous. Not foolish, not silly, not stupid in any fashion, form or way. Her mind often took intuitive leaps that astounded his mind. He admired her for her ability to just "know" that something was the way it was. But he feared because she also had another admirable trait. Courage. Courage of her convictions to act upon her intuitions which often led to her having to demonstrate courage in a more physical manner. But that, by Great Spirit's Way, was why he was there—to watch her back. He, too, had intuitive knowledge which often centered around his lady. And every nerve said she was walking into something that on the surface seemed innocent, but might be roiling with danger beneath.

Wait a minute. He snapped his fingers. She last saw him using the phone in the library nook. Bet she left a note there. Of course. Whew. *Thank you, Great Spirit, and let it be so.* He did an Igor-hitch walk into the nook, flicked on the lamp and stared at the desk. No note. He was about to turn away when he slowly lifted his head, narrowed his eyes. Something. He nodded. Something was out of place.

He shut his eyes and tried to envision the desk as he had left it, not an easy task with the damned effects of Demerol in his system. He touched his pen, the notepad from which he'd torn his notes so as not to alarm Willi if she glanced down at them. What in Black Crow's beak was missing?

The receipt. He dug in his jeans, pulled out the notes with name and address, but no receipt. Had he left the tiny piece of paper here? And if so, it should not have bothered Willi. After all, she'd brought it in to throw it in the trash. Ah. He rummaged through the wire basket beside the desk. Nothing there. Had she . . . had she—? No, surely not.

He hitched his way back into the kitchen, considered the Crock-Pot, peered again at the bread, and rechecked the salads. Quickly he stepped on the lid opener of the garbage can. There fluttered the receipt which he grabbed up. Great Coyote's balls, what was that woman up to? She'd obviously taken a meal to a friend, and he didn't for a minute believe it was the Kachelhoffers, but rang up Frog's End as they called their cottage, on the off chance.

"Nope," Elba said, "didn't bring nothing this-a-way, and I'm right partial to her garlic bread. Reminds me of that homemade I had in Italy. It was softer inside than the duck's feathered behind, was crisp on the outside as a black-edged steak, and as sweet as any honey in Texas, yep. Yes, it does remind me of Italy and the time me and—"

"Did she happen to call and mention where she might be?" he interrupted.

"No, Mr. Fire-In-Your-Pants-In-A-Hurry. Now I do know

where your uncle is, if you were to need him."

With mounting worry, he almost yelled into the mouth piece. "Yeah, where?"

"Him and Agatha is out on the town over to Fort Worth—big city lights drew them in. Some kind of Halloween masquerade party. They did not even—"

"Ah, damn. It's a good week before Halloween. Damn."

"Quannah Lassiter, you are a man of clean tongue. What in hell's wrong?"

"Nothing. I've got to go."

"What's going on? You wait right there. Be with you in five."

With the crumpled receipt in his hand, and the phone in the other, he stood undecided for a minute. Finally he dialed the station, and asked the dispatcher—Zinnia—who the officers on duty were tonight. Calm as always, the sixty-year-old didn't react to his terseness. She languidly answered in a voice that calmed his nerves, "Parva's on. Says if you were to call, we were to let him know. He's pulling extra hours, doing all kinds of duty. Because of the guilt, don't you know. How's your sweet butt doing? Willi kicking it good for you getting in the way of a bullet?"

"It wasn't my—What the hell. I wish she were. Patch me in to Officer Parva's cruiser."

"Done, Investigator. You take care where you sit now, hear?"

When she patched him through, he said, "Parva. Lassiter here. Just want you to check on an address for me, run by and do a welfare check, okay? Who? Uh, just occupants. Maybe there was yelling heard by the neighbors. Yes, Parva, I said *maybe*. Just go by, ring the bell, and see that all is well . . . please . . . and . . . be careful."

Elba's pickup lights flared through the dining room window. Quannah grabbed his shoulder holster from the coat rack by the front door, rushed out without a thought of locking up either garage or front door. Not until he had pulled himself up into the passenger side of the pickup did he realize he was barefoot. Great.

Elba twirled the pickup on the gravel driveway and toward town. He didn't stop her.

"Where to?" she asked, followed by, "What's she gotten into now?"

"609A Fetchwin Way." In response to her second question, he merely tightened his lips.

CHAPTER THIRTEEN

Strange twists of fate are often needed
And when they come should be heeded.

—G'kah'ah
The Book of the Ancient Ones

Earlier that afternoon as Willi had driven the winding Licorice Lane, lightning hop-scotched through the cloud banks. Even at one in the afternoon, darkness had set in. She berated herself for not having left some lights on for Quannah, but then further chided herself for borrowing trouble. But she knew she'd be home before he woke. She wished these dang niggling worries would dissipate along with the rain which slashed down now forcing her to use her wipers.

At the very moment she was adjusting them and finally getting the window cleared, a car slammed into her back passenger side. Willi's forehead thumped against the steering wheel.

"Dang crazy fool!"

The stalking green car, a watery blur along her side window, sped around and out of sight down the far curve. Willi's heartbeat cantered. "You stupid idiot!" Enough was enough. Having many times before foundered on this very road, she stalled a moment before applying more pressure to the foot pedal, but she couldn't let this incident go until Monday. Either she would catch the damned stalker, or she'd go directly to the Sheriff's Department. The Nickleberry PD jurisdiction didn't extend out to her country home, despite her knowing everyone on the force. And even if she could call on them, with her luck, pistol-happy, chocolate-high Officer Smitty Parva would be on duty there, gnawing his fingernails down to nubbins or maybe practicing new ways to sneak up on his appointed partners.

The car's green color worked as ample camouflage in the downpour, but Willi recognized the taillights, a distinctive pattern, as it swerved onto the highway heading toward the high school and the junior college.

With her right hand she scrambled in her purse for her cell phone, got it, and flipped it open just as she hit an oil spot and fishtailed. The phone flew somewhere into the back seat, her stomach seemed to join it there. Willi caught the wheel and got the car under control.

"Hell's bells." The lapse lost her visual contact with the jerk.

Well, she was still going to check out the school on Monday, anyway, so she might as well cruise around now to see if she could locate anyone. The public would be surprised at how many instructors spent hours of their weekend in prep time at the school on Saturdays and Sundays. Something told her this threat came from that arena of her life. If she could find five minutes to think when she wasn't just emotionally drained, she might figure out what told her that.

She circled the school twice and was about to give up when she caught a glint of chrome shining behind the double Dumpsters at the back. The car, parked in the shadows created by the iron monsters, was empty. She tried the door and opened it. She'd let this boogyman scare her too long. Notes, calls, and white shoe polish. Why had she been so afraid so long? Even as the question entered her mind, she answered it. The unknown. Everyone is afraid of the unknown. Well, she couldn't stand anymore. One mystery in her life had to be answered, and this was now. Right now. Maybe it was unlawful to open the door, but the perp had left it open, by daggum. And she had a right to find out what she could. She let this reasoning carry her through the act as she glanced around the inside of the car.

"Great." Now, maybe, just maybe the rain gods would smile kindly on her for a change. If so, she'd find a registration or something in the glove compartment. She took the fistful of papers back to her own car, turned on the overhead and scrambled through the mess, and located an insurance form designating this vehicle and a 2006 Delfin as belonging to the same person. "Oh, my gosh. I never would have guessed. I'm . . . truly shocked."

Willi surveyed the school. Two of the hallways were lit which meant someone had recently walked through them to set off the sensors.

"I've got you now."

One lit area was her hallway, the 300's, and the other the science and math rooms two corridors away. She parked her car outside the 300's, grabbed her pistol and stuck it in her bag. Okay, considering she knew who the car belonged to, this might be an overreaction, but still she was Texan at heart, and she had a license to carry which meant the State of Texas had also trained her when and when not to use that firearm. Whenever there was a question of to carry or not to carry, she'd opt for to carry. Her heart hammered at the idea that she—Sophomore English Teacher of the Year—she, Willi Gallagher, respected leader in the community, was now this very minute breaking a law which could land her smack dab in a cell where she'd be wearing Texas prison orange garb just like any common criminal. Guns were not allowed within so many feet of any public school.

But she'd not face this threatening creature without protection. Hadn't the creep just tried to crash into her car, maybe even kill her? Okay, the use of the gun was a last option, but she'd take it with her until she knew what had caused this jerk to do this.

What the hell motive was there to treat me this way?

She slung the hefty bag of food over her shoulder with her purse. That way, if anyone asked, she was coming for a long stint of paper grading, so she'd brought along her evening meal.

Inside the brightly lit corridor, she brushed her fingers through her soaked ringlets and shook herself before plunging down the hallway that offered no inkling of what rooms were occupied since all were closed. She'd have to pass by and peek in the glass window of each one to see who else might be in the building. She already knew behind which door the owner of the green car sat.

The adrenaline rush moved into her lower limbs, making her knees shake. Just as she was in the cross hall connecting the lower rooms, a momentary lightheadedness seized her.

"Chaucer in the eye, Poe to the head, you beast. Now, try Dean Koontz to the midriff, a whack on the hind side with Agatha Christie."

She rubbed her temples. Why would that line from her vision revisit her? Somehow the words dealt with the skunk, the nasty-smelling vermin that had signaled her for days, chasing her out of the sheds, waiting for her in the form of salt and pepper shakers, and growing huge in the vision. Yet she had overcome it or perhaps frightened it away through . . . through literature, according to the obsidian mirror.

She peered again at the insurance form. Of course, literature. She and the stalker had that in common. The wave increased to nausea and a rising conviction that she was close, so close to unveiling one of the shape-shifters, the sowers of discord in her life. One hand against the wall, she took deep breaths. Yes, so close, but it *wouldn't be what she most expected*. Well, duh-uh. How could it when she didn't know what to expect, but she daggum knew *who* now.

Another thirty seconds and she pushed off the wall to continue down the hallway to *the* room, Ms. River's Junior English class where only a halo of the desk lamp light inched its way to the door. Willi entered and stood on the student side of the desk. Somehow, despite her soaked attire, the ding in her car, the fright she'd been through the last few weeks, she was calm. Why not?

Why not Edie Rivers?

The world had gone crazy, and certainly Edie would not be one Willi would have ever expected. Calmly, she managed to ask, "The green vehicle—it's yours, isn't it?" She dropped the heavy bag on the floor, but her purse, with the gun, she kept on her shoulder and reached in to feel the cold comfort in case one Edie Rivers started acting like a . . . like a . . . *witch bitch.*

Edie Rivers, fifty-plus and not telling, sat in a green sweat suit, the hood lying down her back. She rubbed her eyes as if she'd been grading the stack of junior book reports in front of her. "Willi? Surprised to see you here. You're not usually one to do the weekend stints, opting for those gosh awful early mornings instead. What's this about my second car?"

Willi smirked. "Green outfit to match the green car. You are so anal retentive about the details."

"Excuse me?" Edie said with an edge to her voice, like a crow's caw of danger.

"Why? What did I ever do to you? Why would you visit this horror on me?"

Edie Rivers narrowed her eyes and stood up. "Are you okay? What are you talking about? Do I need to call someone for you?"

"Here. This is what I'm talking about." Willi shoved the note she'd received in the restaurant across the pile of book reports. "Why?"

"Why indeed? Who—?"

Willi flattened the insurance form on top of the note. "And this is proof that—"

The door slammed back and Willi reached into her purse to place her fingers on her .357, but loosened her grip upon seeing Professor Stöhr. Both she and Edie said, "What?"

"Madam Chair, forgive my intrusion. The back door, it did not quite close behind you, and I took the liberty of entering with the hope that both of you would be here. I had, by various roads, come to, I believe, the same final destination as you, Madam Chair. I've intruded into your personal life. Yes, me." He flared his fingers upon his vest, and then raised one finger. "But, perhaps I've saved you from accusing an innocent woman of the harassment you've suffered through for some months. That is what"—he pointed at the note—"the restaurant epistle amounted to, yes, another incident in a line of maneuvers?"

"Yes, I remember meeting you at Catalina's," Edie said, smiling uncertainly.

Willi said, "Yes, this is Professor Stöhr, one of the contenders for the museum curator position."

"Yes, we were introduced at the Mexican restaurant. Delighted to meet you again, Mrs. . . . . uh . . . Ms. Rivers."

"Likewise," Edie said, a shine coming into her tired eyes. She pushed her naturally wavy hair back, allowing her left hand to show that there wasn't a ring. When she turned on Willi, she narrowed her eyes without one bit of fluttering eyelashes. "What is going on? Sit down and tell me, Willi. You're as white as that marker board and look ready to collapse."

"If you would be so kind," Professor Stöhr said, "as to get her a glass of water, and permit me to do the explaining."

Edie smiled, but said, "Leave you two alone in my room . . . the way you all are acting? I don't think so." She opened a cooler and offered each a bottle of Springdale orange-flavored water. "So? Let's get this over with. What about my car and this"—she flicked the note with a French-manicured nail—"ugly missive?"

Willi took a long drink and peered at her watch as she lowered the bottle. "Good grief, it's already three o'clock. I've got to get the chicken to—"

"Pull yourself together, Willi, and stay on the subject; you're a professional, for heaven's sake."

"I myself will tell what the circumstances, I believe, point out." Professor Stöhr strutted behind and around the podium as he spoke, obviously quite comfortable in his position as informant. "Madam Chair, Ms. Gallagher, while graciously playing hostess to me at lunch two days ago, received this note by way of an obnoxious little messenger, who no doubt the two of you will put straight when he advances to your classes. From him, certain facts were ascertained, yes? Yes. The young ruffian informed us that he had received five dollars for his redoubtable deed."

Willi, a bit of fire back in her cheeks with the restorative water, interrupted. "She owns the car that's been following me. It's *her*. We don't have to go through all of this."

"Me?" Edie stood up. "I'm tired of being accused of I don't know what all, so perhaps, Miss High-And-Mighty Madam Chair, you'd better think twice before saying that again. I mean it, Willi."

"Or what? Going to break into my house, my friends' homes, paint my car again?"

Professor Stöhr raised and lowered his hands again and again in a placating way. "Now, now, lovely ladies. Let me finish. Please, a modicum of patience on both sides."

Edie reseated herself. Willi crossed her legs and bobbed one foot, but tightened her lips so as not to speak out of turn.

"Thank you, thank you. So, to continue. When I walked away

from Ms. Gallagher yesterday, I thought to myself: Me? Yes, I do that now and again. The young letter deliverer suggested that the one who had requested he present the note had only given him one of the four five-dollar bills in his possession. I may have mentioned this to Ms. Gallagher, yes?"

Willi nodded. "I sort of recall, but there's really no reason—"

He held up a hand, palm outward. "So, me? I go walking on foot." He laughed. "Of course, on foot, how else would one walk." He shook his head at his own verbal faux pas. "At any rate, I walked down a few blocks, and I see him."

"Little Kit?"

"No, Madam Chair, the black man who gave Kit the money."

"Now, we're getting somewhere." Willi nodded and rested her hands on her knees.

"Just as the young vagabond described him. Quite a good-natured fellow, really, especially after I bought him a beer at the Oxhandlers' place."

Willi's head was swimming again. "So . . . so this man has been chasing my car, leaving notes . . . I don't understand. Who is he? Get to the point, Professor, please. Now."

He smiled benignly upon her and continued in his calm and pedantic vein. "Him? No, he is not the culprit. Only a go-between messenger who was paid *twenty* dollars to deliver the note. He is not comfortable in nice establishments, but, despite his adverse conditions, did want to fulfill his obligation, so convinced a younger and cleaner version of entrepreneurial matter to make the delivery for five dollars. He stayed closed enough to see the job done, or I wouldn't have caught up to him."

Willi stood again. "And he told you someone in a green vehicle gave him the dough, right? And you came into the restaurant, Edie Rivers. Guess you wanted to see the effect this nasty note might cause? I hope you were thoroughly disappointed."

"Absolutely right, Madam Chair. He did say it was a green car, yes."

"Well," Edie jumped up, too. "It wasn't me. For heaven's sake, how could you think that? I drive the Delfin."

"It wasn't out in the parking lot," Willi said, pointing toward the back.

"Because I parked in the front circle. I've not used my second car but once or twice the whole month, anyway, and . . ." Her voice trailed off, and a cloud seemed to come over her features, removing the shine to her eyes, leaving a somber cast to her skin. Slowly she sat down.

"She is right, Madam Chair. It was not her. She is not the skunk stinking up your life."

"But . . . her car, and it's right outside now behind the two Dumpsters."

"Oh, my," Edie whispered, "I begged them to take her back. Too late in the year, you know?"

"Edie, what are you saying?"

"She's not in your class anymore. The exchange student I took in—Selma Hazeltine—from Germany. She did so poorly in your class. It was such a shock because usually our exchange students are scholastically screened so carefully."

Willi said, "I didn't fail her. *She* failed to do anything. She flunked the six weeks all by herself. And you know as well as I this isn't the first exchange student to prove to be . . . a . . . teen, a typical teen. This went a bit past that, of course. We can't have a hundred percent angel every time."

"Oh, I know that, Willi. She pulled the same crud in every class, but you were the only one who didn't let her get away with it, forcing her to change classes or take the failing grade she so richly deserved. Selma let me know the first week here she was in the States for the parties, the drugs, and the rich boys. But, fool that I was, I thought I could change that attitude." She shook her head. Tears of anger brimmed in her eyes. Willi admired her for ignoring them.

Professor Stöhr picked up the tale. "I have done a bit of research, too. Talked with the secretaries, the counselors by way of offering possible jobs for our youth in the future of the museum. Ah, and such things. I discovered that because of Ms. Gallagher's recommendation, the committee of the hosting group put Selma on probation of a sort so that she could not, with impunity, enjoy the parties, the drugs, and the rich boys, huh?" He patted his gold watch chain. "Her anger was channeled most venomously at the one she felt was to blame, her English teacher, Ms. Gallagher. The young woman has issues. On one hand she is brilliant and very adult, on the other a typical teen, but one with anger management problems. Or that would be my opinion with all the facts at hand."

"Hence," Willi said, "the mixed level of messages and anger. I never could quite pinpoint why or who because of that."

"Yes," continued the professor, "problems, I think, dear Ms. Rivers, even someone of your formidable heart and conviction can't help. She should be sent home for some mental evaluations. In fact, that might be a way to get you past all the red tape, and allow you to send her back immediately. Or, you could press charges here, but with it being an exchange student—"

Willi shook her head. "No. If you'll see that she's sent back with a full report, Edie, we'll let her parents take over and get her counseling." Willi touched the frigid metal of her gun, and closed her eyes a moment. Her wet hair clung like damp worms across her neck and seemed to wriggle upon her gooseflesh. Oh my gosh, she was as bad as Officer Smitty Parva, going off half-cocked, not having all the facts. The what-could-have-happened scenarios flashed through her mind, and she asked Edie for another cold bottle of water. Suddenly, an overwhelming need to fall apart, go to sleep for a month, came over her. Now she knew what Dorothy felt like in the field of poppies. So damned drained a real lion chasing her wouldn't even budge her.

Professor Stöhr scrutinized his watch and stuck it back in his vest pocket. Willi blinked. It was the first time she'd actually seen the silver casing. Obviously noting her interest he said, "At my last position, remember, I located the conquistador's helmet, and gold artifacts of those we believe were some of the ancient Aztecs here in Texas."

Willi nodded. "Vaguely, yes, I remember."

"This, the museum gave me. It has one of the hieroglyphics on it—the Aztecan god Chacmool—the one who receives the waters of life—uh . . . in some instances of course that was—"

"—blood," Edie and Willi in unison finished for him.

"Indeed." With interest, he peered at Edie Rivers. "Where is she now? The young girl?"

"Here in the school doing no telling what, or maybe one of her obnoxious and dangerous friends picked her up when she dropped off the car. She prefers her friend's fancy new convertible, although they can't have the top down tonight."

"While we look, let's allow Ms. Gallagher to rest, if there is a place where—?"

"Nurse's office."

"No," Willi said, "I really need to get this to another friend before it goes bad."

"An emergency?" Edie asked.

"Not really, but—"

"A fifteen-minute siesta will do wonders for you, then."

Willi had to admit the crisp clean pillow case sounded awfully good, much better than a field of poppies. Her mind and limbs were drained. Perhaps a few minutes of shut-eye would perk her up. She glanced at her wristwatch. 4:30 p.m. Where had the time gone? No, she'd best take a couple of deep breaths and move on. Since she was already in the building, she took a few minutes to check her teacher's mailbox. There was one last nasty note, but now it seemed pathetic and nonthreatening. So why was she sitting here in the teachers' lounge, tears streaming down her cheeks?

Relief.

Relief. One mystery solved. She put her head on the desk, gave into the weepies and nodded off.

Hours later when she awoke, a note on Edie's door told a story that neither Edie nor the professor had wasted time. Professor Stöhr and Edie Rivers located Selma Hazeltine due to the strobing lights of the cruiser where she was being held. By the time they'd discovered she would be arrested for shoplifting along with two of her less-desirable cohorts, and the professor had helped Edie locate and hire a bail bondsman, it was some hours before they returned. At that time, try as they might, they could not rouse Willi from a sound sleep.

They figured that with the last few days of turmoil over a best friend's passing, Quannah's being shot, and the toll of Selma's nasty antics, Willi needed the extra sleep. Willi glanced at her watch and blinked. 8:00 p.m.

8:02 p.m. Oh my gosh. Quannah might be awake. She'd better call and let him know she was okay and on her way. She pulled out her cell phone. Lots of static came along with the connection, but she had to leave a message on the machine. It clicked off before she had finished, but at least he would know she was on her way home.

Super. Maybe the sleep will have done him some good, too. *He won't even know I've left, much less find out about this horrible stalker. Of course, eventually, I'll tell him. I need someone to tell it to, since I'm talking to myself. Great Spirit, I need help.*

CHAPTER FOURTEEN

That which is buried beneath the ground
Must remain there until the good is found.

—K'a'lane
The Book of the Ancient Ones

"Great Spirit, I need help," Quannah said. Barefoot, hair loose, he knew what any onlookers would say: "Damned naked Comanche. Wild heathen." He'd pretty much have to agree with them at the moment. But nothing mattered except he had to protect that downright certifiable woman who'd changed his life into an emotional roller coaster. Her heart-shaped face surfaced in his memory for a moment and a whimper came from her mouth. Oh, no . . . from his mouth. He tightened his lips, and practiced breathing so he'd sound less like a thundering bull.

As Elba pulled into the driveway of the duplex on the side of 609B, a woman stepped off the porch of 609A, Tattoo's address. Or rather Rhonda Faye Nadge's address. In bangles and dangling earrings, a long, flowing and shapeless dress, she met them on the tiny porch.

"She's not home," said the Hispanic lady with a frown on her face. "I so needed her help with my display." She mumbled this to herself, seemingly not noticing Quannah and Elba in her path until they were almost nose to nose.

"Who are you?" Quannah asked.

"I'm the storyteller, of course, Drianina Manauia. Here's Dr. Etzli who can tell you."

"At the museum? So, you know Tattoo and Willi?"

"Willi? Oh, Ms. Gallagher, yes, of course. She is the *señora* who heads the curator committee."

"What is going on here?" Dr. Etzli got out of his car and asked from beneath his shadowy hat.

"*Querido,* I was about to ask him just that."

"All of you, off the premises," Quannah said. "Elba, move your pickup across the street. You folks head over there, too. I've a few questions for you both."

Mrs. Manauia looked him up and down, noting his bare feet, loose hair, but his double shoulder holster must have spoken volumes. "Are you a *pistolero* or a lawman . . . ?"

Elba said, "Sure is. Special Investigator for the Texas Rangers, that's what he is, and if he says move we ought to make like those Mexican frijoles and clickety clack away, or like jack rabbits and start hopping, or maybe kangaroos and really start to jumping."

"Elba." Quannah's hair, catching the electricity in the evening air, swirled around his head, lifting and settling again down his back.

"Yes, sir?"

"Thank you for your . . . your help." His next inclination was to batter his way into the house, but he calmed his galloping heart, and remembered he was working with that totally unpredictable Gallagher woman. Satisfied upon seeing them huddled across the way, he knocked loudly on the door just to make sure there would be no response. No answer. That meant nothing, of course. If—and he had to admit, it was a big "if"—if it were Nadge and his cronies inside, they'd not likely reveal themselves, but there had been no proof yet that Rhonda Faye Nadge was kin to the criminal. And if she were kin, that didn't automatically make her an evil accomplice. Yet. Other than break down the door barehanded, there wasn't much else he could do until help showed up.

He strode over to the others who stood between Elba's old pickup and the red Jag. He watched for the smallest flicker of light to show behind the window casings while he talked with Mrs. Manauia and Dr. Etzli. "You two come together?"

"Yes," Dr. Etzli said, "Mrs. Manauia had to leave her car in the shop until Monday and wait for a new battery. She wanted help building part of her storytelling display. I believe Tattoo was supposed to have already done this, but—"

"—but, she didn't," said Mrs. Manauia. "Really, the youth of today. *Queridos,* it is enough to make an old woman *loca.*"

"And, also," Dr. Etzli continued, "I had a few questions about . . . Yaotle. He and Tattoo worked so much together out in the sheds. He helped her unload the many deliveries for the museum and vice versa. I thought she might know more than she remembered when questioned by the police."

"Yaotle?" Quannah kept a vigil upon the Fetchwin Way address but said, "Seems a lot has been going on at the museum."

Elba patted his arm. "I'm sure Willi has caught you up on the most important details."

"Uh-huh, but it's always nice to hear viewpoints of others—pass the talking stick, so to speak."

By the time Quannah had heard from their prospective about the demise of Ludwig, the bloody footprints, the trashed museum office, the disappearance of Tommy Balboa—Yaotle—and the discovery of his pickup with a cab full of blood, Quannah's meds had lost all effect, and he was sweating profusely. His side throbbed at a low-level pain threshold. His heart lurched up into his throat, and he had to exert strong self-control not to pull out his hair and scream, "Gallagher!"

What in Great Crow's beak had Willi gotten herself into?

How was he going to keep his one special lady in the whole world safe when she was . . . when she was Gallagher? Instinct told him he'd not yet heard everything. He stared hard at Elba. "Is there more?"

"Well . . ."

"Yes, go ahead. I need to know."

"She didn't want you to worry about her."

"Elba Kachelhoffer, if I have to I'll arrest you for . . . for undercooked scones, burnt beans, something . . . if you aren't telling me everything."

Elba shifted her hefty bosoms into a comfortable position and sniffed. "She might have one other tiny little bitty situation. Not more than a molehill. She seems to be coping real fine with it, too."

"Molehills have a way of growing into full blown volcanic eruptions with her. What else?"

"Stalker."

"She told me a little about it, but acted as if it were some school prankster more than anything else. What didn't she tell me?"

"Now, there you go, rolling your eyes, like she doesn't have sense enough to come out of the rain. And you'd be dead wrong. She's bought herself a high-powered handgun. .398 or something like that, and she's been a-going to the range to practice. Yep, see there. She deserves that name Miss Marple of the Range. She'll be fine."

"She's loose in Nickleberry with a .357? And going to take on her stalker?"

He strode around, circling the Jag half a dozen times. Think. He couldn't think straight. Okay, best case scenario, Willi for once forgot to leave a message. Worse, he left his cell phone beside the bed. She might be now trying to reach him. Elba didn't carry a cell phone but maybe one of the others did.

When he asked, Mrs. Manauia offered hers. He had dialed the cell phone first and after receiving no answer dialed the home number in, when the wind whipped up a cyclone of leaves, and he handed the phone to the storyteller. "Just leave a message when the machine picks up, okay? Tell her the location, that I'm fine and chasing clues to the escapees . . . and to stay put when she gets home."

Mrs. Manauia nodded, and with ear to phone waited for the machine to go through its phone spiel. He stepped across the street to try and peek through a window.

Just when he thought things couldn't get any worse, a deluge broke from the sky. While Elba and Etzli got inside vehicles, soon followed by Mrs. Manauia, Quannah stood, hair streaming down his back, his side now making him take notice by way of muscle spasms. Officer Smitty Parva screeched his cruiser to a sideways stop, lights stippling across 609A, easily alerting any criminals in a three-block area that the law had, indeed, arrived. Elba in her pickup, and Etzli in his sports car drove off at high speeds. Elba stopped a block down, but Etzli cruised out of sight.

Quannah considered the bright-eyed officer. "Oh, great, we're all gonna die." As Parva passed by, Quannah grabbed the bullhorn from him and sprinted across the street into the miniscule garden, his feet slipping in the barren yard now turned to mud.

The duplex came to life for a moment. On the tiny front porch, Quannah ducked down and signaled for Parva to head toward the back. Quannah had no problem hearing the man inside yelling. The curtain of rain ceased as suddenly as it had started a moment ago.

"Tat'? Where the hell are you? What's all this blood? Sonsofbitches!" Curtains parted as Quannah flattened himself against the entryway full of shadows despite the lights. "Damn. I come home to this? Where the hell? Heberly, where is your ass? Rios, damn it, are you all okay? Tat'?"

An answering voice yelled out, "Just come in a side window, amigo. We're surrounded."

Quannah squinched up his bare toes. Yeah, those two killing machines—Nadge and Rios—should really be in fear of one half-naked Indian and a nervous rookie who'd probably think too long before he took aim this time. From the corner of his eye he saw Parva keying in for backup. Quannah nodded and in a well-modulated and calm voice used the bullhorn. "Nadge, we know you're in there. Rios, too. No reason for any of us to get out of control here."

Sweat trickled down his back, and even his toes upon the uneven boards seemed slick with slime. He tried to rub some of the mud off on the wood. "I'm Special Investigator Lassiter. We just want to talk. We don't want anyone in the house hurt, including yourselves." Especially not Willi—please not her. Please let Willi not be in there.

In response, Nadge shot out the front window and blasted away the revolving lights atop the cruiser. One end of the bar managed a weak red glare. The barrage gave Quannah time to bend over and run for cover behind giant oaks in front of the shadowed side of the doorway.

Nadge yelled out, "Can't think with those damned lights. Any more police arrive with them and people gonna die in here."

Quannah's stomach knotted so hard, it twisted him to the ground in pain, but he nodded at Parva beside the right side of the house while he said into the bullhorn. "No lights, no sirens, no police cars. We'll just stay calm and talk. No problem. You got a working phone in there; we'll try to reach you by that." He hoped Officer Parva had a cell phone on him. He had to stay calm, keep them talking any way he could until he figured some way to get Willi out of that house, assuming she was there.

Or any other innocents.

Nadge yelled out, "You just don't rush me, you hear, Special damned Investigator? I need time to think what we need to get clear of this hellhole. You just sit tight and don't try no funny business, hear?"

Quannah breathed a sigh of relief as the figures of lawmen answering Parva's summons quietly circled the house. Parva slunk across to his cruiser. Quannah used the bullhorn again. "The officer is also moving the cruiser out of your way so you won't be bothered by it anymore. That's what you'll hear revving up, no new men on the scene at the moment. Just the few that are already here." He didn't want to tip the perps as to their numbers now gathering all around the site and up and down the block.

Peering at the street in both directions he eased his shoulder muscles and leaned against the thickest oak tree. Cruisers blocked both ends of the street. A few lights in other houses had come on and gone off. The folks at this end of Fetchwin Way, being used to shootouts, drug busts and the like, merely slunk to the rear of the houses and hunkered down or went back to sleep until the excitement was over.

Lt. Bennie Oso de Oro crept up beside him. "Your uncle, Sheriff Brigham, phoned and asked me to take over negotiations. Said you were off-duty due to an injury."

"Yes, but Willi's in there, I think."

"Your partner? How'd they get their hands on—"

"No, not that kind of partner. My lady, you know?"

"Damn. You've got confirmation she's in there?" Bennie put a hand on his shoulder and squeezed.

Quannah told him about the receipt, the supper items gone and what was the probable action taken by Willi.

"I'll do my very best, Lassiter, if it takes hours, we'll go slow and easy until she's released, I promise. We're not exactly the

Dallas SWAT team, but we have good officers."

By the moonlight and the few lamp posts' illumination, he noted Bennie's graying temples, his lined face. Bennie said, "I've been a negotiator for twenty years. I was the one talked the Piney Woods serial killer into coming in last month."

Quannah gulped, knowing the lieutenant was saying this by way of assurance, not bragging. "Not bad for a country PD, or the Dallas SWAT, but I've already opened up negotiations. Told them no lights, no—"

"Yes, sir, I know. But there was a barrage of shots, right?"

"Yeah."

"So we tell them you were nicked, not badly, so if Willi hears, she won't be alarmed, okay?"

Quannah swallowed, but it took him a full quarter minute to do it. "Do what you have to. I . . . I understand. I want to be there . . . when you enter. You got an extra assault rifle to loan me?"

"Against my better judgment, but I know if you really wanted you could pull rank on me." Oso de Oro signaled his second-in-command and gave him orders to supply Quannah with flack jacket and a weapon.

Quannah said, "I'll be in that cruiser." He pointed to the shot-up one Parva had moved half a house away, out of range of the bullets from Nadge and Rios, maybe Heberly, too, if he was inside. Quannah's lip trembled which made him thankful for the cover of night, yet his inching away to where Parva sat was the hardest thing he'd ever done.

To turn Willi's safety over to . . . to anyone, even a seasoned vet like the fiftyish Oso de Oro . . . no, it didn't sit well at all, but he knew it was the right thing at the moment. He didn't remove the side panels of the flack jacket, although they seemed to dig into his bandaged side.

Lying back on the headrest, he moaned.

Officer Smitty Parva, who'd donned his protection too, said, "You okay? That's a stupid question. Of course, you're not okay. Gosh dang, shot up by me, having to come out before you're well. By the way, before you got that flack on, you did notice your side is bleeding through the dressing there?"

"I'll be fine."

"Ms. Gallagher's smart, you know? And they aren't totally stupid, either. They'll keep her as a valuable hostage. You'll see."

Quannah lowered his chin onto his chest. "This is worse than the night of the bat."

"You fought bats?" Smitty pulled two bottles of water from a cooler on the back seat. "Tell me about it. Nothing's happening at the moment. They're giving Nadge and his buddies time to get their list of demands together."

"Yeah, a typical ploy to let them believe they've got some control over the outcome of this . . . horror. Yes, I'll take a water." Quannah sat up straighter. "No coffee?"

"Uh . . . naw, thought I might need to . . . uh . . . change a few habits."

"That's what the night of the bat is about. Changing. Well, discovering what you need to change."

"So, you're talking some kind of ceremony. Ah. Can't imagine that'd be a big, mean ceremony. What? A promise to do better? Drink a little bat blood? Translyvania stuff, huh?" Smitty drank his water.

Quannah intently watched Lt. Oso de Oro and whenever there was communication, he promptly raised a finger for silence, but between times, he welcomed the respite of talking to Smitty. It eased the pain cascading through him from his opened wound which he clamped down on so as not to alert Smitty more than he was already aware. It also eased somewhat the horror of knowing Willi was only steps away, and yet he couldn't get to her.

"So?" Smitty prompted. "The bat thing?"

"Some aborigines refer to such initiations as Night of the Bat, other native peoples refer to it as the Night of Fear. Often the person undergoing the cleansing or the initiation goes out into the forest and digs his own grave during the day; sometimes friends help him. At nighttime, he descends into the grave and lies down, the opening covered by a large tarp or blanket."

Smitty squirmed. "Don't see why anyone would—"

"—to test themselves."

"Against what?"

"Officer Parva, think a moment. You're six feet down, symbolically within Mother Earth, and you are even denied the sight of stars and moon. Total darkness as if you were in the womb from which you came. For us Native Americans, that's *Ina Maka* or *Maka*—Mother Earth. Some even use *Unci—grandmother* as the earth mother name. Sorry, I like to give tongue to the old language now and again."

Smitty rubbed the back of his neck and shivered. "Okay, okay. Then what? So what's the test?"

Quannah sighed. "You listen to the creatures traveling through the brush around you. The night crawlers touch your skin. Scents of freshly turned dirt mixes with blood and animal feces, rotting wood. Scents not normally acknowledged, but now can't be ignored as your sense of smell sharpens with the inky night. The wings of owls on the hunt swish through the darkness above. Is that a snake making its whispering way toward your grave? What's that nudging its nose underneath the blanket, a wild hog or just an inquisitive little mouse? When you think about and face those fears, and you're able to get past them, you go deeper into thought. You face phobias and weaknesses within yourself. You encounter the ideas and ideals that need nurturing or change. When you leave the grave in the morning, you have a rebirth from the womb of Mother Earth.

You have transformed your less decent virtues for a commitment to go toward more noble aspects."

"Oh, okay." Smitty scratched his head.

"Some liken it to the bat because the bat goes into caves, the darkest tombs of Mother Earth, every night, hangs upside down in the position a newborn assumes, and meets each new flight out in that way."

"I guess you'd feel free to accomplish about anything once you survived all that, huh?"

"You've got the idea, Officer Parva, you've got the idea."

"Unless, of course . . . unless . . ." Smitty said with his face screwed up.

"Unless what?" Quannah shifted to a more comfortable position, hoping that Willi was not confined in such a hurtful manner. He shook the mental pictures away. "Unless what?"

"Well, unless, when that hedgehog snorted and blew out breath, you peed your dang pants. I'd be outta that grave long before daylight in that case."

Quannah studied the dark shadow of Smitty Parva and sighed deeply. "You may have a point. What the hell am I doing sitting here when Willi is in danger? I don't care what Bennie Oso de Oro says, I'm going in after her. Let's roll."

"Is that such a good—"

"Start the engine." Quannah sat up and goose bumps traveled over every inch of his body, now all nerves alert, a sure sign that his action was right on and timely. "Oh, Great Spirit, don't let me be too late."

"You ain't."

"What?"

"Too late."

Quannah grasped Smitty's arm so tightly the man yelped. "What do you know?"

"Didn't want to say earlier. I told the lieutenant. Didn't want you worrying more than—"

"Spit it out. Now!"

"At the side window I saw a woman on the floor, injured but moaning and okay. Could be that Tattoo girl."

"Or Willi. First or second window on the right? Describe her."

"First window. Living room. She had a shirt on. Looked like an Indian blanket."

"Damn you, Smitty Parva. That's Willi's. She keeps it in the car for chilly days."

Just as Smitty turned on the ignition, the van at the side of the 609A driveway backed out fast, the stench of burned rubber on the drier asphalt beneath the carport hitting Quannah's senses strongly.

"How did they let them get to the van?" yelled Smitty. The van kept on backing down Fetchwin Way, swerving as two men let loose with a barrage of bullets in all directions.

"Go after them. You're the only one ready. Don't lose them. I'm betting they left Willi here." He rolled out the side and slammed the door. Smitty hit the pedal and was off. A quarter minute later, the foot officers raced from behind the house and dove for their cruisers. The race was on. Quannah jogged toward the duplex. Oso de Oro was barking orders and relaying to the higher ups the mishap, all the while signaling to his own driver to pick him up.

"Yes, I had visual at the last," he roared. "All three, I repeat, all three—Nadge, Heberly and Rios—escaped in the museum van. Officers are in pursuit."

Quannah leapt across the porch railing, crashed open the door with the butt end of the assault rifle and slammed his way inside the house before the lieutenant could turn around. He ignored the glass and splinters as best he could. "Damn." He bent down to pull out a small shard. A trickle of blood oozed across his hand. He kept on the move. No lights. He fumbled around on the wall but couldn't locate a switch, but by the illumination now bursting through the windows from the ambulance and a cruiser Oso de Oro must have left behind, he managed to see shadows here and there. He scrambled through each room, finally got a hallway light to flick on. Nobody in any of the other rooms. He checked closets and the back porch before coming back through the front room. He hollered out the door. "Clear. Get the medics in here. Now."

Huddled in the center of the living room, she lay face down, the flannel shirt over her shoulders and head like a blanket. Blood pooled at the corner of one temple.

"Gall . . . Gallagher?" He placed a hand on her back. "Help is on the way." He bent closer to the prone figure, touched her hair, and his senses signaled him. He pulled the jacket back for confirmation. At last a medic with the sense to pull the overhead light string switch, eased down beside him, and Quannah peered into the drained face of Rhonda Faye Nadge—Tattoo. "It's not . . . not her. Not my *Winyan*. Thank you, Great Spirit. If . . . if Willi's not here, she's . . . they . . . oh, Great Spirit." His knees buckled, but he used the assault rifle to balance himself. "They *did* take her."

He rushed out the door, told the officer with the cruiser. "Let's get going. They took a hostage. They took Willi."

Stunned, the officer stood a moment with mouth agape. "Can't, sir. They shot out the tires."

Out in the middle of Fetchwin Way, he let out a bloodcurdling war whoop, a cry of anguish, and one foretelling death for the three in the van if he could get to them.

Lights flickered as a vehicle backed up to him. Elba swung the side door open. "Damn it, burn heel leather, boy, and let's go." Quannah jumped in and Elba careened around the corner and pushed the truck for all it was worth. Unbelievably, Elba and he were on the tail end of the chase and in sight of the final cruiser in the long line within five minutes.

Quannah said, "I shouldn't put you in the line of fire."

"Why the hell not? I stopped for you, didn't I?"

With no answer and no time for other options, Quannah kept his eye on the lights of the last cruiser. He had to trust that that officer was in contact with the cruisers closer to the escapees.

CHAPTER FIFTEEN

In anger and malice the Jaguar leaps
But harms not one who true faith keeps.

—Lan'a'cat
The Book of the Ancient Ones

Willi ran into the house just as the phone jangled to life, pitched her purse and keys and grabbed up the handset. "Yes, Mrs. Manauia? Yes, the storyteller from the museum, of course, I remember. He said what? Thank you so much."

She hung up the phone before she wandered around to the living room. Sure enough, Quannah wasn't there. Well, now what exactly had the storyteller said other than ridiculousness about Willi staying put at home? Right, sure. While he's out chasing those killers and probably thinking they were at Tattoo's like Mrs. Manauia indicated. Willi wrung her hands. She couldn't just sit here. No way. She had to find out more. Mrs. Manauia was at the museum with Dr. Etzli, and . . . now why wouldn't she have stayed on the scene if she thought one of her colleagues were in trouble? Just human curiosity would have kept most folks glued as close as possible. Humph. Anyone who didn't have more curiosity than that was just beyond belief. Willi snorted her disgust in as ladylike a way as possible while grabbing up her purse and keys, scrambling back into the car and heading out to ask Mrs. Manauia more questions. Shed number seventeen, wasn't that what she'd said? Or maybe nineteen. Dang old numbers anyhow.

Well no matter. She'd locate Quannah, get him resting as per medical instructions, and have a calm evening of Country and Western music at home. But it wouldn't hurt before heading to the museum sheds to just check on Tattoo.

In the 100 block of Fetchwin Way the Halloween decoration competition was well underway. The old Victorians lent themselves to walkways of jack-o'-lanterns, porches strung with spider webs, and even bubbling caldrons, smoke whirling through the night mist. The Dalrymples' yard now also had background music coming from somewhere on the porch to accompany the dancing skeleton couples under trees of twinkling lights. More than likely they'd win in the "enchanted" category for the third year in a row. "Macabre" would probably be taken by the house across the way with life-sized figures of the McAdams family posing with their fire-breathing pet. Dinosauro.

She drove on down to the 600 block of Fetchwin Way. Ohmygosh. 609A Fetchwin Way didn't require any Halloween trappings to be a winner in a special category of "gruesome." The crime scene tape, taut around front yard trees and porch banisters, enclosed the house of shattered windows, busted out doors and an eerie silence.

"Oh my gosh. What in the world went on here?"

For a moment she stood beside her car, unsure whether to approach or not. Where . . . where was Tattoo? Her visitors? Maybe, maybe the décor truly was a grotesque attempt at Halloween decorations. She swung under the yellow tape and her foot crunched upon broken glass. Who was she kidding? She placed a hand over her chest, the better to still her pounding heart. Something really bad had happened.

"Willi? Willi Gallagher?"

She shifted around and ducked back under the crime tape. "Officer Bourne? Is that you, Karon Bourne?"

"Yeah. You know better than to traipse through a crime scene. Get out of there."

"What's happening?"

With her baton Officer Bourne pointed toward the cruiser, one door askew, tires in rubber shreds, and windows mere shards of glass poking out of the frames. "I'm holding the fort until the forensic van and team—that would be Ostendorf—gets here. Probably be corralled into staying and helping him."

"What . . . exactly happened here? Halloween vandalism? Was anyone hurt?"

Officer Bourne's face lit up, her eyes sparkled and her voice grew animated as she said, "Unbelievable shootout. Bullets flying. Like awesome. My bad luck my cruiser got totally disabled, and I wasn't quick enough to fight my way out of the backyard brambles to scrounge a ride with another one."

"Yeah, tough. Who was shooting at whom?"

"The killers—those escaped convicts—Nadge, Heberly, and Rios—they made a getaway in one of the new museum's vans. Believe that Tattoo girl—Rhonda Faye Nadge—worked there."

Even with her hand over her heart, Willi couldn't slow the drumbeat of her heart down. "So, was anyone hurt? Did they catch them? Where's Tattoo? And was Quannah . . . was Quannah Lassiter here?"

"Calm down. He's fine. Well, I guess. He was a wild man. Whew. Barefoot, long hair flying. Slammed that door to smithereens. I tell you, Willi, you got you a man what is a man, even if he did get butt shot. Only one taken in an ambulance was the Nadge woman. She was coming 'round, though. Talking a little."

Past the cotton suddenly growing in her mouth, Willi managed to say, "Where . . . where is he now?"

"Don't know. When he scrambled out of here, he said he'd left another museum person with a message for you if you came home."

"Oh, oh, yes he did. What's the matter with me? That's where I'm headed." She twirled toward her car. "One more thing. Is he in a cruiser with that . . . that . . . with Officer Parva?"

"Nope. Believe Lieutenant Oso de Oro said he was riding shotgun with one of the ladies that runs the tea shop."

"Which one?"

"Short. Round. Loud."

"Elba."

"Guess so. Oso de Oro could've told you, but he's gone back to headquarters waiting until they get the three cornered again. My bet, they'll go down before being talked in."

"That's fine as long as my man doesn't go down, too."

"Wouldn't worry about it. That old pickup was in the tail end of the chase."

Willi waved a hand in farewell. "Thanks, Karon. Later." Well fried armadillo feet, she couldn't get in the chase, but she knew from Mrs. Manauia's message where they might be headed.

Revived after the afternoon siesta, Willi's ebullient mood kept her from too much worry about Quannah, especially seeing as how one Elba Kachelhoffer was a far better watchdog than Officer quickdraw Parva.

Although intermittent rain meandered downward, her drive to the museum was relaxing. Yep, and Officer Karon Bourne was right. Willi grinned, envisioning the soon-to-be meeting between her hombre above all men. So, Mrs. Manauia, I hope you're right. Willi would meet him at the museum.

Tattoo—she was also upset about and thoroughly disappointed that the young girl was involved with the murderous trio. Could be she was truly an innocent relative, who had no choice but to let him hole up there. Willi banged a fist on the wheel. Dang, life could get as creepy and messy as those make-believe spider webs in the Dalrymples' yard.

Lots of lights were on in the back sheds and Willi pulled the car before the one with number seventeen. Seventeen or nineteen? She'd check this one first. Nothing seemed amiss there. Outside she paused. Elba's old pickup wasn't out here in the work yard. Maybe she'd driven on into shed number nineteen. Willi pulled out her cell phone, pushed the fast dial for Quannah's, remembered he didn't have it, and grumbled at her phone.

"Dang. No signal out here in the sheds anyway. Oh, shoot, my fault. The battery is about gone."

She shoved it back in her purse and went into the lit shed nineteen. She vaguely remembered Yaotle worked there in Dr. Etzli's office. Wonder if Yaotle had gotten in the way of the killers, because that sure as heck would explain why his pickup cab was filled with blood, and why he couldn't be found. Idiots. Today's forensics would pick up hundreds of clues to Heberly, Nadge and Rios if any of them had been breathing close to Yaotle's pickup.

No large train parts in this shed. Number nineteen had been cleaned entirely of the railroad remains of years past. The cavernous area had been broken up into offices and storage rooms in the front area. Maybe Elba had driven far back into the shed. Walking down an eight-hundred-foot hallway between those led her to the area with shelving all around and up to the ninety-foot ceiling where muted lighting cast a comforting nonworking glow over the entire shed. The numerous units in the center five aisles had room for a forklift to traverse. And many of the smaller sections were mobile atop industrial-sized mega wheels. Sure enough, to one side sat a huge yellow Caterpillar forklift with an hydraulic lift, the better to reach the boxes at the very top.

She sauntered back down the long corridor, but goose bumps rose on her neck; she shivered and returned to the Caterpillar. She squinted her eyes. Surely, she had not seen it move. But something drove her to inspect it further. Something ran across her foot. A tiny mouse—not more than a one-inch baby—skittered toward the yellow monster. Where in dark Hades were the light switches? She made her way out to the middle support pole. Sure enough, just as in shed seventeen, the switches were located there, one of the few leftovers from the railroad history. A momentary triple heartbeat of flickering preceded bright light flooding the area. That was better.

"You better stay hidden, little mousy. I don't think these museum folks will take kindly to your type of critter. I'm sure they have periodic infestation control, or will when the museum opens."

Daggum, had she gotten Drianina Manauia's message wrong? Willi reviewed mentally. *Querida. This is Mrs. Manauia. Officer Lassiter asked me to relay he is fine, and is in pursuit of clues to the killers at 609A Fetchwin Way and perhaps later in of all places the number nineteen shed—where I have an office. No criminals can get in those buildings. I will be there. They cannot disturb my props. Ah, anyway. He wanted you to stay put and out of harm's way. He said stay home. Sí, sí. I think that is all he said.*

Short and to the point. Willi shook her head. Like anyone who knew her, would expect her to . . . duh-uh . . . stay home. Okay, so he'd gotten waylaid by the chase after the van, said van not having made a trail to any hidey hole here. Fine so . . . this was . . . a dead end.

Maybe not. No convicts, thank goodness, since there were no squad cars anywhere near the buildings. With all that went on at Fetchwin Way, Willi understood that Mrs. Manauia might have gotten a few details confused. She tried her cell phone, but the weather high above was still not allowing connections. So, maybe she could still use the time in the sheds. Maybe she'd talk to Mrs. Manauia. Sometimes older folks noticed more going on around them than they got credit for. Mrs. Manauia had noticed items of hers that had been stolen. If Tattoo were the culprit, would Mrs. Manauia be amenable to restitution and giving Tattoo a second opportunity? And the old storyteller might more readily talk about things she noticed concerning Yaotle's disappearance. Many times the Hispanics in the community did not trust law officers and did not tell them things they would readily share as just general gossip. For some reason, Mrs. Manauia seemed to fit this old-time cautionary attitude. But perhaps she'd talk to Willi. If the old lady were still here. She might have checked her office and props and already left.

All the horned toads in Texas knew she was not one to let an opportunity slide by. Could be there were clues in here to Yaotle's disappearance. While Quannah had the three killers at bay elsewhere, she'd be perfectly safe in searching out Dr. Etzli's office, supposedly the last place where Yaotle was seen.

Head high, and with purposeful step she trod toward the offices at the front. The doors were all unlocked. How odd. In fact, some were slung back against the inner wall, as if the occupant had just left, meaning to return after digging up paperwork elsewhere. In the first ten-by-ten room she saw the tiny hand-painted nameplate on the desk. TATTOO with a rose and vine surrounding the name. Willi had to give the girl marks. She had a high neatness quotient. Papers stacked in boxes of in-out-mail, file cabinets labeled and locked. Nothing out of place.

Moving on toward one of the open offices, she met with literal chaos just as it had been in Anastasia's office. Papers had been pulled out of files, which had been broken into with a crowbar. She shoved the tool aside with her foot, careful not to touch. Holding her hands together in front of her, she peered at the big squares of the desk calendar with October at the top. A coffee cup had spilled over it. She used a pen from her purse to shove that aside, along with numerous folders. In the corner where the triangle held the calendar pages in, she saw a host of scribbles. She inched up the containing triangle of cardboard to pull out a tiny sliver, a partial piece of an invoice. She could have sworn it was the second half of one she had in the debris of Anastasia's papers. But this section clearly indicated it wasn't something coming into the museum but rather an item going out of the museum. What? They sent something back that had not been ordered, an item that had been damaged in shipping? Why place such importance on such an invoice? She pocketed it. Pieces would eventually fit together.

Those dang goose bumps made a beeline down her back. She peeked outside the office door. All was as bright as a lit jack-o'-lantern. She moved her shoulders in circles and then her head. Just tenseness, that was all.

As she moved back into the office to inspect more debris, the tiny mouse ran into a cubbyhole behind a bookcase. She peered toward the area. "You are one traveling critter. Whoever had this office must have been asleep half the time to miss you . . . or maybe just had his mind on other things."

She bent down to see behind the bookcase, but the slit was too tiny. Lying up against the wood was a book. She picked it up. One on Aztecan Jaguar clans. A leather bookmark, with many years' wear upon it, marked the reader's spot. YAOTLE. So, this was his cubbyhole. Or rather Dr. Etzli's and his together.

She eyed the phone, really wanting to check on Quannah even if she had to call dispatch at the sheriff's and the PD. Lifting a tiny sliver of paper was one thing. Leaving her own prints over this—naw, not going to happen. About to head to a third cookie-cutter office, she was attacked by the mouse. No other way to put it. He ran toward her foot, screeched to a halt, tried to bite her leather shoe, and skittered along the way down the long corridor.

"Yikes." Willi backed up toward the outside door. Hairs on the nape of her neck stood up, her limbs shook. "It was a little mousy, for gosh sakes." She stopped. Okay, okay. This wouldn't be the first time one of Great Spirit's creatures had kept her out of harm's way. Uh . . . it wouldn't be the first time one of them had led her down some downright dangerous trails, either. But, three encounters.

"All right. You little cheese-chewing, Camembert-loving, cheddar-crazy critter. Show me what you need to show me." She eyed the yawning maw of the open storage. No little mouse in sight. Thank goodness no one else would ever have to know of this incident. "I need a big piece of yellow cheese, don't I, for negotiating? Well, you're out of . . ."

Big.

Yellow.

Caterpillar.

Hmm. She'd thought that had moved before. Maybe . . . maybe what was being shipped out was on the forklift. Or at least, perhaps the paperwork would be in the cab. Right. Like she wanted to climb up into that monster.

She twirled around as if one foot were stuck in place. She did it again. "I've got to get over this curiosity bent. I do not need to be climbing up into machines I know nitwit nothing about." She did the one-foot-glued-to-the-floor maneuver again. "No one is here to help me if I fall off the thing. My luck I'd hit the wrong button, thingamajig and take off into my own destruction derby. No. Common sense is going to win out on this one, you hear me, little mousy? Forget it. This girl is out of here." She twisted around a last time, to face eyeball to eyeball with the tiny baby. On one of the shelves at shoulder height a cat blinked, the mouse caught neatly between its teeth. Willi's heart zoomed up to her throat. "No, no, no." She swatted the cat's mouth. The mouse dropped and ran back toward Yaotle's office. The cat snarled and bounded off the shelf in the opposite direction.

Willi stood staring at the cheddar-colored, wheeled mega lifter. Hell's bells and rats' tails. Sheesh. One solid foot in front of the other, she steadily approached the damned forklift.

"Kitty, just please don't be mad and jump out at me."

She gulped and put her foot on the first step up into the cab. "It's going to be okay. Quick glance inside. Step down. Don't even get into the cab. It'll be fine. Rush out of the building. Find a working phone and get ahold of Quannah. Easy. Piece of cake. It'll be fine. Saying something three times is powerful, so say the Kachelhoffer sisters. So once more ought to make for perfect insurance. It'll be fine."

She grabbed hold of the hand bar to help hoist her up to peer into the window. She froze. She leaned her head against the pane. "No, no, no." She had to find the strength to make herself open the door against all the strong inclinations to just run, forget what she'd seen, and call anonymously from a pay phone. Oh, it was tempting, but . . . but he might need medical help.

She pulled off his wide-brimmed hat and eased him off the steering wheel. She slapped his white face. "Dr. Etzli? Dr. Etzli, can you hear me?" She grabbed his hand, which pulled his cape away from his chest. "Just squeeze my fingers if you can hear me. I'll go get . . ." She swallowed three times and blinked back nervous tears. "Don't guess . . . don't guess you can do that. Squeezing of the hand thing. Oh my, dear Lord." His white shirt, covered in blood, was open, revealing an horrendous wound to the chest area. No pathologist her, no forensics expert, but she'd swear on ten stacks of Bibles or a dozen of Great Eagle's feathers, that the man's heart wasn't in that cavity.

Willi's knees buckled, and she wanted to turn loose of his cold digits, but couldn't seem to move her own for the longest time. Little mousy must have felt like this frozen in the cat's jaws, totally helpless, stifled with fear, afraid to move; after all, there might be something even more horrifying over the other shoulder.

Finally, she eased down from the forklift and stood in the glare of the intense lighting, pulled in a half dozen good breaths and swallowed. She could handle this. It wasn't, for gosh sakes, as if she'd never encountered a . . . a dead body before, but it was the first one to be so . . . so bloody . . . so horribly mutilated. When she got her breathing under control and her legs able to move correctly, another unwelcome thought struck. Was someone still in the shed? Who knew, after all, that Willi might be here? Mrs. Manauia and anyone who'd overheard her phone message as everyone was in a tizzy fit outside the Fetchwin Way address. "Anyone there?" The two words came out as a whisper. She recalled the phone message. Was the storyteller somewhere in shed number nineteen incapacitated—translate that deader 'n a doorknob—inside another machine or . . . one of the hundreds of containers . . . or . . . in one of the office cubicles not yet opened? "Mrs. Manauia?" Hell, it could be any of the museum workers.

Willi eased down the long corridor and tried again in a stronger voice. "Mrs. Manauia? Drianina Manauia, are you in here? Make noise someway so I can find you? *If you can, please, please make some noise.* "Okay, well, don't worry if you can hear me. I'm going to call the police right now." At the door to Dr. Etzli's office she eyed the phone three feet from the door. "Thank goodness." Gulping, she ran in, grabbed it, dialed 9-1-1 and raised the receiver to her ear. "Hurry. Answer. Please, hurry." A full thirty seconds passed before she realized there was no ringing. Her fingers trembled as she punched in the three numbers again. "What the heck?" She eased the phone down, lifted it again and listened before dialing. "Lots of things deader 'n doorknobs around here."

273

Get out of shed nineteen. Get in the car. Hightail it out and find a phone.

She'd almost made it, had in fact had her fingers around the door handle, when something slithered around her ankles snapping her down hard on the ground. Before she could twist her body more than just to see the rough rope wrapped across her ankles, someone jerked her arm back and wound the rope around her wrist and upper arm, trussing her as one would in a rodeo bulldogging contest. Grit met her mouth and then a hand with a cloth clamped over her nose. She breathed in noxious fumes.

None of this made her lose total consciousness, merely incapacitated and blurred her vision. Her hand banged back against one of the museum carts, and her attacker, now driver, careened through the old train house doors and into the museum proper until coming to a halt before the Aztecan pyramid with Chacmool's statue.

Her assailant shoved her out of the cart onto the cold stone floor, pulled on the rope and dragged her up the steps. Dear Lord, he had to be as strong as one of the Oxhandler cousins. Each step caused pain to shoot through her shoulder and neck. Her head connected with one step so hard, she tasted the blood trickling down from her temple. For a fleeting few seconds she could see out the tall glass front of the museum as if she floated over the town and in the far distance lights blinked and she imagined that the sirens wailed, although no sound came through to her.

But the cruisers weren't concerned with her. Probably, they were the ones chasing the convicts. *Quannah, please, please, get in my head. Come this way. Lassiter, I need you.*

Next thing she remembered was being lifted onto the sacrificial slab. No, no . . . impossible. "Why?" she managed to get past an uncooperative tongue. "Who?"

Mrs. Manauia's face floated above her a moment. The woman pulled cotton out of her cheeks, rubbed away the heavy makeup, and grinned.

"You're . . . you're the yard girl . . . Día Muñoz."

She brushed her hair back, and pulled out a double set of side dentures, completely transforming her face. "No . . . you're . . ."

"We've not met, Ms. Gallagher, although I think I was not careful enough, and you caught a glimpse of me at Ernesto Etzli's. I'm also Nina Ricardo."

"Dr. Etzli?"

"Yes."

"He's . . . he's dead."

"He had to be sacrificed just as Yaotle was, just as Anastasia Zöllmer was."

"You're . . . the shape-shifter, the horrible one." Willi could barely get the words past her dry tongue. "Why?"

"Stop struggling, Ms. Gallagher. Won't do you any good, *querida*. Why? Because your blonde spiky-haired friend discovered things missing from the museum. Things not belonging here. Artifacts taken from the warriors and they will be returned to the true Aztecans—the clan of the Jaguars—to protect them. I'd set it up that she would blame that Tattoo girl, but Yaotle and she working together came across some of the crates and the invoices. Well, sometimes the gods call us to a bloody war."

"I don't understand."

Mrs. Manauia—Día—Nina Ricardo leaned over her again. This time she had on the jaguar costume Willi had seen at Dr. Etzli's. Her costume, or her breath, stank so badly, Willi tried to twist away.

"It's the fresh blood you smell, *querida*. Etzli's. His heart lies in Chacmool's bowl even now. Yours will join his soon." She frowned. "I regret Etzli's demise. He was such a good cover. A boyfriend who was constantly on the move from one museum to another, and his sun phobia kept him inside, leading a quiet life otherwise. He never questioned where I went at other times, thinking I was always in my persona as international buyer. An easy man to fool until Yaotle went missing."

"All that blood in the cab . . . you . . . Yaotle, too."

"Tommy Balboa should have minded his own business. A few more months, and I could have replaced most of the artifacts with fakes before the museum even opened. It's much harder after they've been enclosed in the cases. Not impossible, but difficult, depending on the museum's level of security. I even had hopes he could truly become one of the Jaguar clan, not just a wannabe."

Willi swallowed, which popped her eardrums. A distant wail reached her. The cruisers? Were they coming this way? No, now the sound receded. Her heart hammered in her chest. "Lassiter will hunt you down to the ends of the earth."

"*Querida,* how melodramatic you are. He won't even spend a month in mourning, men being what they are."

"You old witch. You're nothing but a pathetic old . . ."

Drianina raised an obsidian knife. "I can make it quick. I can draw . . . the . . . moment out to excruciating eons. Be right back."

"Where?" *Be right back? Oh, dear Lord.*

Willi twisted, scrabbled with her fingers for a hold on the cold stone, managed to twist to the side just as the front door was shot out. Two men ran past her below the pyramid. They dragged another along with them.

Willi had no doubt she was viewing the three escapees.

Rios said, "Hey, your *prima,* she said that old storyteller woman, she has a blue Volkswagen and a pickup. She's always around here. We'll take her hostage, and take her cars, amigos. Vámanos."

Drianina stepped out from behind and down the pyramid steps. Rios jumped back from the jaguar vision before him and crossed himself. Even from her upper vantage point, Willi could see he was covered in sweat, blood, and fear just as the wounded Heberly and the boot-kicking Nadge came into view. Rios said, "Old woman, you scared the hell outta us. You wanna live, you hand over your keys and get out of the way."

"*Idiotos.* Killing for a reason is a god-given right from the ancients. What you do is pathetic. No, you will not use my vehicles. I will have need of them myself. Move on, now *estúpidos,* move on."

In answer, Rios shot her just as she let fly with the obsidian knife. They both collapsed.

Oh, hell. Willi must have said it aloud, because Heberly looked up and locked eyes with her. With Herculean effort, she fought her restraints, used her one free foot for leverage to try to roll over and onto the offside of the sacrificial stone. Intense pain slammed into her back, taking her breath away, taking her into a black tunnel she'd never come out of, and yet she could still hear. Sirens wound up to rapid-fire megahertz, gun blasts, pinging of bullets ricocheting, and finally quietness for a moment. Then again, the sound of running feet, men barking out orders.

Oh dear Lord, don't let them chase those creatures up here. Despite the blackness and the wound, she wanted to face the action. Maybe the lights from outside would help her see. Again, she rolled over to face the front of the museum.

She still couldn't see, and somehow the initial pain had ebbed, but when someone bent over her and pulled at her ropes, she used all her might to rear her free foot back and kick. She made resounding contact and the man whimpered. Finally, though horribly woozy, she could see through a haze.

A bit more lucid after the initial shock of being shot, with hands and feet untied, she could see a man coming up the steps toward her, his hair flying outward, his T-shirt soaked and matted with blood, and he reached for her. No, she'd not be taken hostage by the last of that murderous trio, not a hostage twice in one night. When he bent over her and pulled at her ropes, she used all her might to rear her free foot back and kick. She made resounding contact and the man yelped. He buckled and fell backwards down, down, thumpety, thump, thump down the pyramid steps.

Landing spread-eagled on the museum floor, he yelled, "Gallagher."

She whimpered, "Oops."

Beneath the crisp white sheets in her hospital room, Willi sat up in bed and surveyed the facial damage in a mirror Tattoo held up.

"Glad you're okay, Ms. Gallagher, and sorry again I couldn't tell you about my cousin and his buddies. They swore up and down they'd kill my mama and little sister in Itasca if I was to snitch on them. I had the inclination and the time, but I sure didn't have the guts. Guess it would've saved a lot of folks heartache and lots of injury, if I'd told, but then my mama . . ."

Quannah placed a hand on her shoulder. "Willi knows, and we know your heart was in the right place. Officer Parva has a crew fixing your windows and doors right now. Those folks who Rios, Heberly and your cousin lifted things from—the Kachelhoffer sisters, Rasco Coontz, Emmett and Ilene Hawley at the gift shop—are letting you make up for those items through either returning them or cooking up batches of your homemade cookies or handiwork. How does that sound?"

"Fair. I can work, given the time and inclination, which I've got right now despite this wrapping." She pointed to the bandage circling her head. "You all take care, try not to get butt shot again, hear?" She tromped off in her no-nonsense way as if she had places to go, people to meet.

Willi sat the mirror down, and a tear trickled down her cheek.

"Winyan," Quannah said, "is that a happy tear?" He wiped it with his finger and left his hand cupping her face as he sat down on the side of her bed.

"Yes, I'm glad she wasn't involved. I've grown to like that young woman despite those wild tattoos. I'm just glad you're okay. Sorry about . . ."

"Not to worry. The two days with the chiropractor got me aligned again, more or less."

With her nose in the air, and eyes slightly crossed from the medications, she asked, "Did you finally call Sydney Curry for me?"

"Yes. While you were in two days of La-La Land after they dug the bullet out of your derriere." He rubbed his chin. "Sydney Curry had discovered the cigarette butts which Ludwig swallowed had small traces of poison. Your storyteller, Drianina Manauia, had obviously been cornered and made to answer questions she didn't want to answer. As we've finally pieced it together, in that crazy woman's attempt to get back all Aztecan artifacts and turn them over to this so-called Jaguar Clan of investors, she left no witnesses, no one to question. Anastasia was smart, and finally had figured out that as the items were shipped in, Manauia was shipping them out. Many times in her role as Nina Ricardo, overseas purchasing agent for textiles and homewares, she herself carried them out. Manauia had a receipt for a special shipment of a canister of vials of a particularly interesting gas from the caves of Mexico. This gas, when mixed with smoke, is deadly if given in the correct dosage."

"Ludwig. Is that what killed him?"

"Yeah, the poor pooch. Kind of a slow death, since he didn't get a big dose and not always a still-smoking butt of the cigarette." Quannah folded his arms across his chest and frowned. "Manauia knew Anastasia was on to her and doctored the ends of the cigarettes with the gas, thinking eventually Anastasia would smoke one down at a time when the storyteller would not be anywhere near. But back to that night. Manauia had her cornered and was about to do a sacrificial number on her, rather than let Anastasia reveal her deeds and multiple identities. Anastasia ran, managed to get in her car and on the way to the police station, smoked and without Ludwig in the car to nip up her butts, she smoked the cigarette down. Her last minutes were horrendously frightening, I imagine when she realized she had been poisoned. Hence her erratic driving, her crashing into the pole."

"But she didn't die then," Willi said.

"Again, due to the storyteller not soaking the cigarettes long enough."

"But, she came back and . . . and finished the job."

Quannah uncrossed his arms and patted her knee. "Exactly. She was strong and a lot younger than her storyteller persona. After all, she was Día Muñoz, the yard girl and Nina Ricardo, the elitist traveler. She worked with the Clydesdales, too."

"And what happened to them?"

"Like any good gypsy caravan, the mobile home, caravan and horses disappeared. Obviously, there is a network of her co-Jaguars."

Willi wedged a pillow on her bum side and moaned. "I should have told you about what was going on."

"Not your fault. I was out in the field."

She ducked her head and twisted the sheets. "I should have let you know about the stalker."

"I was in the hospital then. You didn't want to worry me."

"I should have left a message on the white board."

"You thought I'd be asleep until you returned. Things happen." He squeezed her knee. "But . . . in future, leave the notes.

I . . . I've grown accustomed to them." He winked.

"No comments about my hiney boo-boo. You're giving me an out for everything." She looked him in the eye.

"Guess so, *Winyan,* lady of mine, but just this one time. Now, you need some rest." With an evil grin he reached toward the med pump.

"Wait. You all got Manauia or Ricardo, whatever her real name is . . . you got her in jail for the murder of Tommy Balboa, Dr. Etzli and Anastasia, right? Or did Iago Rios take care of her for good with that bullet?"

"Nope. She escaped. In the chaos surrounding taking the convicts out, she managed to leave in her little blue minivan which we've never located. Must be big money backing her shape-shifting scheme."

"So she goes free?"

He sucked in his lips and slowly blew out air. "For the moment. We'll either run her to ground, or she'll reappear for another scam, and we'll catch her then. Not to worry. Three murders—two with mutilations, hearts ripped out—she won't ever go off the radar."

Quannah reached over and this time gave a good punch to the button.

"No, no, not yet." Willi took a deep breath. "Iago Rios?"

"He died on the spot. Heberly died in the operating room."

"Tattoo's cousin, L.T. Nadge?"

"We cornered him in one of the outer buildings. He 'fessed up he had nothing to live for, especially after he and his girlfriend got in a fight and he sliced, diced and hid her body."

"Oh my gosh. What happened? Did you all have to . . . to—?"

"Nope. He told us where her body was. Wanted her to have a church burial, believe it or not. He said he was headed for Hell and shot himself. We've got a team out searching the woods where he said she's buried."

Quannah reached behind her, fluffed her pillows and said, "Enough, Gallagher. These aren't thoughts to bring sweet dreams, and you're overdue for a few."

"One last . . . let me see now, what . . . what?" Her eyelids fluttered, she got a dreamy look on her face, almost gave up the fight, but finally rallied just as Professor Stöhr and Parker Nolan walked in, each bearing a beautiful bouquet of flowers. The professor set the daisies upon the windowsill, and Parker Nolan placed the pink roses upon the side table.

"Lovely. Thank you, gentlemen."

"Indeed they are, and you'll soon have the bloom back in your cheeks, no pun intended," Parker said, twirling his cane around. The grin on his face belied his remark, but Willi let it pass as it seemed harder and harder to form clear thoughts.

"Madam Chair, we come with an offer we hope you'll consider. We know the stipend quoted for the curator position. We also know that you have the authority to double that stipend if you think one of us is ready immediately for the job." Professor Stöhr stuck his thumbs in his vest pocket.

Willi blinked, trying hard to keep up with his proposal, the meds starting to work.

Parker Nolan leaned upon his cane. "We propose that for the first five years of the museum, you hire us both. I will take on the artistic procurements, the museum loan-outs and such, while the professor will work with the natural museum items. Both of us will handle the finances, therefore providing a system of checks and balances I'm sure the committee, community and yourself need after what has happened."

"So, Madam Chair, what do you say?"

Willi, eyelids so heavy she could only manage looking at them through slits, nodded her head.

"Ah," said the professor, "always regal and simple. I do so admire your style. We shall take our leave and see you in a few days, Madam Chair."

When they left Quannah climbed up on the bed and cradled her head in his arm. On his side he began to sing softly to her as she drifted off. Willi crooned the words, too, words found in a hundred different versions in a thousand love songs. "*I make it through my day because of you.*"

Quannah sang, "*. . . and at dusk I dream of you . . .*"

Together they ended the song, "*. . . always in my arms . . . always you . . .*"

ABOUT THE AUTHOR

Kat Goldring lives in Cleburne, Texas, surrounded by wildlife and country folks. She enjoys playing guitar and singing with a country and western band, artwork, and learning about the many wonders of nature and the universe—especially those most unusual of all creatures, the Two-leggeds.